THE CASTAWAYS

Lion or Panther?

THE CASTAWAYS

JESSIKA FLECK

Entangled Publishing, LLC
2614 South Timberline Road
Suite 109
Fort Collins, CO 80525
Visit our website at www.entangledpublishing.com.

Entangled Teen is an imprint of Entangled Publishing, LLC.

Edited by Theresa Cole
Cover design by Erin Dameron-Hill
Cover art from iStock and Shutterstock

Manufactured in the United States of America

First Edition April 2017

For the Olive Gagmuehlers of the world.
Just be.

Chapter One

A Name

I used to have a smile. A real smile. All teeth. All cheeks. The kind that makes your eyes go squinty and pinches your nose.

But I lost it.

I've tried finding it — really I have — but it always comes off fake and forced, or, as my mom reminds me, like I'm in pain.

I blame my name.

My smile disappeared slowly, over time, like the old Jackson farmhouse in the field east of downtown.

God knows how long the place had been there. The fence was nothing but broken posts poking out of overgrown weeds. The once jolly red paint on the house had peeled and chipped away, leaving only rotting wood.

It had started with kids daring each other to go in and steal old doorknobs, broken dishes, and other unidentifiable, rusted treasures. Then the windows went — a fun Friday night in Hillings was a drinking game of throwing rocks at the glass: you miss, you drink.

The thick front door disappeared. Next, the shutters went missing, along with much of the interior, forcing one side of the roof to collapse in on itself. Before long, the place was gutted—its joy snatched away plank by plank during the night. What was once someone's home had become a moldy, decomposing shell. Then it was bulldozed to dust. Gone. Nothing to show for its existence except an empty, weedy, weedy field littered with soda cans and chip bags. Now it's a super-market attached to a mega church with a Subway sandwich shop in the lobby.

That's how it happened with me. First, they picked and prodded, threw stones, and pulled at my hair. Then, piece by piece, they stole it—my smile, my joy. Now I'm being bulldozed.

All because of a name: Olive Gagmuehler. A smelly food plus the word "gag," which quickly morphed into Olive McGaggy for funsies.

My middle name is Maxi. Once *they* got wind of this information, I was all variations of *Maxi Pad* from grades six through eight.

They're family names. I know—I should feel honored. But couldn't I have paid tribute to my great grandmothers in some other way? One that didn't predetermine my social fate?

Olive Maxi Gagmuehler.

Thank you, Mom and Dad.

Chapter Two

A Norman Rockwell Moment

It's forty-five minutes before school, and my brother, my dad, and I sit at the breakfast table eating overcooked waffles that are basically large crackers. The sun casts a spotlight through the window, so I'm forced to squint across at my brother through the blur of my eyelashes.

"O-live! Stop hogging the syrup!"

My little brother's going through a growth spurt. At least, that's how Mom justifies his constant need for food.

"Jeez. Chill, buddy. Here, it's all yours." I push the syrup across the table. Lucky grins at the bottle, gazing at me through the amber glass, one eye scrunched shut. The weirdo then proceeds to pop the lid, dump the thing upside-down, and drown his waffle. Taking a heaping, sticky bite, he stops mid-chew, examining me with suspicious eyes.

"Hey, where's your black sweater? You're *supposed* to wear it today!" Damn it. Cute as he is, the eight-year-old sneak notices everything. It's spirit week. Today is "black sweater day." Something about "black out the Wrens." "You know I don't get into that stuff."

He snorts. "Well, *I* would."

"Then you can when you're in high school. But today, I'm wearing my white sweater." What he doesn't know is that my black sweater was stained with mustard when they tried to squirt it in my eyes.

"You know Olive's a rebel, Luke. She's not at all about the status quo," Dad cuts in, trying to relate to my "angsty teenage ways." I roll my eyes. He winks. I smile back.

Mom peeks her head in from behind the pantry door. "Where is your black sweater?" Great. Double interrogation. "I haven't seen it in a while."

"I-I must have left it at school in my gym locker."

"Olive—"

"I'm sorry. I forgot to grab it, but—"

"Oh! Wait—" Lucky jumps up, runs past Mom and straight to the hook where we keep our backpacks, furiously digging into his. He comes running back, waving a flier in his hand. Mouth still half full of slimy, syrupy waffle, he mumbles, spewing crumbs, "Look!" and thrusts the paper in my face. Then, pulling off his shoe and dumping whatever lives in there into his hand, he reveals a gold coin. "I also got this! It's a doom-bloom."

I hold my hand out and he tosses it in. "It's doubloon, weirdo. Pirate money."

"Yeah! Well, yesterday, we had assembly, and the carnival pirate guy said I could use it to get into the ship or the maze! Can we go? Pleeease?"

Mom, coffee cup in hand, joins us to investigate. "What's all this?"

Phew. If the sneak was good at anything, it was diversion. Black sweater forgotten. For now.

I tear a piece of waffle off with my fingers and dip it in syrup, staring down at the flier. "The frickin' Castaway Carnival." I nearly choke.

"Olive…" Mom motions to Lucky like he's never heard

such vulgar language.

Dad snorts behind his mug.

"What?" I lower my voice. "That place is a death trap."

The Castaway Carnival is held one weekend a year and is known for its over-the-top pirate themes and world record-holding corn maze where children disappear. Last year, it was a nine-year-old boy. But he wasn't the first. Back in the sixties, when the carnival had first opened, two high-school boys also went missing. The same way. Vanished.

She gives me her evil eye, tucking a piece of dark, short hair behind her ear. "We promised him," she sing-songs. "Besides, there's a logical explanation for where those kids went. They just haven't found them yet." But the worry lines between her eyes say otherwise.

"Yeah… *Death trap*," I sing-song back. She takes my plate away. I pull Hazel, our ten-year-old cat, up onto my lap and let her lick syrup drips off the table. Mom groans. She hates it because it ruins any hope she has of a Norman Rockwell moment.

"Can we go, Olive? Can we?" Lucky is literally licking his plate clean. Mom groans again. "You pro-missss-ed," he begs, stretching the word out as far as possible.

Yes, I had. Months ago. I'd needed his last piece of gum before school. Total desperation move. I breathe in, then release a long exhale before I answer. "All right." I hand the paper back to him. "When's the big day?"

"Tonight!"

I stare at my parents.

They stare back.

The three of us know *they're* working late.

Perfect.

I sigh. "Fine. I guess I can take you by myself. It'll be a first for both of us."

"Yes!" Lucky makes a fist, yanks his elbow in, then flings himself away from the table.

The coin, still in my hand—and heavier than a piece of

junk like it should be—has a skull and crossbones embossed into it, and the word CASTAWAY along the top. I hold it up between my thumb and forefinger. "Forgetting something?"

Lucky stops in his tracks, pivots on his heels, and faces me. He holds out his hands, smiling, all teeth.

I toss the coin back to him. "For the pirate ship, *not* the maze." No way will Lucky be the next kid lost to the Castaway Carnival.

Chapter Three

Three hours later…

I'm not here. I'm somewhere else. Anywhere else.

"Smash it in her face!" Hannah screeches through her teeth.

No. This isn't happening.

"Shove it up her nose, Les!" Dillon chants.

Laughter. Snickering. Evil heckling.

No.

I cough, choke, and shake my face from side to side to avoid the blood clots that formerly resided in Lesley's upper vag region.

Oh God.

The thought tugs a familiar heat up from my stomach.

Lesley's straddling me with her volleyballer's thighs, waggling her used tampon across my face. Hannah and Dillon stand sentry on each of my wrists, their wedge-heeled shoes smashing my hands into the floor, pinching my fingertips.

Lesley squeezes the tampon.

It drips.

Small red tears plunk along the bridge of my nose. It's all rust and sour, and that acidic warmth rises higher into my throat.

"Stop!" I scream.

"What's that? I couldn't hear you, Olive. You know, over all of the *gagging*!" Lesley has that trademark sneer stretched across her face.

"Get off—"

The tampon's jabbed against my mouth. Thank God I clamp my lips closed. But the damage is done.

Stringy, wet cotton sticks to my face. I twist my head to the side to get it off me.

Then I puke.

A chorus of "*Ewww!*" is followed by the scattering of two pairs of wedges and one pair of lime green Chuck Taylor's.

I force myself up off the floor and wipe my mouth with my sleeve. The three of them stand in a line facing me like a firing squad. They're blocking the door. I realize there's a greater plan and I'm about to find out all about it.

In a split-second decision (probably my animal instincts to flee impending danger), I bound between them, shoving through Lesley and Dillon with my shoulders.

I don't make it far before my arms are grabbed. I'm not super tall or super strong, and I'm definitely not athletic, so they far outweigh me on all counts. Despite the losing battle, I jerk my arms, trying to rip free of their claws, when something snaps inside me. Maybe it's that animal instinct again, because, for the first time, I fight back.

"What?!" I scream. "What do you want from me?!" I shout with everything I have from someplace deep down inside me. It must unnerve them because there's a pause.

Somehow, I pull one arm free, ball my hand into a tight, solid fist, and punch Lesley straight in the nose. Sheer shock pales her face and she stumbles several steps back.

Blood dribbles out both of her nostrils.

My hand stings with electricity and pain.

I swear Lesley's eyes go red. "Oh, you're gonna pay for that, Olive McGaggy!" she yells, blood running over her top lip and into her mouth so her teeth are a horrible shade of pink-red.

Stunned at what I've done but knowing I should run for my life, I hesitate a beat too long. They catch me as I flounder, pinning me to the floor and assuming their usual and perfected positions of restraint. Lesley straddles my thighs and leans over, her face inches from mine, her blood, for the second time in mere minutes, dripping down my nose.

Then her eyes switch from wild to wide. I'm not sure which is more terrifying.

She clears her throat, spitting a bloody chunk to the side.

The bell rings.

"Time's up," she says, and Hannah and Dillon move away from me.

Lesley moves off me, but not before clutching hold of my jaw. "You just wait—" She smirks. "You won't even know what hit you."

Shoving my face away so my head hits the floor, she stands and leaves, her minions following.

I lay there, dazed.

The door swings shut.

I'm alone.

The stained, aquamarine tile of the girl's bathroom is hard and cold beneath my back. A pile of vomit sits festering much too close to my face, a bloodied tampon the cherry on top. Just as the stink oozes toward my hair, I manage to sit up with a grunt.

I glance down. A rusty red stain streaks across my uniform. I stand, wobble, then stagger toward the mirror and gasp.

It looks like I've slaughtered a pig with my bare hands and eaten its entrails. Instead, it's Lesley's period spattered all over my face and chest, on my lips.

I dry heave into the sink, my hands shaking, clutching the

sides of the porcelain.

My throat tightens and my breath wheezes.

Not daring to make eye contact again with the mirror, I turn on the water, swiveling the knob all the way to the left. Steam rises from the sink as I work to lather the soap into a thick foam. I then slather my face, rubbing it raw. The water burns, but I don't care. The hotter the better.

More soap... In my mouth, my eyes, my neck, I scrub between wheezing and hyperventilating. I spot my necklace, the one I never take off, the one I got from my favorite market stand in Portland. There's a splattering of blood across the simple, silver disk and the sight sends a coursing rage through my body. Using the sleeve of my sweater, I wash it clean. Then I cup my hands under the faucet and dump soapy water over my head and scrub, scrub, scrub with my nails until my hair is drenched and my face is so red my freckles vanish into my skin.

I stop and clutch my chest, trying to catch my breath. A string of high-pitched hisses leaves my throat in fast succession like a blocked flute. The painful tune continues but soon slows until I'm just breathing heavily, the whistling in my throat gone.

"Okay... Hhhh... I'm okay..." I've managed to tame the attack. The monster.

Hair wet, it sticks to my scalp, soap suds showing where I didn't rinse well enough. My sweater, the white one, the one with the expensive, embroidered emblem on it (of course) is now soaked. The stains smear and seep outward like a bad tie-dye job. I reach into my backpack and switch it out for my maroon gym T-shirt, throwing the soiled sweater into the trash. Mom won't be happy—that's two sweaters in one semester—but the stains will never wash out, and I don't want any reminders of this moment.

Balancing on my toes, I step over the spreading puke, Lesley's tampon bleeding red into the chunks. The image of her with a bloody nose flashes behind my eyes.

What the hell did I just do?

Made things one hundred times worse, that's what.

At the door, I grab a couple paper towels and dab my face, hoping for more of a fresh-from-the-shower glow instead of the I-just-ran-a-few-miles-and-puked look I'm probably sporting. But when I go to toss them in the trash, I see a large clear tube smeared with red liquid. I lift it out. Across the front are the words "Stage Blood," and in smaller print, "Realistic qualities, including: metallic scent, deep color, and medium flowing viscosity." Then, under that, "Warning: Will stain most light materials and fabric. Test first. Not for use in mouth. Do not ingest."

Great.

I might be poisoned, but I'm oddly relieved.

Chapter Four

ASSHATS!

When I enter English outlandishly late and wearing a gym shirt, Lesley sneers at me from the back row.

"Why's your hair wet, Olive?" she calls out. "Oh. Did you just get out of gym?"

Everyone looks at me. Some laugh. Others whisper. Because they all know gym isn't until the end of the day.

I skulk to my seat, the desk behind Tawny. Wide-eyed, my best friend stares at me with her sweet, round face, cheeks flushed from walking across campus, sweat beading her forehead.

"What happened?" The familiar rasp of her voice hugs me.

"Trio."

"Again?"

I nod.

Throughout class, she keeps her eyes narrowed on Lesley, who only responds with eye rolling. Luckily, about the time it seems Tawny's taken her last eye roll silently, the bell rings.

"Asshats! They're total asshats!" Tawny has a mouth like a sailor, *asshats* being one of her three favorite expletives.

"I know." I stare ahead as we walk to our next class, cutting through the courtyard, the bizarrely-too-warm, October wind hitting me in the face. What I wouldn't do for five minutes of cool, Oregon coast sea spray.

"I mean, sweet Jesus! A *used* tampon? They can't get away with this!"

"T… It was fake blood," I say, shaking my head, still a bit dazed.

"It doesn't matter!" She clamps her lips together, breathing out her nose until she calms down. "Olive. Seriously."

"What?" I glance over. Tawny's curly black hair whips around her head. Part Japanese, more parts Samoan, she's tall, strong, has a gorgeous, full face, and her skin is warm like sand on a beach. Tawny was teased as much as me growing up, maybe more. But she always held the power; she fought back and won. Somehow, despite my luck, she picked me as a best friend.

"You. Have. Got. To. Do. Something." She stares me down with her dark, all-knowing eyes, pulling the emotion from me like my mother does, somehow reaching in and plucking it out thorn by thorn.

Memories of the girls' bathroom, the blood I'd thought was so very real, the tampon, my stained sweater…come clawing up my throat. I try choking it back, but several tears escape despite my hold on them.

"Listen," Tawny lowers her voice. "It sucks. This sucks. *They* suck. But you can't keep letting them walk all over you. It's not right." She spits the words out as if Lesley stands inches from her lips. "You have to tell someone."

I release a long sigh, then wipe my budding tears with the backside of my hand. "I know, I *know*. But…" She side-eyes me. "I can't. Seriously, how could I possibly explain what happened to me today without an epic parental freak-out bomb over it?"

"But, you—"

"Like, mushroom cloud epic."

"Seriously, though—"

"You know they'd go to the principal, to the Trio's parents, the media… It'd be all over the internet—"

"This is serious. Stop joking."

My shoulders fall. "I know. Trust me, I know. Truth is, I'd be in a far deeper crap hole than I already am."

"Not necessarily…"

"But likely."

"Yeah, all right, it's likely. As usual, you…win…" Something catches Tawny's eyes. "What the? No way they're still having it after last year!"

Following her stare, I see a poster plastered on the bulletin board next to the door:

Castaway Carnival
This weekend ONLY!
Come, if ye dare!

"Oh, ballz no!" she answers the poster with another patented Tawny cuss.

"They never found that kid last year, eh?" I ask.

"Nope. Went in the maze and never came out. Vanished. Just like the other two from way back when."

Death. Trap.

Tawny shivers. "The place creeps me out. Something's not right with that maze. I swear it."

"It's just a carnival. There's an explanation for it, we just don't know what it is." I shake my head, because, beyond all reason, I'm repeating my mother's words from this morning. But, despite my logic, a shiver runs down the back of my neck, too. Though, it's not all fear. Oddly, there's excitement mixed in.

An idea hits me over the head like an anchor. I skid to a stop, grabbing her by the arm and pulling her away from the door. "I've been thinking…"

"Shits." There it was. Fave cuss number three.

I laugh. "Shut up. Listen."

She giggles back, her eyes going all crinkly.

"I need to get my mind off all of this. Do something… uncharacteristic. Fun. A little…rebellious."

She raises one eyebrow. "I like it. Go on."

I inhale deeply in preparation. "I'm taking Lucky to the carnival tonight. You want to meet me there post eight-year-old bedtime and go through that maze?"

"Hmm, let me think… HELL NO! Have you lost your mind?" Her voice goes raspy, classic Tawny *are you effing kidding me?* style.

"What? Where's your sense of adventure? It's just a field of corn. Come on…"

She sighs heavily, tightening the straps on her backpack and shoves her hands into her pockets.

"Please? It'll be fun."

I have no idea why this is such a big deal that I'm begging or how a stupid carnival attraction is going to solve anything. But the more I imagine that dark field, the corn, and trying to find my way through it, the more important it feels.

She narrows her eyes down on me. "Damn it. Only for you would I do this."

Chapter Five

The Trio ignores me the rest of the day.

The few encounters I have in the halls with them are absent the usual eye rolling and smirking. Their silence is worse than the torture because I know… Something is fermenting.

This year I have the misfortune of schedule. Lesley, Dillon, and Hannah workout — gossip, check themselves in the mirror, flirt with guys, and generally plot my demise — during fifth period. Coincidentally, the same class block I have required PE.

When I return to the locker room after a thrilling forty-five minutes of yoga — Sinclair Private School, always keeping with the trends — I've lagged behind, hoping the Trio has already showered, mascara'd into oblivion, and moved on to sixth period.

When I enter, I'm welcomed with an empty space, save for a few girls talking in front of the mirrors.

I exhale.

I go to my locker, open it, and pull out my boots and my uniform. I fasten my skirt, pull on my knee socks and boots, then tie the —

Footsteps stomp up behind me, and before I can turn, my locker door slams shut.

I barely get a glance over my shoulder to confirm what I already know.

"Bitch!" Lesley yells. Her nose is red and swollen, and the sight fills me with simultaneous pride and dread.

The primping girls grab what they can salvage and leave in a rush. *Thanks a lot.* I want to yell at them for taking off. I want to scream at Lesley and Hannah and Dillon for being such supremely horrible human beings. But I can't. Because the monster is closing my throat in on itself.

I gasp. Wheeze. I try to cover it up by coughing, but it only makes it worse. I've always been able to hold the worst of the monster back until they've disappeared.

When Lesley realizes I'm having an attack, a twinkle glints in her eyes. She laughs. "What the hell?"

Hannah and Dillon snort-laugh.

My hands go numb and my head swims and, despite my efforts, I slump to the floor and start making the noise. The one that sounds like I'm totally geeking out with laughter, but it's really me trying to hold on to each breath mixed with complete and utter anxiety and fear.

Their eyes go wide in shock — not concerned shock, more like embarrassed-to-be-near-me shock. More like what-the-hell-is-wrong-with-her shock.

With the hyperventilation peaking, I know it's about to get its worst, but also, that it'll be over soon. The "geeking out laugh" turns to more of a barking as I work to slow my breathing. Somehow, I wiggle enough to turn onto my side and try to curl up. I squeeze my eyes shut.

"What's wrong with her?" I hear Hannah say. Was that a bit of remorse? "Let's get out of here. Now." Guess not.

I'm able to climb onto my knees and tuck my head down

against the linoleum floor. It's gross and dirty but I'm thankful for the cold.

My breathing already calming, back to that choppy wheeze I'm so familiar with, I dare a peek up. The three of them are leaving, rushing out the door, when Lesley stops and squints down at me. "You're such a loser, McGaggy. God, you can't even breathe without messing it up. Don't think you can fake not breathing to get out of what's coming."

They leave.

Everything's blurry and topsy-turvy.

Several girls in absurdly short running shorts enter.

"You all right, Olive?" a girl from my economics class asks in a bizarre and far-off voice. I didn't know she ran cross country.

I nod. Or at least, I mean to nod.

As if I'm watching a movie, I see myself stand, look back at the faces staring at me, then run…

Out of the locker room.

Down the hall.

And out of the heavy double doors.

The world screams gray, the sun covered by thick clouds.

Chapter Six

The Run

My boots clap against the sidewalk, the laces snapping at the leather. I'm not a runner.

How I got here, I'm not sure.

I freaked out.

Took off from the athletic wing and didn't look back.

Now my legs ache and I can't breathe, but I don't care. The rain from last night left everything a muddy brown mess. The clouds still hang low in the sky and a brisk breeze reminds me it isn't always sweltering hot in this hell hole.

I round a corner, passing through a neighborhood and toward the open field. I don't know my destination.

But I know why I'm running. What and who I'm running from…

For over six years, I've endured the taunts and torture orchestrated by three girls.

"Why me?" I whisper under my breath.

At those two small words, my chest tightens and my throat closes around a knot. My eyes sting and prickle in the corners.

I let the tears fall, all hot and salty. Down my cheeks, over my lips, under my chin and neck.

The concrete beneath my feet morphs from cement to muddy, dry grass and my boots sink in as I enter the open field. I slow my pace, knowing I'll have to stop soon for fear of a collapsed lung or two. My eyes search the space. The open field isn't open, but full of trucks and workers setting up tents and rides. To my right, I spot the infamous corn maze, all fenced in to protect it from intruders, but it'll come down this evening—opening night.

I slow to a quick walk and stride right up to the fence. When I go to wipe the sweat and tears from my eyes, a bit of red catches my sight. Yet another reminder of earlier and a creepy preview of what, without a doubt, awaits me still. Wiping my hand clean, I shudder. It had been so real. Leaning forward against the portable chain-linked barrier, trying to catch my breath, I see movement in the maze.

From where I stand, it's a thick golden wall of leaves and dried corn, but if I squint, I can see several men swerving in and out, clearing the paths of debris and trimming the stalks. Oh, how I'd love to get myself lost in there right now. Just hide in some corner, pull the stalks down over me like a blanket, and curl up where no one would ever find me. I'd stay there for days, weeks, months. Hidden.

"Hey!" A low voice shouts. I jump at the noise. "You can't be here!"

I back away from the fence and turn. A mammoth of a man stands before me. Easily over six feet tall, he's thick with strength; not muscled like a bodybuilder, but I have no doubt he could uproot a tree. His head is shaved and the side of his neck is an old canvas of blurred tattoos. Half his face is hidden beneath an unruly dark, wiry beard.

"Well, go on now. Come back tonight when we're open." His beard moves along his gruff words as one puff of hair, and he tosses something at me. The gold disc flashes once and lands at my feet. I pick it up. A doubloon.

Unable to pull my eyes from the mangy creature, I nod. He raises his eyebrows, nods back, and returns to his work, disappearing into the maze.

I turn, making my way toward the neighborhood, focusing on walking, forcing my legs to move one step at a time.

I don't stop until I'm home.

When I walk through the front door, the house is still, quiet. I stall in the entryway. The stained glass window casts multicolored rays past me and onto the tile floor. Hazel greets me, weaving herself around my legs. I bend down and pet her between the ears.

I make my way through our living room, the amount of beige suddenly nauseating, then I go down the hall, passing through my room, walking straight to my bathroom.

I stop.

I cry. For real this time. My face crumples into a horrible, messed-up version of myself. I wrap my arms around my middle, slide down to the floor, and ball up. The soft turquoise bathmat sticks to my wet cheek, a fake pirate coin still clutched in my hand. I whimper. Whine. Let it all out until I've got nothing left. Empty, light as a feather, I take a shower, dry off, and dress.

Hazel is on my bed in a perfect, furry, ball of warmth. I curl up next to her and shut my eyes. But there are words behind my swollen eyelids. I think they're written in Lesley's blood. Or perhaps it's only stage blood. I lean over to my side table, open my journal, and in drowsy chicken scratch, jot down two words in hot pink ink: *Just be.*

It's all I want. To just be. What did I do to deserve the wrath of Lesley Dawson? Will it ever stop? The name calling and the being held down and the horrible things those girls put me through—it's wearing on me. Ruining me.

There's only so much a person can take.

Tears flood my eyes as I tighten my arms around my knees.

Hazel's rhythmic purrs envelop and soothe me. Eventually, I drop off to sleep.

Warm breath. Against my face.

At first, I assume it's Hazel's kitty breath, but it smells too much like chocolate. I don't want to, but I pry my eyes open. Lucky's blurry face rests on my mattress, his blue eyes bulging back at me, melted chocolate caked at the corner of his mouth.

"Hey, buddy," I mumble, allowing my eyes to close again.

"O-live…" He shakes my shoulder.

I open my eyes.

"To-night's the carn-i-val!" he sings, waving the golden chocolate coin wrapper at me.

I groan. "I'm not feeling so great. Can we go tomorrow instead?"

His body falls limp as he dramatically melts to the floor.

I scoot to the edge of my bed and peer down at him. He's dressed in full-on pirate gear and rolling back and forth on the carpet, moaning.

One eye squinting open, he spots me watching him. He stops writhing. "The first night is the best night to go. All the coolest stuff is the first night! You promised!" He digs in his pocket then presents his folded fist before me. "And…" He pops his hand open. "Now I have two coins! Found this one on your bathroom floor. I think the pirate's left it for us!"

I flop back onto my bed and stare at the photos aligning my walls: trips, our old home in Oregon, parts of the Texas landscape I've found photo-worthy.

"Argh!" Lucky jumps up.

I startle.

"Look, you little sneak—" I'm about to say something mean, but I stop myself. I sigh. "You're right. I promised. We'll go tonight."

"Yes!" he yells, a huge grin stretched across his rascally face.

I glance out the window, then to the clock. It's five thirty and I can smell the faint aroma of lasagna cooking in the oven. My favorite. Though, as much as I love it, everything feels different now. Bland. Things changed this afternoon and nothing, not Lucky's grin, Hazel's soft paws, or Mom's lasagna is quite the same. I look at Lucky, who's staring at me, counting down the seconds until I say we can leave.

"We'll go right after dinner, okay?"

"Really?" He hops in the air, landing in a scissor-legged stance, and grabs my black slouchy, knit beanie from a basket on my shelf. "You can wear this hat!" He flings it my way. "It looks kinda pirate-y." And he runs from my room, shouting, "*Argh*."

Pulling the hat over my head so it flops, I can't deny it's comforting and cozy. Right now, I need all the comfort I can get. That Lucky. Bless him.

I switch on the lamp. My journal lays open beneath it. The pink words I scribbled earlier stare back at me.

Just be.

Wanting to both appease Lucky and not make a total fool of myself, I settle on a pair of black skinny's, my brown leather boots, a tunic-style top, a light jacket that fits me like a perfect hug, and my knit hat courtesy of the shrimpy rascal pirate himself.

Dad's working even later than mom had to, so it's just the three of us at dinner. Mom questions me about leaving school early. She got a message on her cell that I wasn't in sixth or seventh periods. I tell her my lunch didn't sit well and I came home early and napped. Anything stomach-related usually cuts her right off. The woman has the gag reflex of an infant.

It seems I've gotten away with it, but as I'm walking out the door, Mom asks, "Olive, what's with the hat?" It really is too hot to wear, but I feel all smushy and snuggled in. So very cozy. Or, wait. God, am I acclimating?

I turn my head back and wink. "Pirates."

She smiles.

Chapter Seven

PIRATES

Lucky and I park and walk across the field, taking the same path I ran this afternoon. What was a barren pasture with a pile of chaos in the middle of it has been transformed into a glowing, flashing, caramel-corn coated, pirate wonderland.

"Hurry! Let's go!" Lucky shouts, pulling me along behind him. The kid is freakishly strong and fast for an eight-year-old.

When we approach the front gates, we both slow, mouths dropping as we stare up at the bright yellow and red light-bulbed sign: *Castaway Carnival*. The metal around the bulbs is rusted, the paint peeling away.

"Genuine sign, circa 1962," the man in the ticket booth calls over to us, his voice scratched with age but with an air of gusto in regard to the old sign.

"Oh?" I reply, walking to the window. By the sight of him, he's been sitting in this booth as long, his leather hat worn and weathered, matching his speckled skin. "Two, please."

"Ten dollars."

"Is that price circa 1962?" I laugh under my breath.

"Ha-ha!" He guffaws, humoring me as if it's the first time he's heard that joke.

I hand him the money.

He gives us the tickets, glancing up at me, dark, wrinkled skin hanging under his eyes like a basset hound's.

Lucky swipes his ticket out of my hand and sprints to the entrance.

"Thanks," I say, glancing back at the man in the booth.

He tips his hat.

Lucky waits for me on the other side of the gate, jumping up and down like he needs to pee and clutching his golden coin. "I wanna see the pirate ship first!"

"Settle down, buddy. We have plenty of time."

I scan for the ship—which can't be missed—and am bombarded by game booths, food stands, red-and-black striped tents, and a handful of rides, all of it dipped in pirate. Hooped earrings, beards, hats, boots, even some peg legs and lots of scallywag talk abounds. It's a Renaissance fair, pirate, and theme park mash-up.

"The ship!" Lucky spots it and is off running, his black cut-off pants swishing at his ankles over his tennis shoes.

"Lucky, wait up!" I call after him.

He slows, bouncing up and down from the knees, waving his hand out. We close in on the ship, scents of turkey legs, popcorn, and cotton candy all mixing into one heavenly, salty-sweet concoction.

The un-seaworthy monstrosity grows larger and larger until we're at the roped ramp. A woman, corset busting at the seams, long black hair setting off her very red lipstick, sits on a stool. She opens a black velvet bag for our coins. We drop them in one by one.

"Welcome aboard the *Queen Anne's Revenge*. Enter at ye own risk. And—" She leans in, chest bulging, begging to spill right over her top (I'm tempted to cover Lucky's eyes with my hand). "Mind the plank and keep on the lookout for old Blackbeard himself!" she warns us in a bad British accent.

"Cool," Lucky whispers as we walk past.

"Thanks," I say.

She nods.

As we head up the ramp and into the ship, I'm impressed at the attention to detail. I'd expected it to be pieced-together plastic and cardboard, but the thing somehow feels authentic. Metal cannons line the sides and the wood creaks under our feet as we walk. We bump shoulders with other carnival-goers who are in just as much awe. Lucky hasn't uttered a word, a feat in itself.

After we explore every room, hatch, and galley, we reach a black door with a crude painting on it: a horned skeleton holding an hourglass in one hand and pointing a spear at what looks to be a bleeding heart with his other. The wood across the top of the door has the name, *Captain Blackbeard* carved into it.

Lucky puts his hand on the ornate brass door handle, but hesitates.

"We don't have to go in, buddy."

"I know. I want to. I just think we should knock first. You know, to…be polite."

"Ah, of course." I nudge my head toward the door. "Go ahead."

His pale knuckles barely make a sound against the thick door.

"Enter if ye dare!" booms a voice from the other side like clockwork.

Lucky peers up at me, then opens the door.

Before us sits Blackbeard. He's behind a desk, piles of gold towering all around him. The room is rustic but fancy, all wood and plush carpet and candlelight. Books and maps adorn the walls and cover the desk. Blackbeard holds a large compass in his hand. He stares back at us and… Wait, I recognize old Blackbeard. We met a few hours ago, in the field. He winks at me, confirming it. I flush.

"What brings ye scallywags to Blackbeard's personal

quarters?" he grunts.

"We just wanted to see your room, Captain Blackbeard." Lucky's voice—bless him—is sweet yet confident.

"Aye. Well, come closer. All young pirates who find me be deserving of gold doubloons."

Lucky stares up at me and smiles.

I stay at the door as he marches up to the pirate. Blackbeard picks up a handful of coins and dumps them into Lucky's small hands. "Share with ye sister now."

"Oh yes, sir. Thank you, Captain." Lucky turns on his heels and I'm witnessing a new obsession developing in Lucky's smile—spy gear traded out for swords and maps and eye patches.

We make our way out of the ship, Lucky's pants jingling, my back jeans pockets overflowing with doubloons. He insisted I take half or "Captain Blackbeard would know because he's magic." How could I argue?

It doesn't take long for the kid to realize the coins not only grant access onto the ship and into the maze, but also buy food and games. Two hours, one cotton candy, two hot dogs, two sodas, countless ring toss attempts, and one stuffed parrot later, only a single, lonely doubloon rests in my back pocket. I pull it out. "Last one, bud. What's it gonna be?"

Lucky looks up at me, large parrot tucked under one arm, his eyes glazed over and coming off his cotton candy high. "You can have it. I'm ready to go home now."

I finally broke him.

"You sure?"

He nods in slow motion, a line of ketchup dried under his bottom lip.

"All right, let's go, then." I shove the coin away.

Several steps toward the exit, I notice he's fallen behind. I turn around. "Lucky, what are you—"

He's stopped dead, staring at the entrance to the maze, the corn stalks so tall they'd easily tower over my head. I can only imagine they seem like skyscrapers to him.

I walk back and stand next to him.

"Can we go in?" he whispers, not sounding so sure.

"Well, we only have one coin, so you'd be on your own. Cool?"

I hear him swallow. "No." But he walks closer.

I follow.

He steps to the side of the entrance, pushing his head between two stalks. "It's dark."

"Can be pitch black in some spots. That's why we give you one of these." The same leathery man who took our tickets sits next to the entrance on a stool, holding up a lantern that flickers as if there's a real flame but is obviously battery powered. "You going through?"

"No, just checking it out. Maybe next year, right, buddy?"

I look down at Lucky.

He stares up at me. "Can we go home now?"

"Of course."

He makes it halfway to the car. I carry him the other half, and he's asleep the minute I put the car into drive, parrot pushed against his cheek and the window.

Chapter Eight

THE MAZE

For the third time in one day, I make my way across the field toward the maze. It's cooler now, that storm from earlier returning for another round.

Once again, the bright carnival lights are overhead, creepier now that it's completely dark out. I walk up to the booth.

"Forget something?" the leathery ticket man asks, pushing a newspaper away and removing a pair of glasses then folding them into his breast pocket.

"No, just came back to meet a friend." I give him a five-dollar bill.

"Mmm-hmm. Well, you've got a coupla hours till closing." He hands me my ticket.

"Thanks," I say.

Again, he tips his hat. He's creepier in the dark, too.

I enter through the gate and there are more people here than I'd expected—the late-night crowd, hardly anyone under the age of twelve. Cliques of guys and girls checking each other out, couples, groups, older kids with their parents…it's a mixed bag and things are hopping.

When I arrive at the maze, it's deserted. No line. No old man. In the solitary chair is a handwritten cardboard sign that reads: *Be back in five* in black marker.

I check my phone. T and I had agreed to meet here, but I'm fifteen minutes early, so I decide to grab a soda.

I take all of three steps and a familiar, shrill laugh slinks up my spine.

"Well, well, look who's here!" Lesley says.

I glance over my shoulder to see the Trio standing firing-squad style. They're all carrying lattes and wearing fingerless gloves, despite that it can't be below sixty-five degrees.

Lesley's nose has grown angrier since the locker room. A purple bruise has bloomed across the bridge and under one eye. The corner of my mouth inches upward.

I turn around and swiftly walk away like buying a soda is my one and only goal in life. I'm not doing this. Not here.

"Olive! Wait!" Lesley calls.

I walk faster.

They stampede and are on top of me within seconds.

Three pairs of hands drag me to the ground.

I try to yell for help, but a palm smacks my face, covering my mouth. It smells like mocha.

"You pushed it too far today, McGaggy. I told you I'd get you," Lesley seethes.

I shake my head, screaming into Hannah's hand, my voice muffled by her stupid, knit glove.

Lesley laughs and then that sneer curls the sides of her lips right up toward her eyes.

"Dillon. Clippers," Lesley demands like a doctor in surgery.

A small black machine with sharp silver teeth flashes past my eyes.

Kicking my legs as hard as I can, digging my heels into the dirt, and pulling my wrists back, I try to escape their grip, try to get away. But they've got this perfected. I can't move.

This is happening. Here. Now.

"Your curls are getting a little unruly, *Olive*. Let me help you out." Lesley winks and then raises the clippers.

She flips the switch.

The quiet hum buzzes in my ear like a hundred angry wasps.

Dillon grabs a thick chunk of my hair, just above my ear, and holds it up for Lesley.

Again, I shake my head from side to side, pulling the hair out of Dillon's hands.

"Uh, uh, uh. You move, I'm slicing your fucking ear off."

I stop. Dead still. Because I believe her.

My heart pounds against my chest as I hold my breath.

A group of carnival-goers laughs in the distance. But they're too far... Too distracted... Too much carnival noise booms between us.

"Hurry!" Dillon says, glancing around.

"Come on," Hannah adds.

The thick, long wavy section of hair is pulled away from my face. It tugs at my temple.

Lesley grips the clippers and then brings them to my head. *Zzzt. Zzzt. Zzzt.*

The wasp has its way and wins.

Beneath Hannah's mocha hand, a whimper escapes my lips.

The switch clicks off and the buzzing stops.

Lesley puts her mouth to my ear. "Don't you EVER touch me again. Because I promise you"—she clenches her teeth—"it'll only get worse." She punctuates her threat with a kiss to my ear.

They let go of me.

I stand up on my knees, biting back tears and hate and everything that's built up all these years.

I was wrong. The bomb isn't in the reaction my parents might have. It's inside of me.

Lesley throws the cut tendril of hair. I catch it against my chest.

Staring down at the clump of auburn, I touch the side of my head. Where the hair should be, it's all stubble. Rough. My scalp right there beneath my fingertips.

The bomb goes off.

I run straight toward Lesley and push her so she stumbles backward.

Her eyes go wide.

Shit.

She bounds back toward me.

I search for an escape route, but my only option is the maze.

I run straight for it.

"Olive!" I hear Tawny call, but she's far away. Too far to save me. Too far to do anything.

Without hesitating, I grab a lantern, scale the closed gate, and take off.

I hear Lesley follow, but it sounds like she trips on her way over.

Not a thought as to where I'm going—except that I've got to lose her—I sprint through the maze, curving here, turning around there, hitting dead ends only to flip around and double back.

Making my way deeper and deeper into the stalks, I notice things grow quiet. I can no longer hear Lesley's footsteps crunching fallen leaves. I risk slowing down to catch my breath.

Everything appears the same—all tall stalks of corn and dirt paths. It's the maze, me, and the night sky above. The moon is a perfect crescent smiling down on me, half covered by clouds. The wind picks up, shaking the dried stalks that surround me. They jingle and whisper and hiss all at once. Pulling my hat down over my ears, the breeze licks along the path, kicking corn husks and leaves into my face.

I hold the lantern out in front of me. It's pitch black except for the six inches of light the sad thing provides. The blowing leaves have grown so loud I can barely make out sounds from the carnival: muffled voices, muted music, the smells barely sticking in the air, now overpowered by the earthy scent of plants and dirt.

Rounding the corner, I risk a glance back to be sure I've

truly lost her—

I hit a wall and fall back onto my butt.

It's Lesley.

She sneers.

I glance to my right and spot a low tunnel in the corn where the stalks are separated and bowed above the ground.

I chuck the lantern at Lesley but don't wait around to see if it hits her.

Bounding into the tunnel, I scurry like a small animal along the dirt. It's pitch black, but I keep going, hoping beyond hope this is a magic wormhole out of here.

I don't hear Lesley behind me but don't dare assume she isn't.

Speed-crawling, dried corn husks rustling beneath my knees, I think I see something ahead, a black hole that must lead back to the path or, *please*, the exit.

I scoot out under the tube of stalks as fast as I entered it.

Standing, brushing off my hands and knees, readying to resume sprinting, I stop. A bird sings loudly above me. Something scurries from a branch. The bird squawks.

I look up.

A thick canopy of trees towers over me. But there are no trees in this field, only grass, cornstalks, a carnival. Taking a step to the right, I catch a bright light peeking through a break in the leaves.

The moon stares down on me as a perfect silver circle in a cloudless sky.

Chapter Nine

THE MOON

Wait.

I spin in a circle.

No corn.

No stalks.

No carnival sounds or smells or lights. All I see are shadows, silhouettes of trees against the dark sky. And the moon? It's no longer a crescent. Somehow, it blew up into a bright bulb.

I turn around and glance back. I try to gain my bearings because I've obviously gotten myself lost.

But there's nothing. Only more trees. A large boulder. I touch it to make sure it's real. My hand shakes as I graze the top with one finger, careful, as if it might burst like a bubble. It doesn't. The rock is smooth, covered in soft, slimy moss. I jerk my hand away.

It can't be.

A far-off whimpering sends a shiver down the back of my neck.

But I recognize the voice. It's mine.

I spin away from the boulder. My heart beats and beats, threatening to jump out of my throat and run for its life.

"Okay. It's okay," I whisper, swallowing back the hyperventilation monster I know is on the other side of my words. There's got to be an explanation. It's some kind of illusion.

But the sky…

Again, I stare up between the trees.

I fall to my knees.

Pulling my eyes from the sky to my surroundings, I take things in. I'm in a moon-lit, dense forest boxed in by trees and plants and god knows what else.

I listen: birds, bugs, and…water?

A damp, cool breeze brushes past my face, dousing me with aromas of the ocean and honeysuckles. But there is no ocean in Hillings. We're lucky to have a pond people like to call a lake. Having lived in Oregon most of my life, the difference between sea-smell and pond-smell is like fresh pine and those blasphemous, tree-shaped car air fresheners.

All of that aside, I stand, determined to find my way out, convinced that this must be a dream or hallucination or an extravagant Castaway Carnival prank. I walk forward, but instead of cornstalks bowing around me, I now have branches waving and stooping above, as if the tunnel from the maze only grew and morphed.

I raise my eyes to the sky. The full moon glares down at me through blowing leaves like a large, silver eyeball.

Something catches my foot.

I trip and fall. Tumble. Twist. My ankles become more tangled in the "something," then I hit the rocky ground with the side of my head.

Hot pain spreads from my temple to my ear to my face. Once it hits my eyes, the forest spins upside-down like a carnival ride. The strange, foreign world goes fuzzy, then flickers out like an old, crappy battery-operated lantern.

"Where do you think she's from?" A boy's voice, masked with a barely there southern drawl, creeps in through my ears, stirring the fuzzy into froth.

I chance a tiny peek through dim light and the dark wisps of my eyelashes.

A fire. Dancing shadows on earthy walls. Four figures huddled into a circle: a boy with glasses, an older boy with nose and lip piercings that reflect the fire, a girl with unruly red hair, and another guy, his dark hair carelessly a mess, who wears a black patch over one eye. Something springs deep in my gut when I search him further. When his good eye focuses right on me, the spring in my stomach flings to my throat and I squeeze my eyes closed.

"She's probably from the caves," Lip Ring Guy says, his tone undeniably pissed. "I'll bet my share of pork she's a spy."

"She's quite pretty." The girl, British accent lacing her gentle voice, breaks in.

"All right. Where'd you find her again?" Eye Patch Guy asks, his voice just as low as Lip Ring Boy's but softer and more commanding.

"We were doing the nightly perimeter check, just up the ridge, and we found her, out cold and caught up in one of the pig traps. Jude helped me — " the boy with glasses answers, but is interrupted by the one with the lip ring.

"Yeah." He laughs. "I helped all right. After you begged me and threatened to do it on your own, which would have been an epic disaster. Dammit, Lewis!" There's a pause and a crash like he's thrown something. "There's no telling who she is or where she's from."

The two argue over me and the noise shoots into the side of my head like jagged metal. I don't mean to, but I moan in pain.

The room goes silent.

I hold my breath.

The fire crackles.

My arms and legs are tied with rope and I'm lying atop a soft, furry mat on the floor.

Something pokes me in the shoulder.

I pry my eyes half open.

Eye Patch Guy stands over me, pointing a long, carved stick at my neck.

"Who are you? Where are you from?" He jabs me with each question, the stick barely making contact, but just enough that I know it's sharp.

I open my eyes fully. Behind him, stand the others. They all stare at me.

I focus back to Eye Patch Guy. The black leather over his eye is so worn and weathered it could be a hundred years old. His face is filthy and his dark, coarsely cut hair falls onto his forehead, but is short, nearly to the scalp over his ears. His face is stern, his jaw tight, but there's something else there. Kindness? A bit of sympathy, I think? Despite the weapon pointed at what is probably a main artery in my neck, my stomach does that springy thing.

"Well? Can you speak?" He nudges the stick so the point makes contact with my skin.

"I—" I cough, clearing a knot of emotion and confusion and fear. "My name is Olive. I'm from Texas."

"Oh! Same as you, Will. You and Charlie and Duke…" The girl widens her eyes.

Eye Patch Guy—Will—yanks the stick away from my neck.

"*That's what I said to Jude!* I found her near *your* place!" The boy with glasses throws his hands up in surrender to Will who seems to be in charge.

"*Lewis*," the girl whispers his name under her breath to shush him.

Lewis is younger, though nearly as tall as the other two boys, but he's quite wiry, his pointed features only exaggerating it.

"My God, man! She could be lying!" Lip Ring Guy—Jude, I'm assuming, adding it to the short list in my mind—is muscular, his strength showing through his very worn T-shirt, a thick neck tattoo peeking out of the top. He pushes through the small crowd, wielding a shorter version of the spear. It's in my face before I can flinch. "Who are you? What's your business on this side of the island?"

"I…I don't know." My voice quivers. I'm going to cry. The knot in my throat burns and my breathing is uneven and wheezy. "I was running through the maze and—"

"And you ended up here." Will pushes Jude aside.

I nod, several tears escaping and streaming down my cheeks.

"Untie her."

"What?" Jude looks from Will to me and back.

"*Untie* her," he repeats through clenched teeth.

Lewis rushes to free my wrists, Jude reluctantly doing the same at my feet, then moving away when he's done. Lingering to help me sit up, Lewis's face is covered in a thin layer of grime and his hair is dusty brown and roughly cut in a similar fashion to Will's. "I'm Lewis. That's Will." He points. "Jude and Matilda—"

"*Tilly*," she corrects him, forehead furrowed, eyes not leaving mine.

"Sorry, that's *Tilly*." He wiggles his fingers at her. "Welcome to the island." Lewis straightens his shoulders like he's expecting a reaction. Like this is some sort of big announcement. Like this is really happening.

Nervously, I smile at all of them, unsure how to respond. How does one react to a situation when they can't tell if they're dreaming, awake, or caught in some bizarre hallucination. Is this what limbo is? Did Lesley finally do me in for good?

Jude snorts and strides away, leaving the room without glancing back.

"I get your pork!" Lewis shouts after him, then motions to me. "Don't let him get to you. He gets cranky when he's tired."

"All right, let's give her some space," Will says, pulling Lewis away from me.

My head is spinning. I take a deep breath and more intently inspect the room. The floor is pebbly sand but has been covered with large woven mats. The walls and ceiling are smooth, deeply grained wood, shadows from the fire reflecting on them like dancing figures. It's a decent-size space and other areas branch off this one through arched openings. The stone fire pit stands as a centerpiece and there's a sort of ventilation system built above it—a hole in the wall with a large tube of what looks like bamboo going through it and extending into a makeshift cone over the fire.

Several torches hang along the walls, which are barren save one section. It's covered with black chalky drawings, tic-tack-toe hashes, and what appears to be a calendar and a list. Glancing from wall to wall, I don't see a door.

My breath hitches.

Will stares over, piercing me with his one good—and very green—eye. The color is like sage, but darker and a touch brighter all at once.

"The door's hidden and in a different room." He exhales, shrugging. "We won't keep you here. If you want to leave, you're free to go—"

I stand and my head swims, stars polka-dotting the space before me. I sway. My knees buckle. I attempt to grab the wall, but miss, and instead land within a strong embrace. Warmth.

When the stars clear, Will stares back at me. He's close. *Close*, close. I'm not sure if I'm about to hyperventilate, scream, or faint, but I don't dare move.

"Before you go," he says, voice low, inexplicably calm compared to how my heart pounds inside my chest. "I should explain a few things."

Chapter Ten

LUCKY 13

I agree to hear Will out and put off my escape attempts until I've gotten the details and I can stand without buckling under my own weight.

Tilly brings me a cup of tea that tastes more like dirt and an ice-cold clump of moss for the wound on my head, which she examines and explains is only a bump and a small scratch.

My shoulders instantly soften and, as if beyond my control, my body leans back against the wall. I'm not sure if it's the moss or the tea, but my injury numbs and a sudden calm overtakes me.

Will sits cross-legged in front of me, barefoot, his worn jeans frayed around his ankles. He's wearing a faded black T-shirt that's been stitched up in several places. Lewis and Tilly sit a little behind and to each side of Will.

I stare back at them, glance toward the fire, then follow the shadows up onto the ceiling, mesmerized by their silky movements. A loud sigh slips from between my lips as I bring my attention back to Will, my eyelids as heavy as rocks.

He glares at Tilly. "How much moon root is in that?"

She straightens her shoulders, one eyebrow cocked up. "What? Don't question the Brit about the art of tea-making, thank you very much." She smooths her stained and tattered dress. It's old-fashioned and similar to a porcelain doll that's somewhere in the depths of my closet.

"Yes, but we need her to at least be coherent, so—"

"There's not that much," Tilly snaps, her crooked strawberry bangs swaying with the jerkiness of her words.

"Okay." Will looks to me. "Sip slowly."

I nod, the cup at my mouth. I only allow the liquid to splash my lips then pull it away.

Will runs his hands through his dark hair, leaving it sticking up in places. His jaw keeps flexing.

Despite the heavy relaxation of my body and mind, my heart races in anticipation.

"We should get on with it before the Littles wake," Tilly breaks in, her voice both sarcastic and sing-song.

Will clears his throat, shooting her another look.

"Just a thought," she murmurs under her breath, winking at me.

"I'm going to give you a speech like the one I gave Charlie, who you'll meet in the morning. He joined us most recently."

Tilly's eyes dart to a nearby doorway while Lewis chews a fingernail.

Will takes a deep breath and continues. "You're on an island. We call it the island because none of us ever planned to be here long enough to name it. We don't know what ocean surrounds us. We don't know if there are other islands nearby, but none can be seen from the highest point and on the clearest day." He exhales. "You are the four—I mean—" Will eyes Tilly. "The thirteenth person on this island—"

"But how?" I interrupt.

"No questions until I'm finished." He puts one hand up. "It'll make more sense to give you all of the details first."

I answer by taking a gulp of tea, cringing at the bitterness as it bites its way down my throat.

"Six of us live in this cave-tree. I found it years ago after I arrived. It's several hollowed tree trunks that have grown together to form a shelter. It keeps us dry and warm at night and cool during the hot days. We've found ways to make it livable. Using bamboo, we collect rain water for drinking and ventilate our fire, among other things." He pinches his brow. "You following all of this?"

I nod, taking another sip, the tea beginning to taste more appealing in a medicinal sort of way.

"Good. As I was saying, there are six of us here: Tilly and Lewis." He tilts his head to each side.

Tilly scoots forward. "I'm sixteen, from Sheffield, England, 1940."

I choke on my tea. "What?" I manage between coughing and spurting. "Did you say 1940?"

She smiles back at me the way I smile at Lucky when I'm about to tell him Mom says he can't have dessert. Gently. Timidly. "I know it's alarming. Just listen, okay?"

I say "okay," but all I can think is, *What's happening?*

Lewis picks back up like they've given this speech before. "I'm fifteen, from Memphis, Tennessee, '53."

I force myself to sit up straighter. "*Nineteen fifty-three.* Like, the year."

"Uh-huh."

Will lightly squeezes Lewis's shoulder. "And I'm eighteen. Hillings, Texas. 1962." He watches me intently.

I can't speak because I know I must be on a reality show or something. Finally, after I don't know how long, I find words. "This is a joke, right?" I glance around the cave. "Am I on camera?"

Will raises an eyebrow and shakes his head no.

Despite the calm-inducing tonic, my head and stomach spin. "Come on." I look to Tilly.

Her mouth is set into a grim, pale line.

"Really. I mean, *really*," I sort of say to Lewis, who gives me a crooked smile.

I stare back at Will. "So… You're telling me… I'm…" I can't spit the words out, my mind a mush of moss, that post-Trio anxiety slowly building in a new way—closing my throat up, speeding up my heart rate. Quickly tossing me into the throws of the monster.

Out of nowhere, Tilly shoves the tea in my face, shushing me like my mother would, urging me to drink. "Breathe. It's all right. I promise you."

I take another sip. And though her presence is comforting, her promise of "all right" doesn't calm me much.

Will scoots in closer. "I know this is a lot to take in. And, trust me, we've all been where you are. Just…try to stay with me here, okay?" He leans in even closer and despite that I'm somewhere between fainting and losing my mind, my cheeks warm at the impossibly short distance between us. "You're familiar with the Bermuda Triangle?"

"Yeah." I take in a deep breath that steadies the whirling in my head and almost turns into a yawn.

I swear I catch the corner of Will's mouth turn up a bit, and it's like he has to backtrack to remember what he was saying. "Bermuda Triangle… Think of it this way. Instead of a large triangle, it's little pockets—for you and me, a corn maze. For Tilly, a bomb shelter. For Lewis, a chain-link fence. Instead of planes and boats, it's kids that disappear." I glance from one face to the other. They all share the same sad and tired heaviness in their eyes.

"But… How? Why? Have you tried to escape?" I ask, wondering if my eyes are already showing early signs of that same burden.

Will laughs under his breath.

"Sorry." I bite at my bottom lip. "Of course you have."

"We've tried it all. Rafts—"

"They come right back." Lewis jumps in. "There's no way around it, the tides won't allow anyone past a certain point. Not on a raft. Not swimming. We found that out when Jude swore he'd swim out of here." Lewis rolls his eyes. "Pfft. The ass."

Tilly side-eyes him, swatting him on the knee.

"Olive." Will places his hand on mine and, again, my face prickles with warmth. Stupid face, this is serious! "We've done everything from sending smoke signals to nearly burning the island down to, yes, trying to swim away. The island won't allow it." Will sighs. "Another thing we've found is that there's no ticking clock. Time doesn't pass. While the sun still rises and the moon still shows itself each night, life, as we know it, is on standstill. Each of us showed up at random from our own times only to be frozen here." My eyes flick to Will's. He nods as if to confirm my doubt, to shut me down before I cry "It's a joke, right?" again.

"Also," he continues, "we were all running away from something."

"I wasn't," I say, no idea why I'm lying, suddenly protective of the truth.

Tilly and Lewis whip their heads toward Will.

"You sure about that?" he asks, a glimmer of humor itching the corners of his mouth like he doesn't believe me. Which, of course, makes me more defiant.

"Yes."

He studies me intently, working something over beneath the surface of that serious, piercing stare of his.

Tilly stands and walks to the list on the wall, picks up a piece of what must be charcoal and, under the heading, *Connections*, strikes a line through the top sentence which reads: *Running*.

Will only reacts by raking his hands through his hair.

I yawn, shutting my eyes just for a…

"Wait—" Will shouts.

I rub my eyelids and strain to keep them open.

"I said you were number thirteen, but there's only six of us here—" He pauses for breath. "Our population has been divided in half by necessity and a sort of…war."

"War?" Half asleep, I bite my tongue on the word, the

metallic bitterness of blood filling my mouth.

He nods. Tilly and Lewis's faces are serious, eyes unblinking. "I didn't come here alone. Duke followed me. He and five others live on the other side of the island. They call themselves the Panthers."

"Panthers? That's my school's mascot. Weird…"

Will stares into my eyes, so deeply my stomach not only springs but full-on flips. "It's not… Duke and I attended the same school you do, just decades apart. He was the definitive jock and wouldn't consider any other name for his group."

Then it hits me. "You don't age." I say the words more to myself as if confirming the unbelievable.

"No ticking clock."

That makes me wonder if time at home keeps going. Are my parents going to freak out tomorrow morning when they find I'm not in my bed? "What about—"

"Time at home keeps passing."

"How do you know?"

"Charlie confirmed it when he showed up last year. He knew about the maze sucking Duke and me into it decades before it took him."

My poor parents. Lucky. Oh my God…

"The war…" Will brings me back, lowering his head to mine, forcing eye contact. "The Panthers want control of the island and refuse to let up. Our last encounter with Duke cost me my left eye, but gained us these…" He stands, walks to the fire, picks something up, and comes back. "Flint. For quick and painless fire-making. And this—" He pulls a small metal bat from behind his back. "Aside from wanting control, I fear the island's worn on Duke's mind. He's… Well, he was always bad, but he's since gone mad, too. He beat me with this one too many times." Will whacks the bat against his palm, a far-off look in his eye. I can't help but wonder if there's more to the story. "So I took it from him."

"He and his group have the absurd idea we're onto figuring out how to get home and they'd like more than anything to torture it out of us."

My brain shudders awake at "torture" and I manage to sit taller despite the jelly that is my body.

Will shakes his head. "We're not, though." He laughs airily under his breath, but not in a funny way. "No one is."

We share a moment of silence where I begin to fall asleep and dream I'm rowing a boat off the island.

"Any more questions?" Will's voice yanks me from the boat and I jump. Only partially awake, I do have one question on my mind.

"What is our, I mean, your group called?"

"We're the Lions. Each must earn his place among us."

"Why…lions…?" I say through a yawn, my body slowly sliding down the wall.

"Because lions are strong, keep their families close, and are one of the few predators of panthers."

I nod. My eyes shut.

"You sleep. We'll talk more in the morning."

I mean to say "okay" or "thanks" or "good night," but only sigh in response. When I finally give in and lie down, I curl my hands beneath my head as I always do, but something's missing.

My last thought is a fleeting one: *my necklace…*

Chapter Eleven

Lion Cubs

The soft rhythm of warm breath blows like steam against my nose. I know it's either Hazel or Lucky and the dream I had was so real my head actually aches from my "stumble" in the forest. My eyelids are heavy, and as I strain to open them the fishy breath grows more sour and moist. I focus on the face before me.

Two big brown eyes stare back at me like beautiful twin cocoa truffles.

I sit up and scoot back in one quick motion.

It's a little girl with a dark halo of hair, her skin nearly the same rich brown. I take in my surroundings. I'm in a tree. A cave. A cave-tree.

It wasn't a dream.

My body shakes. I'm terrified, confused, exhausted. My stomach growls, but I can't fathom the thought of food.

The girl scuttles closer, no sense of personal space. Poised on hands and knees atop the fur where I slept, she studies me over, searching me with her eyes, repeatedly going back to my hair.

I throw my hand over the stubble above my ear.

She jerks back. Still staring at me with those eyes that remind me of Tawny's, she's sitting cross-legged, back perfectly straight. "I like her!" she shouts.

I jump at the shrill noise.

"Oh, very good. We always wait on your approval, little lightning bug," Tilly says, huddled over the fire.

The girl leans in once more. "I'm Bug," she whispers, an accent I can't place barely clutching at her words.

Bug continues staring, eyes wide. "How old are you?" I ask, cringing, my head aching from the inside out, my own words cutting between my ears.

"Seven." She sits even taller. Bug wears a patchwork dress and short pants made of leather and suede and other woven fabric all sewn together.

"Here you are." Tilly hands me a bowl. "It isn't much, but its lunch around here."

"Lunch?"

"You had a good sleep." She smiles. "Come Bug, give Olive a chance to breathe."

I wince at the sound of my name—though, I'll admit, it does have a certain ring to it with the accent.

Bug jumps up and follows Tilly.

The sight of food, as bland as it looks, triggers my appetite. It's fish and coconut and some kind of plant in a gray liquid. I eat, all of it tasting similar, having been cooked in the same pot, but with different textures. I finish every bite despite how it even tastes gray.

Lewis, wire glasses sliding down his nose, strides over, sitting next to me with his food. "It's no steak, but it'll do."

Not looking at him, I smile.

Another younger boy—Charlie?—sidles up next to us and my sacred personal space is once again challenged. Unlike Bug, who has a childish playfulness about her, Charlie seems wiser than he should. Sad. Eyes set on his bowl, he picks out a few bits of coconut with his fingers, plopping them into Lewis's bowl. Lewis doesn't flinch and keeps eating. Then, not using the spoon-like wooden utensils the rest of us have, Charlie tips the rim to his lips like a cup, and bits of fish and stringy vegetable hang down his chin. He has the same build as Lucky: scrawny, probably small for his age, with blond, overgrown, hardly brushed curls falling all over his head like a sheepdog. He, too, is barefoot and wearing a pair of black cargo pants and a T-shirt with a parrot on it that reads in faded, cracked red lettering: *Castaway Carnival*.

I drop my bowl. The half coconut shell bounces, spilling fish juice and the spoon onto the floor.

Everyone in the room stares at me, then quickly goes back to whatever they were doing like nothing happened.

I pick it up, not taking my eyes off the shirt or the boy wearing it. It's him. The boy who disappeared last year. Will had said something about it last night, but it hadn't registered. Much of that conversation was a total haze.

"Charlie. He's from the same place as you and Will and Duke," Lewis says between bites, wiping his mouth on the sleeve of his heavily stained, once button-up shirt. "He doesn't talk," he adds, looking over at Charlie.

Charlie stands, walks to a vacant corner, and squats facing the wall.

I lean in toward Lewis. "Could he ever speak?"

"We're not sure, but we think so because he talks in his sleep all the time. Will found him huddled in a ball, down by the beach, what we can only guess was days after he got here. He wasn't speaking anything but gibberish by that point." Lewis shakes his head. "Poor damn kid."

He barely finishes the sentence when Will and Jude bust through the door. They pant for breath, faces red and dirt-caked.

"Take cover!" Will yells as Jude runs full force toward Charlie, pushing him to the floor and hunching over him. Before I know it, I'm flat against the floor, too, Lewis above me.

"Hey—" I begin to say when an explosion sucks my voice away with a crack and a boom that shakes the entire cave.

The floor, the walls, the ceiling. Even my teeth chatter from the blast. My eyes strain to look up. Dirt falls down on us like a light dusting of snow. Just how strong can a cave-tree possibly be?

"They're getting closer," Will says, Bug curled on his lap, a ball of rags resembling a doll gripped at her chest. Tears fill her blank eyes as Will gently strokes her back. I follow her stare and see it's trained on Charlie, who's in his corner, mumbling and picking at his toenails.

The rest of us are scattered before Will, a captive audience.

After cleaning up the few things that fell and broke and sweeping the dirt that rained from the ceiling during the blast, we're once again in the common room. It's cool and dark, aside from the firelight from the few torches.

Now that the literal dust has settled, the weight of what just happened hits me full force. A bomb! A freaking bomb just went off. My hands are shaking and my shoulders are tremoring and my throat is as dry as sand and my breathing, as much as I try to keep it low and calm, is growing closer and closer to wheezing.

Will, his one good eye a shade darker than before, somehow stares at each of us. "Jude and I were doing a perimeter check when we heard the bomb flying through the air, whistling down toward us like a dying bird."

I jump under my skin, remembering the blast. The way it shook the floor beneath my knees.

Bug gazes up at Will, tracing his eye patch, black dirt stuck under her fingernails. He smiles down at her.

I take a deep breath and swallow to wet my throat. "What is it? Where did they get a bomb?" I need answers. Now. Everyone looks at me. I shrink under my skin. Was I supposed to request permission before speaking or something?

Will answers. "A type of island-made bomb—coconut shells filled with an explosive. We have no idea how they're doing it, what they're using to make them. The one's we've found have only been remnants, burned to bits."

I gasp for breath, releasing a long wheeze I hope no one else notices. "So we're sitting ducks?"

"Until we find a way to counter the attacks. But, to our advantage, we're hidden. To their advantage, they've got the high ground, the mountain caves."

I'm trying to get a feel for all of this, a mind's eye layout of the land. Partly to distract my nerves and partly to make some sort of sense out of everything, I close my eyes. Inside my head, I draw a map based on what I've been told.

Jude loudly clears his throat. I open my eyes to find he's striding toward Will. "Now that we've got an extra mouth to feed"—he eyes me—"we're extra low on rations. I'm going for water and food. Lewis?"

"Yep!" Lewis jumps up, brushing the sand off his pants, and then gives me a small smile.

They turn to leave without another word.

"Take weapons along!" Will shouts after them. "And stay near cover."

Jude glances over his shoulder. "Done and done."

Will stares down at me, but speaks to Tilly. "Do you mind holding down the fort? It's time I gave Olive the grand tour."

"'Course," she says it in a distracted way, her eyes gazing in the direction Lewis and Jude just went. But she pulls herself out of it, smooths what's left of her cardigan, and smiles a composed smile at Will, then me.

When I start to get up, I'm distracted by my hands, the dirt already caked under my nails, but mostly how they shake all on their own, as if they know something I don't.

Chapter Twelve

As I follow Will through the cave-tree, I try my best to regain control of my anxiety. To rein in my instinct to either flee or slap myself across the face and wake up.

He's casual as he guides me, showing me what's what, as if we didn't all nearly just get blown to bits.

The first room we walk through is the "kitchen." Makeshift bowls, a rough-edged metal pot made from something that must have washed up on the beach, carved utensils, and rags torn from pieces of clothing fill one corner of the space. The rain collecting system is here, as well, water dripping into a hollowed and sanded tree trunk. It's shiny, smooth. I stop to touch the outside of it. It's hard like plastic. When I pull away, my fingers are still shaking. Will notices. I shove my hands into my pockets.

He ignores it. "Many, *many* coats of bee's wax and coconut oil and Lewis finally found something that would seal the wood, keep from soaking up the water. Another one of his ingenious inventions."

"That's amazing."

"Yeah, well, we have a lot of time on our hands." It would be funny if it wasn't so true.

He walks on.

The next room is covered in charcoal drawings and something resembling paint, with two furs on the floor. "Charlie and Bug's room," Will says.

"The fur?" I ask, remembering how surprisingly soft and warm and welcoming my sleep mat was last night.

"Wild sheep. They're assholes, but they provide soft bedding and good meat."

"Huh." Asshole sheep?

"We also have chickens and pigs running rampant, along with fish, fruit, roots, and greens. I suppose if one is to be stranded on a secluded island, this one isn't so horrible — aside from our enemies on the other side, that is." This time, when his mouth turns upward, it's less restrained, more real.

I find myself mesmerized by how this smile of his is genuine, how my own mouth is lured into following along, when, as if he catches himself, his crooked grin disappears and I force my lips to stop short.

Will takes me through two more rooms. The first is another bedroom, the second is full of things ranging from shells and firewood to a bizarre collection of material items, my purse and jacket among them.

I run over, digging through my bag for my cell phone. Once I find it, I hold down the power button. "Come on... Come on..."

Will walks up behind me. "It's no use." With his breath on the back of my neck I simultaneously jump and shiver then turn and face him. "Charlie had one, too. It ended up more useful pulled apart and re-purposed as a game for him and Bug to play."

He's right. My phone's totally dead. I toss it back into my bag and spot some gum. My mouth goes dry. I pull out the pack.

Will's eye widen. "Whoa!" he shouts, then catches himself. "I mean, I can't believe Jude didn't rummage through your things and swipe that."

I pop a piece into my mouth, then tilt the pack his direction. "You?"

"Only if you have some to spare."

"It's a full pack. Here." I wave a piece at him.

He hesitates, then takes the stick. "Thanks." Will smiles, shoving it into in his mouth. "You'd better hide that if you want it to last. If found, it'll be up for grabs and gone before you know it."

I shoot him a questioning glance.

"Nothing's sacred here. We share everything out of necessity and survival. That leather jacket of yours? If you're asked to stay, and accept, it'll be made into something else — shoes maybe, a wrap for the handle of a spear. Everything is put to best possible use."

"Makes sense," I say. Will creases his brow. "What?"

"Sorry, that's just not the response I expected. Tilly cried for days when we had to use her shawl for fishing."

"It's just a jacket." I pause, a memory hitting me. "Hey! Is that where my necklace ended up? Re-purposed?" If they even...

"Not that I'm aware of, sorry. I'll ask around, but it's probably gone."

"Maybe it broke off when I fell." Grazing my fingers along my neck where it used to hang, I add, "It's okay." I try to convince myself it's just a necklace like I did my jacket, but it's not as easy. I never take it off. It's like a piece of me. A piece of my past that I was able to carry with me.

He stares for a minute, that hint of a crooked grin teasing at his lips, then peers down at the floor, clearing his throat. "The front door."

I search the space but see nothing resembling a door. The only indication this might be the way out is the row of shoes sitting along the wall, my boots included.

Will bends to his knees and brushes some sand away to reveal a metal ring. He pulls it, lifting a wood-planked door that leads into a dark tunnel.

As he stands, a grin forms on his face, as if to say, *See? You weren't trapped.* That's when I realize how tall he is—six three, maybe? He makes his way to the shoes and slips on a pair of over-worn black lace-up boots, rolling his pants to the tops. I follow his lead and reach for mine, my beanie balled inside. I remove it and slide the boots on. I reach up and feel the stubble above my ear and lift the hat to my head.

"You won't want that. It's a hot one out there." My fingers freeze, grazing the rough nearly bald spot. He adds, "Appearances don't matter here." And he taps his eye patch.

I nod, exhaling, folding my beanie in half and shoving it into my back pocket.

"Shall we?" Will asks.

"I think so."

"We have to crawl. It's a tunnel, but it won't take you home, just into the forest." He laughs under his breath then clears his throat. "Follow me."

Will lifts the door and the space is just wide enough to squeeze through on hands and knees. It's a slight descent and then we climb upward and through an identical door. There's a large-leafed branch above us. Will pushes it aside and helps me up out of the hole, his hands warm, coarse. "You all right?"

"I'm…fine…" I'm taken by the daytime version of the forest. The sounds of bugs and birds and waves mingle nearby as the scents of flowers and earth and salty moisture fill the air. Everything is bright and vivid, the colors so brilliant it's blinding.

I spin in a circle, to find we're surrounded by large bushes and several mossy boulders, the door to the cave-tree truly hidden. I make my way back around to Will. He's staring at me, taking me in, looking through me, a confused grin on his face.

I stop spinning, completing the circle. "What?"

He snaps out of it, blinking several times. "Huh? Oh, it's nothing."

"Seriously, what?" I run my fingers over the shaved side of my head, suddenly self-conscious, and notice my hands aren't shaking anymore.

"It's just... Duke and I were the first ones here, and I've seen or heard most everyone's first days on this island. But you're incredibly calm considering the circumstances. It's like...like..." He just shakes his head.

"Like?"

He laughs under his breath. "Like you're okay about being here. Like you're on vacation. Not as if you've been taken from everything you know and are now stuck on a secluded island and might never get home."

Taken aback by his words, I think on them, on the situation. My throat tightens and tears well up. "No. I don't feel that way at all. I have a little brother back home, parents who love me, the best friend in the world, a cat..." Now I'm crying. "But I'm good at keeping things in. At hiding. I'm good at staying in denial. So, yeah, I'm looking around, amazed by the beauty, but I'm not totally convinced it isn't a dream. And on the inside? I'm *definitely* freaking out." I inhale a shaky breath, surprised by the first truth I've spoken in longer than I can remember.

Will, still staring, confused grin gone, puffs his cheeks out then back in. "Good." I glare at him, wiping my face with my fists, noting how my fingers are all tremor-y again. "All of that? It's normal. You were beginning to freak *me* out." And he walks away.

For hours we explore the island, collecting tree fruit, roots, and anything else of use along the way. Will carries it all in a brown net-like bag—what I assume was part of Tilly's shawl.

The forest goes on forever until finally the sound of waves crashing along a shore grows louder and truer.

We pass through a line of palm trees and collide with sand. The rocky beach leads to an ocean that pitches and sways and endlessly expands until it meets the sky at the horizon, blue on blue. The island literally drops off into nothingness.

The wind whips up off the water and hits me, giving me a slap in the face that takes my breath away.

I gasp.

This is real. I'm on an island. Stuck with a bunch of kids and teenagers. In the middle of a screwed-up, real-life, Lord-of-the-Flies situation.

What now?

Frantic, my internal freak out works its way out. I search for a place to run to or from. There's nothing: water, sand, rocks, the forest behind us, a mountain in the distance, then more beach, nothing but water in all directions until the blues meet at the edge of the earth. If I'm even still on earth.

I'm hyperventilating and don't realize it until I'm on my knees, the warm sand radiating through my jeans.

"Huh…hhh…hhhh…" My breath wheezes as it works too hard to go in and out.

"Olive?"

"Don't say it. Not now." I gasp for breath. "I wouldn't be here if it wasn't for that damn name."

"What?"

I don't want to answer and I can't on account of the rising hyperventilation—monster it is—taking over.

"It'll be all right. Slow down. Breathe." Will moves closer and rubs my back. Despite the numbness taking over my body, I can feel his warmth and am torn between curling up right there on the beach and taking off.

In the end, the choice is easy.

I stand. Then run. It's like I'm floating—no feeling in my feet—all numbness. Behind me, Will calls, "Wait! Olive! You don't know where you're going!" Then I hear, "Shit—" and footsteps after me.

But everything's clear. I do know where to go. "I'm going

to find that boulder—" I suck in shallow breath. "The…hhh…maze."

"It's no use. We've tried everything. It doesn't work! Wait!"

But I'm not listening because it *has* to work. It's the only way. If it got me in, it'll get me back out.

I run until my body, my mind, and, mostly, my lungs give up. Because, problem is, Will's right. I don't know how to find it.

I stop.

Will stops.

Bent at the waist, hands on my knees, I cough and spew, trying to catch my breath. The hyperventilation has passed, but my insistence on sprinting like I'm a track star when my lungs and legs have no business running, has taken its toll.

I look up.

Will isn't fazed. At some point he took off his shirt and now stands with his hands on his hips, chest rising and falling, barely winded. His abs flex with each effortless breath. "Get it out of your system?"

It's when my stomach springs that I realize I'm staring at his body. I quickly glance away and completely ignore his question. "Take me there."

"I told you. It's no use."

"Please," I whimper. Tears race down my face.

Tucking his T-shirt into the back of his pants, Will walks in another direction.

"Where are you going?"

"I'm taking you. But don't say I didn't warn you."

With Will now leading the way, I watch his suntanned back, the sweat beading at his shoulders and slowly, one by one, how the beads roll down the center crease. I'm in a daze or a haze or a trance because all I see is his back, his muscles contracting and tightening with each step, and, like magic, we're there.

The mossy boulder stands before us and, I swear, it mocks

me in all its ordinary, commonplace glory.

Will stops, then steps back. My forehead creased, I glare at him, then at the boulder.

"You need some time, but I won't be far. Call if you need me or when you're ready to go back to the cave-tree."

I nod.

He sighs, gives me a look I can't decipher as annoyance or concern, then he leaves.

I want to call after him. So much so I can taste his name on my tongue. But I don't. Instead, I watch as he walks away until he disappears behind the trees.

Chapter Thirteen

The Boulder

With one hand resting on my hip, the other holding my forehead, fingertips squeezing my temples, I stare at the boulder. Then I breathe out and gaze up toward the sky. It's peaceful here, with the sun already setting behind the sharp, pointed mountain where bombs come from. My throat burns, and I'm still working to catch my breath from the hyperventilation and running. I've run more in the past two days than I have my entire life. Well, physically anyway. I've been running as a means of escape and avoidance for seven years.

I shut my eyes, closing out the forest before me. I think of home, of Lucky's eyes and Tawny's turtle figurine collection, Mom and Dad sitting on their bed behind their laptops. Tears collect beneath my lids. My eyes shut yet overflowing, I slide down the boulder. Its mossy blanket pads my back, and my fingers leave tracks, green fuzz catching under my nails until I'm on the ground.

I open my eyes.

Tears spill down my cheeks, into my hair.

I stare into the forest, resting against the moss blanket until my tears dry and my lungs settle. Inhaling a long breath of fresh island air awakens me as unexpected emotions wash over me—relief and freedom. But just below is a knot of guilt coated with fear. Because I shouldn't feel anything but fear right now. I'm stuck on an island with a bunch of warring kids for Christ's sake. I have no idea how I got here and no idea how to get home.

Still…

I can't help feel my chains have been cut. As if poor, Olive McGaggy was left behind in that corn maze. No one here knows me. I let out a sigh that almost sounds alarmingly close to an airy laugh, and a smile tickles the corners of my mouth.

I glance in the direction where I exited the maze tunnel into this strange place that is half dream, half nightmare, but all reality. From dried corn stalks to moist grass to the boulder behind me in all of its unmistakable landmark splendor.

With a long sniff and a swipe of my face with my sleeve, I sit up straighter and crawl toward that place, stopping when I reach the spot where I think I entered. I poke at the air like there might be an invisible barrier, some indication there's more than nothingness. But that's all it is. Just ordinary air and space. I scoot back to the boulder.

Okay.

I was at the carnival and now I'm on an island. The island. I've gone over the many negatives and it's getting me nowhere. And I can't ignore that tiny spark of relief still warming my chest, the faintest sense of hope blooming within it. Because this island may have a lot of horrible things going for it, but there is no Trio. And there is food. Shelter. A group of kids who seem pretty cool. I've never been the outdoorsy type, but with their help, I can figure this out. And maybe I can help them, too.

Maybe, just maybe, this isn't so awful.

My body is utterly depleted and my mind, set on permanent fight or flight since arriving, isn't far behind. With thoughts of escape plans, and brainstorming, and—if it comes to it—living off the island for God knows how long, I begin to succumb to the exhaustion. Before I know it, the warm breeze, the dimming daylight, and the faint whisper of ocean waves lull me to sleep, so many *maybes* swirling around me like a giant whirlpool in the even bigger sea that threatens to swallow me whole.

Morning comes like someone clicked the spacebar and made the starry screensaver disappear. The sun burns warm and orange through my eyelids and I don't have to open my eyes to know nothing's changed. No magic door to Texas scooped me up and took me back. It hadn't all been a weird dream. It's real. As real as the sticks and leaves stuck to the side of my face. As real as it was yesterday and I can only assume just as real as tomorrow.

I open my eyes and sit up. Something falls off my shoulders. A fur. I scan the space, but there's no one to be seen. Nothing but me, the boulder…and a bowl of fresh cut coconut along with those same roots, all soaked in juice.

I lift the bowl into my lap. "Thank you," I say as if speaking to the trees.

After I eat, it's painfully obvious I haven't used the bathroom in over twenty-four hours. I haven't had much to drink, either, it all working out. But now I fear my bladder might burst. I stand, setting the fur on the ground. "Will?" I whisper like it's some huge secret. "Will?" I call louder.

"I'm here," he says, but I can't see him.

"Where?"

"Here!" He jumps from the bottom branch of a tree.

"Oh!" I gasp, hopping back a step. "Were you up there all night?"

"Best place to keep watch."

I look up into the tree, lost in how he could have possibly stayed up there for so long.

"Olive? You called me."

I pull myself away from the tree. Will is cleaner, his hair less stiff, his face no longer striped of dirt. He's beautiful, but also very real with a small scar that cuts one side of his jaw, the eye patch that covers who knows what, and his nose is the tiniest bit crooked like maybe it was broken once. He catches me staring again and my cheeks go all hot and itchy. But, as embarrassing as that is, I have bigger problems. "I… I need to… Well… You know…" My face grows even redder and I'm all stuttery.

"Yes?"

"The bathroom?" I mostly mouth the words.

His lip tugs upward into a humored half smile, but he catches himself. "Oh! My God, I can't believe I didn't… I'm so sorry."

"It's all right. I mean… I've been better, but I'm okay."

"You're really okay?" He raises his eyebrows, no doubt thinking of my freak out on the beach yesterday. We're no longer speaking of my bodily needs.

My insides barb and twist thinking of Lucky, Mom and Dad, Tawny. But there's that warmth again, that deep-down relief that wants so badly to burst free. It pokes at me, screaming, *This is real!*

And it is, right? I glance around. It's as real as the trees surrounding us. The sun beating down on the top of my head. The salt in the air tingling up my nose.

"I'm getting there," I say, partially present and partially still in denial as if I'm on the other side of a screen, watching this whole thing play out on TV.

I look to Will. His gaze is distracting like he's trying to pull me in. It pierces me in a way I've never known, but I hold it, having to take a breath to keep talking, "I want to be okay." I break the intensity, glancing at the boulder like it's going to give me my next line. It just sits there all big and hard and mossy. I inhale again, steeling myself to face the intensity. "I mean, I'm here. This is real, I get that now. And I want to help figure out how to get out of here and back home." There's a spiky knot lodged in my throat that I manage to choke back. I refuse to cry in front of him again.

Will steps closer. He places his hand on my shoulder and peers into my eyes. My stomach flips at his touch and I stare back into his eyes, wondering what's under that patch. "Don't rush it. It took me years to come to terms with everything."

I inhale. *Years.* A knot of doubt pinches that bit of hope.

With a small squeeze, Will pulls his hand away. "How about that bathroom?"

"Yes, please." I blush again despite the barbs and knots.

He laughs in that small way under his breath and picks up the fur and bowl, but doesn't move.

I glance around. "I'm ready."

"Great, pick a tree. Or dig a hole and grab some leaves. Depending."

"Oh. Really?" God.

He gives me a look that clearly disputes any grandiose ideas I had of an outhouse.

"All right." I take a deep breath, nodding my head and straightening my shoulders. "I've been camping. Once. I can do this."

"I'll wait here." I swear he's about to laugh—a real laugh, not the airy one I've come to expect.

I skulk off in search of a tree and quickly find a big one that offers ample cover.

As I head back, feeling proud of myself, high-pitched laughter shoots down from above. I assume it's a group of monkeys or bats or some mystery animal that only lives here.

My eyes dart upward.

Two boys climb and jump from tree to tree, cackling like crows, hopping from branch to branch like squirrels, and chanting down at me. "New blood! New blood!"

"Olive?" Will shouts.

"Will?" I yell.

"Olive, Olive, Olive!" One of the boys screeches. He has long, matted hair and scraps for clothes, but that's all I see because he's moving so fast it's unreal.

"Olive." Will's found me. He jerks his neck back, peering up at the trees. "You know the deal! Get back on your side of the island!"

"Who's gonna make us?" One of the boys sing-songs, hurling a coconut to the ground, barely hitting Will in the head. In response, Will pulls out a slingshot and a sharply carved wooden stake. My heart starts racing and my face goes pale.

This is no reality show.

These kids are part wild animals, part boys. Wildlings.

Will nudges me out of the way, loads the stake, and aims. He pulls the sling back so it's stretched next to his ear, but stops. "Damn it. They're moving too much." Another coconut comes down, this time grazing my shoulder.

It's then I see the intensity in Will's face, the urgency that we need to move. Fast. He grabs my hand and jerks me along, and the heckling follows us. As we run, Will keeps turning his good eye back and up, searching out the Wildlings.

Running, dragging, and tripping, he takes me back toward the beach. *Get to the water.* Like running from bees?

We hit the beach and collapse behind a large rock, out of breath. Our chests rise and fall as we search the trees. Will has his slingshot out again and is aiming at the forest, his eye squinted, brow sweaty, dark hair stuck against it.

"Who are—"

"Shh!"

I give him a dirty look he doesn't see. He peeks at me from the corner of his eye. "The twins. They're animals." Breathing deeply and lowering his weapon, Will turns his head toward me and leans in. "I didn't tell you everything."

My stomach catches on a barb. "Like what? Now? We've gotta get out of here!"

"Shh. Calm down. It's all right. We have boundaries. And, while they don't always keep to theirs, they aren't stupid. Especially the twins."

I only stare at him, my chest rising and falling.

"We'll wait here a bit longer then head back." He makes sure to connect with my eyes. "It's okay. You're okay." He clears a couple of tears away from my cheeks I wasn't aware of, and his touch leaves tiny sparks that help wake me up to the present.

"You were saying?"

He pulls his hand back quickly as if he just realized it was still at my cheek. "Right." He sighs deeply, checking the tree line again before continuing. "You're the second number thirteen we've had here. The first, Annabel, was captured by the Panthers. She refused to tell them where our camp was and they pushed her off the cliff." He swallows hard, Adam's apple dipping up then down. "Jude found her. They were… close…" His words fade. "Well, more than close."

Oh. Imagining Jude being close to anything other than a block of ice is hard. But. Okay. I can handle this, I can handle this, I can handle this. Despite repeating the words, I'm thrust into the present because I feel like I'm going to faint.

"The truth is ugly. I'll do you no favors sugar coating it. But the more you know, the better your chance of survival."

I swallow. Now is as good a time as any. "And your eye?" I wince.

Will doesn't take his sight off the line of trees. The spiky mountain looms in the distance — the cliffs where innocent girls get tossed over like rag-dolls.

"Like I said, Duke and I were the first ones on the island. He chased after me through the maze and followed me here." Will shakes his head, flexing his jaw, as if reliving the memory. "I used to wear glasses — thick, goddamn, dark-rimmed glasses. Magnified my eyes like Coke bottles. Anyway, Duke and I rolled down the hill from the boulder, punching, kicking, falling until we hit flat ground. When we stopped, he landed on top of me. Pinned down, he took his bat and slammed it into my left eye, breaking my glasses and, well, you can fill in the rest. That's when something snapped in me. I pushed him off, pried his bat away, and hit him on the side of his head." His eye flickers to mine, then back at the trees. "Duke's deaf in his right ear, I'm blind in my left eye. It seemed we were even. We each ran in different directions, living on separate sides of the island until more kids started showing up. Sides were formed. Then Annabel… The bombs… We're at war, Olive."

He turns his head and really stares at me, gazing into my eyes like he did yesterday in that way that made me feel naked.

"Why was he chasing you to begin with?"

Will clenches his teeth. "It's complicated. Duke and I have never gotten along."

I can tell by the way he does a full stop, that's all I'll get out of him on that subject. Pulling my eyes from his, I glance up toward the trees. "And the patch?" I ask.

"I had it with me when I arrived. I'd bought it at the Carnival." He does his airy laugh, this time out his nose. "Kind of funny…the irony of it." I glance back at him and his small smile fades, face becoming serious, jaw again flexing. "Olive?"

My stomach drops when he speaks my name. "Yeah?"

"What were you running from?" A different intensity now masks his face.

"Nothing. I told you, I was just going through the maze." Technically true.

He stands. "If you have any hope of making it here, you're going to have to be honest—not only with us but with yourself, too. Yesterday you said something about your name being the reason you ended up here."

"I… That was just…" I shake my head, not ready. I refuse to be Olive McGaggy here.

With an exaggerated exhale, Will surveys our surroundings, breathing out his nose, nostrils flared. "Should be safe now." He stands and walks away, saying, "If you plan to join our group, you have five days to prove your worth. You fail, you're out. Nothing personal, just a rule."

"Anything else you haven't told me?" I say to his back.

"You have no idea."

Chapter Fourteen

Two of my five allotted days pass in a blur of trying to "prove my worth" because it's no secret I need them more than they need me.

I go with Lewis to collect firewood, help Tilly with the cooking and constant mending of clothes, and I even try to make amends with Jude—because clearly my being here angers him. Still, he and Will stay distant and by day three I'm sure I haven't begun to prove I'm worth anything but an extra mouth to feed.

Currently, we sit around the fire, a nightly ritual. Will tells stories and Jude sings, playing the out-of-tune guitar he carried with him the night he drunkenly arrived here.

Nineteen seventy-nine. He'd played a gig at a bar in some mountain town in Colorado, drinking between sets with a couple of magicians going on after him. When he left, a few guys jumped him and tried to steal his guitar. Jude ran into the woods, tripped over a branch, and literally fell onto the island.

The cave is dark. Orange firelight licks at Jude's face, bringing the tattooed dragon on his neck to life. He sings and plays a sad, folksy song about a girl he wished he'd known, white-capped waves, hot sunny days, and sharp pain—*the sharp, sharp, pain of falling*. His voice breaks with emotion. I can only imagine it's his personal homage to poor Annabel, the original number thirteen. When finished, Jude simply sets his guitar to the side. The instrument groans with a twang and Jude leaves.

Tilly's eyes trail after him, Bug's head resting in her lap. The lion cub's small arm reaches up and twirls the red curls hanging past Tilly's shoulders.

I sit in my usual place—not quite a part of the family, set back far enough so I'm not included, but close enough to observe.

"Tell us a story, Will?" Bug asks within a long yawn, eyes shut, her brown hair a soft shadow around her head.

"Nice try, little lion. Time for bed."

"Aah-aww," she whines.

"Unless you'd rather take a bath," Tilly adds.

"Bed!" Bug shouts, sitting straight up, ball of rags clutched to her chest, eyes wide and shifty—ever the comedian.

Everyone laughs in the reserved way they all do here. Even Charlie cracks a smile, or does he? It's gone before I can make the call.

"Go on, you two," says Tilly. "I'll be back to tuck you in soon." Charlie and Bug race toward their room, everyone mumbling goodnights after them. All I see is the back of Charlie's ratty hair disappear through the doorway.

Tilly sits down next to Will and begins to make tea as they quietly talk; Will glances around Tilly, catching my eye every so often which unnerves me, but also makes my stomach go all springy. Doing what any self-respecting teenager would do, I pretend not to notice.

Instead, I pull my knees up and rest my head on my legs. Bare footsteps approach. My chest tightens at the chance it might be Will, but when I peek out, I see Lewis's knobby, scabbed knees, then his lanky form, and finally, those dark eyes behind wire-framed glasses as he crouches down to my level.

"Hey there," he says, sitting right next to me. "How you coping?"

"I'm doing all right."

He smiles and it's clear to see he'll be handsome, more a man, in a few years. Then I remember. He's likely stuck this age forever. Forever fifteen. What a nightmare.

"It gets better," he says. "I promise. I mean, sure, it's not the best situation, but take Bug for instance. When she got here, she barely spoke a word of English. Now, we can't get her to shut up."

I smile. "Where's she from?"

"No one knows. We think another island, from long ago. She knows a lot about survival—it's like instinct for her. She was the second one here. It was only her and Will for a long while. Then I showed up, then Tilly, Jude, Charlie, Anna—" He swallows back the word.

"It's okay. Will told me."

He exhales. "Oh good. Well, her, then you."

I can't help but stare at Will from across the room. Can't help thinking of him all alone on this island, nursing his injured eye, then a seven-year-old girl showing up. How they must have been forced to learn to communicate.

Will looks back at me.

I glance away.

"Anyway, we all learned to find our place. You'll find yours." He leans into my ear. "No one's ever been sent away. Will's tough, but he's a good guy. The best, just had it rough there for a while."

"What do you mean, he had it rough?" I lower my voice like I shouldn't be talking about such things, even though there's no way Will can hear us.

Lewis leans in. I guess he feels the same way. "He and

Duke, well, they have a sort of long history. Longer than just being on this island."

I wait, my eyes intent on Lewis.

"Duke used to do horrible things to Will back at school in Texas," he whispers so I can barely make out his words. "Will was like a punching bag for Duke. The guy pounded on poor Will every chance he got. Tortured him." Lewis glances up. "He doesn't talk about it much."

"I can understand that," I say, that place above my ear tingling with memories.

Lewis nods. "Hey, Olive?"

"I won't say anything."

"Good, thank you." He breathes a sigh of relief.

I give him a grateful grin that doesn't begin to reach my eyes.

Lewis stands. "Well, good night."

"Good night." He's already walking away, so I touch his calf to slow him down. "Hey, thanks."

He stops and glances down at me. Taking a deep, shaky breath, Lewis says, "Anytime." He swallows and I swear I can feel the heat of the blush that's taken over his face.

As Lewis walks away, Tilly, too, says good night and follows him back to put the kids to bed. My eyes move toward Will, who's sitting in front of the fire, poking at it with a stick. The room is suddenly so very empty besides us.

Once again, he glances up as if he knows I can't keep my eyes from finding him. But there's truth to it and, this time, I don't look away because all I can think about is what Lewis just shared with me. How could this strong, confident guy be so much like me? Is he all mixed up on the inside, too, slowly chipping away like the old Jackson farmhouse? Maybe. I would have never guessed it, though. Perhaps he's just learned to hide his broken pieces better.

Will smiles crookedly. "You can come closer, you know. Must be cold over there in that corner of yours."

It is. I stand, walk over, and sit in front of the fire.

Will sets a small log over the flames. "Looks like someone has quite the crush."

Oh God. I'm so thankful for the darkness, because my face flushes several shades of total mortification. "No, I just…" Keeping my eyes down, I draw squiggly lines with my finger in the sand. I can't look at him. "I mean…"

"Lewis? He's got it pretty bad for you."

"Oh, yeah. Well, he's a nice kid." I exhale, trying to keep it from sounding like a huge sigh of relief.

"He is that." Will smirks as he pokes at the stones at the bottom of the fire with the stick.

"So, Lewis mentioned it was just you and Bug for a while?"

"Two years. We taught each other a lot. I helped her learn English and she showed me how to do things more efficiently around here. Fish, build fire. I swear she's a little genius."

"And a comedian."

He laughs and it's a notch above his airy, sad version. "Definitely a comedian. If it wasn't for that crazy little kid, we'd all lose it—if we haven't already."

"You all seem to have things pretty together" —I raise my eyebrows— "considering."

"Ha!" he laughs. It catches me off guard and I jump. "Yes, 'considering,' I suppose we're all right." He nods, lips pressed together, thinking on something. "Most of us," he adds and I know who he's referring to.

"Charlie?" I whisper.

"Mmm, poor kid. We don't know what to do for him."

"Will!" Tilly calls.

Will jumps up and runs to the other room. I follow, unsure whether I should or not.

"Ugh! Momma! Ugh! Momma! Momma!!!" Charlie's asleep, but screaming, thrashing and kicking on the floor. It's the first I've heard his voice. It's high-pitched and boyish, reminding me too much of Lucky. I'm pulled toward him, wanting to comfort him like I would my little brother, but

Will and Tilly are right there with him and Bug catches my eye. She's balled up in the corner, hands over her ears, eyes squinted shut. I walk toward her.

I place my hand on her head. Her curly mane is both soft like baby hair and stiff from dirt and sand and coconut soap. She stares up, eyes wide, afraid.

I bend down next to her.

She jumps into my lap.

"Oh!"

"Make him stop, make him stop," she chants into my chest.

"Shh. It's all right," I repeat, smoothing her hair, rocking her back and forth. I keep at it, like it's routine, until Charlie calms back to sleep and Tilly comes over.

"Back to bed, little Bug."

"No. I'm sleeping here!" she calls into my shoulder.

"Well, I don't believe that arrangement would suit Olive now, do you?"

Bug nods her head.

"Come now." Tilly's tone is stern.

Bug releases her grip and gets up.

I stand. "'Night, Bug."

She gives me a defeated smile.

As I head toward the door, I pass Will. He stares but doesn't speak a word. I leave.

Settled back in my corner of the common area, I curl up, knees pulled into my chest. Images of Lucky's soft earlobes, the scent of fresh linen that clings to my comforter, the cold, roughness of Hazel's wet nose...all color the dark space behind my eyes. Then I think of the souls who share this strange cave with me. What lights their darkest of shadows?

I vow to do what I can to make this better.

"No! I won't! You! Can't! Make! Me!" jolts me awake. Bug runs through the cave-tree completely naked and screaming between diabolical giggles.

I sit up.

Tilly runs past, Bug's clothes a bundle at her chest. "Child, you have got to bathe! You smell like a fish!" she shouts, a couple strides behind the small sprinting flash of a girl.

They make a good three rounds until finally Bug spots me. She runs full force—all arms and legs—and hops behind me. With the burst of energy, I swear I pick up the faint scent of seaweed. Tilly crouches in front of me—the wall between them.

"This is ridiculous. You know it's bathing day."

"I. Don't. Agree!"

They shout back and forth to no avail until Bug relents with conditions. "I'll bathe. If! Olive takes me." The little beetle bends her upper body around so she can see me. Both she and Tilly stare, the same hope filling their eyes.

"Um, okay," I hear myself say.

"You're sure?" Tilly asks, already passing me Bug's clothes.

"Yeah, I don't mind. How hard can it be?"

To that, Tilly gives me a regretful and apologetic look.

What have I gotten myself into?

"I'm sure she'll behave for you," Tilly says, speaking to me but staring at Bug.

"Give me five minutes and we can go."

They both nod.

I set Bug's clothes bundle down, then I stand and stretch. On my way to the door I grab a toothstick, a wedge of coconut, and my boots. Once outside, I go to the small stream that runs parallel the cave-tree. Kneeling before it, I squint to make out my reflection. My hair is a mess of tangles, my face dirty, clothes stretched out and stained. Stick in hand, first I rub it in the coconut, then scrub my teeth with it. It's not minty or foamy and doesn't leave my teeth feeling smooth, but it does the trick. I wind my hair into a braid, and it's so dirty, it stays on its own without a tie, the shaved part growing a little softer and less pokey.

I "do my business"—as Bug refers to it—behind a tree, then make my way back to the cave. Bug's waiting for me when I arrive. Still naked. Still ornery.

"Ready?"

She nods, shoving her clothes and a pouch of what feels like sand at me.

"It can't be that bad," I say, following her.

"It's worse," she replies, her skinny brown figure, all lean and muscle, taking short steps.

When we reach the stream, we're at a wider area than where I was earlier. The spot is all boulders and sand, and the sun shines down just so, making the water sparkle like a pool of diamonds. Bug stops. Then she stands still peering over at me. "Well?" she asks.

"Well, what?"

"You have to get in with me, or else how will you scrub me?" She holds up the pouch.

"Oh. No. I'm sure you can do that yourself."

She crosses her arms and points her nose up.

I look down at myself. My fingernails are black, my jeans and shirt caked in places with mud and God knows what else. I bring my braid to my nose and flinch. Ew. Maybe it was me I smelled earlier and not Bug.

"Fine. I guess I could use a bath, too."

She smiles in triumph, then, without warning, hops in, splashing me.

"Hey!" I shout, half laughing.

Bug giggles.

I strip down to my bra and underwear and make my way in. The water is warm and more wonderful than I'd imagined. I have no idea why Tilly made such a big deal out of this.

A thick wave of water douses me. Any place on my body that was remotely dry is now saturated.

Bug kicks and splashes and giggles, dunking herself under as if in getaway.

Instead of getting mad, I decide to play along, the scene taking me back to a few summers ago and my daily excursions with Lucky to our neighborhood pool.

I plunge underwater and swim to Bug, popping up behind her and spraying water at the back of her head.

She squeals. "You're more fun than Tilly!"

"Well, I don't know about that, but we should bathe and wash our clothes. Let's get that over with and then we can play."

She nods.

Bug scrubs herself, a luxury Tilly doesn't allow her—apparently, I'm winning all sorts of points—while I scrub our clothes, then lay them on a rock in the sun to dry. I walk back to the water, entering, welcoming its warmth, when Bug stops mid-scrub, eyes wide. "Your underclothes, the colors, they're *beautiful*!"

I glance down. Somehow, by sheer luck, I'm wearing a matching turquoise set that more resembles a bathing suit than underwear. "Thanks, Bug. Bug... Where did you get that name?" I swim to her and take over scrubbing her hair. She doesn't complain.

"When I got here, I didn't know much English, only my people's language. My name was Lee-teeg-buk. Will couldn't really say that, so he started calling me Lightning Bug since it sounded kind of the same. Also, he says my hair reminds him of lightning and I bounce around like a bug." She turns her head and glances over her shoulder at me, her eyes like huge Texas June bugs.

"Well, I love it. It suits you. A name is a big deal, you know?"

"How'd you get yours, Olive?" My insides twinge at the sound of it.

"I'm named after someone in my family, but I've never really liked it."

"Why not? Family is special. On my island, I was an orphan. I ended up here running from the mean man who was supposed to take care of us, but beat us if we didn't work hard enough."

"Us?"

"There were a lot of orphans. More came in than went out. We were always trying to run away, but I'm the only one who ever made it out—only because I ended up here." She gazes out into the forest, probably imagining another scene. "One night, I'd finally had enough, so I decided to run away, but the master chased me. I jumped over a rock, then *poof*! I was on the beach." Head down, she swirls squiggles on the surface of the water with her finger. "You guys wanna get home, but this is my home."

I don't know what to say to that, so I smooth her hair, filling the coconut bowl with water and rinsing the dirt and debris from her tangles. Poor Bug. Seven years old, but goes back and forth between acting her age and speaking like she's much older—I assume the result of living with only Will and those older than her for so long. I clear my throat. "All clean. We should dry off and head back."

"Okay."

We get out and settle on large boulders in the sun. It beats down on us like a tiny piece of heaven in all of this chaos and confusion, orphan stories, and names. Bug puts on her sun-cooked clothes while I switch out my soaked undergarments for my dry shirt and jeans, laying them out on the rock to bake. Bug admires the turquoise again, grazing it with gentle fingertips like its gold.

After a while, I shove my damp bra and undies into my back pocket, lace up my boots, and hear…whistling…

Whistling down toward us like a dying bird.

"Bug!" I shout. She runs at me, eyes wide like saucers as she searches the sky.

Shouts and coconuts rain down on us. The twins. We run, dodging coconuts and "New blood! New blood! Olive-Olive-Olive!" It occurs to me we can't return to the cave-tree.

I stop, switching directions, when an explosion erupts in a

cracking, *ka-boom.*

In the distance, the whistling bird hits the ground, a small tuft of smoke resulting.

"Olive, where are you go—"

"This way!" I try to convey with my eyes that we can't go back, can't lead the wildlings to our home.

She follows. So do the twins.

Head for the water, like running from bees.

I don't know if it makes sense, or is why Will went that way during our last wild-tree-jumping-twin encounter, but I'm low on options.

The ocean is far-off but within sight along the horizon. I run toward it, pulling Bug by her small hand. But it isn't too long before she slows.

The twins are no longer in the trees, they're now on foot and not far behind, their whoops and hollers growing louder.

I glance back and don't see them, so I cut left, hoping to lose them. But no more than three steps out, Bug and I skid to a stop. A cliff.

"Shits," I swear, out of breath, panting, my legs on fire. Shits is right. Oh, Tawny. What would she do?

She'd face them. Fight.

Searching in all directions, I bend down and grab the first thing I find—jagged rocks. Heavy. Sharp. They'll have to do. I push Bug behind me and we silently move away from the cliff's edge.

"New blood! Come out, come out, wherever you are!" The wild-twins sing in rounds.

I yank my bra from my pocket and quickly fasten it into a circle as tight as it will get, trying to duplicate Will's slingshot. I plop the biggest rock I have in it and pull the thing past my shoulder. I'm ready. Terrified, but ready. I think.

"Olive-Olive-Olive!" one sings.

"We saw you! Na-ked!" the other taunts.

Their words fill me with a blood-curdling rage. I'm angry. Violated. Protective over Bug. And I'll do what I must to get us home in one piece.

"Come on!" I shout. "Let's go!"

Plants rustle and I can't help wonder what the hell I'm doing.

I peek around the corner where we veered left. I spot two identical boys, around the age of fourteen. They wear what was probably once shorts, but now are nothing but dirty shreds. Their tangled hair falls well past their shoulders and they're silent, bent at the waist, and searching for us like animals on the prowl.

I breathe in. Then out. Confident they don't see us yet, I set my eyes on the one who's slightly closer.

I aim.

Bug holds her breath.

I release the rock.

It flies about halfway and falls to the ground with a sad *thump*.

They jump back, then take slow, calculated steps toward us.

I load another smaller, sharper rock.

Please work.

I stretch the bra back until I fear it'll snap. Aiming for one of their bare chests, I release.

A high-pitched yelp pierces the air.

I load another and steal a peek around the corner. One boy is on the ground, the other standing over him.

The one on the ground makes a pained, gurgling noise that quakes the air between us. The one who isn't on the ground holds a sharp bloody rock up over his head. He turns to face us. Beady eyes wide with fury, he sets them right on mine. His brother whimpers on the ground, a wound bleeding from his head.

I hit him.

No time to be stunned. The beady-eyed one sprints toward us and again, I release another smaller rock. It flies through the air. Aiming for his middle, it hits his bare knee and he stumbles to the ground with a cry of pain.

I grab Bug's hand. We run past, not daring a peek back at the scene. As I pull her along, we hear a wailing scream from behind us.

We don't stop until we literally run into Will and Jude. Jude picks up Bug like she's nothing more than a kitten. "What was it?" Will asks.

"A bomb, then the twins. I—"

"Go back. I'll be right behind."

Jude runs away, Bug scooped into the crook of one arm. Will goes in the opposite direction. I stand still.

Jude looks back at me. "Come on!" he shouts.

I don't move.

"Forget it. It's on you." He turns and runs off.

Torn, looking from Jude's back to where Will's disappeared, I sigh and follow Jude and Bug.

Once back, Bug sits in Jude's lap as he winds her poof into tiny little braids. She gives an accurate, yet overly dramatized account of our adventure, not omitting my turquoise underwear—to which, I swear, even in the dim cave, I see Lewis's cheeks turn bright pink.

It's only moments later when Will comes bounding in. "Well, I'm happy to report we won't be bothered by the twins for a while." He walks straight up to me and I can't tell if I've done something wrong or right.

I stand to meet him. Will takes my hand and pulls me to the side. Lewis watches us.

Will leans close, gazing into my eyes. His stare is more serious than ever, a hint of something I can't quite place within the sage. My forehead warms from his breath. "You've earned your worth. We'd be honored to have you stay," he says just above a whisper.

Something in my heart both warms and breaks.

Because, isn't this the peaceful side?

Chapter Fifteen

My Place

My violent act wins my acceptance. Acceptance into this group where honesty is everything, family comes first, and violence is a last resort.

Something doesn't add up. Why should I be granted anything? Yes, I got Bug and me out of a potentially horrible situation, but at what cost? What of the boy I injured?

Will says I thought quickly by leading the twins away and fashioning a weapon out of practically nothing—I choose not to get all caught up in the implications of my bra being "practically nothing."

Still, things feel off. How many years has this fight gone on without any prospect of a solution? Clearly, something isn't right, and I'm going to find out what it is. Because in a group where honesty is rule number one, a lot's being hidden.

Will's fingers find my chin, lifting it so we're eye to eye. "I thought you'd be more pleased."

"I am. I'm just…" Overwhelmed. Freaking out. Confused. "I accept." I force a smile.

He cocks his head to the side. "But?"

"But are they badly hurt? The wildlings…er…I mean… the twins?"

"Ha!" A second time, he nearly loses composure. Everyone's eyes shoot toward us then back at the fire. "Wildlings?" He flashes a wide smile I can tell he's trying to make disappear but can't. And that pang tears at my heart again. He's too pleased. Going too easy on me by rewarding me with his almost-laughs.

"Yeah, that's all I could think the first time they chased us. The name just stuck in my head, I guess." I gaze at the ground. "Are they injured?" My eyes sneak back up.

His smile disappears as if he catches himself enjoying things too much. "Mmm, yes, well. Tommy, with the large, jagged scar on his right shoulder—the one you hit in the leg— he seemed all right and was carrying his brother, Jack, who, I'm going to be honest, didn't look good." Will's eye sets on mine, searching for a reaction.

"Is he…" The words barely come out, my throat closing.

"I don't know." He puts his hands on my shoulders. "But *listen to me*." His stare is intense and the look in his eye… I know whatever he's about to say, whether truthful of not, I need to believe. So I listen. "You did what you had to do. For you. For Bug. For us. There was no other way. Do you hear me?" I blink. I do. Still, as his words soar over to me they drop one by one at my feet. "It was either a fight, or you and little Bug would have gone over the cliff." He exhales and his breath smells like fresh mint. I notice he's tossing a couple of leaves around in his mouth. "You had no choice. You have to believe that or it'll consume you."

I don't say anything.

"Olive?"

"Okay," I whisper, lost in the way he says my name, how it's laced with mint, broken wildlings, and near-laughter.

Six days pass. I know this from Tilly's hash marks on our shared wall.

I'm an official Lion now, and I've been moved from my corner in the common area to Tilly's room or "the big girls" room as Bug refers to it. The little sneak often finds her way to my mat during the night, and if Tilly doesn't wake up, neither of us says anything. I've taken to calling her Bed Bug.

Bug's soft touch against my cut hair wakes me up, but I don't open my eyes. The spot is growing back in a way I can only imagine isn't at all attractive because I can feel it skimming the top of my ear as Bug tries to tuck the tiny pieces behind. Each time she brushes the short hairs with her fingertips, it triggers my memory of the carnival, the clippers, the Trio. It feels like another lifetime ago, yet the pain is still right there, right beneath my hair as it's growing, trying to erase the evidence. My mind back in Texas, I can't help but think of my parents...Lucky...Tawny...even Hazel's stinky fish breath. God, I miss them.

Tears prick behind my closed eyes. I rub them and glance over at Bug, hopeful she doesn't see my pain. "Snuck in again, eh Bed Bug?"

She smiles, her teeth so white, so perfect. It's miraculous, considering the lack of dental hygiene here.

"Olive?"

"Mmm hmm?"

"What happened to your hair?"

"Oh. Well. Someone cut it." I can't lie to her.

"Who? They didn't do too good."

I can't help but laugh. "No, they didn't."

She nods. "Who did it?" I'm not fooling her.

My smile fades. "Some really mean girls." She stares, waiting for more. "Um, they're kind of like the twins. They just do mean things."

"Well, that sucks." She raises one eyebrow.

I laugh under my breath. I can only imagine she picked that term up from Jude much to Tilly's chagrin. Bug smiles in her mischievous yet knowing way.

"You're right, it really does suck," I say. And in the words of a seven-year-old, everything feels lighter.

"Did you throw sharp rocks at them, too?"

"No. I ran away."

"Oh." The disappointment on her face, the way her mouth pulls to one side as she considers that version of me and the one she saw the other day, makes my stomach tighten.

"Ow! Jesus, Tilly. Be careful!" Jude shouts from the other room.

Widening our eyes at one another, Bug and I jump up and run to see what's going on.

In the common room, Jude lies on the floor, a bowl of water and another full of what I recognize as melted coconut goop next to him. Tilly leans over his face. "Sit still, we're nearly finished!"

I move closer and see that Tilly is holding a sharp blade to his cheek. She lathers some of the goop on, then runs the sharp edge of the knife from his chin to his cheekbone. Bug and I both cringe. Jude holds his breath.

"One more pass and then I'll tidy your neck," Tilly says.

Jude jumps up, tossing Tilly onto her backside. "No neck! I'm done!"

"Hey! You asked me!"

"That was before you carved me like a turkey!" Jude's face is raw like sunburn. He glares at us, then at Will, who's sitting in the corner, sharpening another blade and laughing his airy laugh to himself. "I'm going out," Jude announces.

Tilly stands, hands on her hips. "You're welcome! Keep the coconut on, it will—"

Jude turns and leaves the room.

"—help with the burning," Tilly finishes near-whisper. With a deep breath, she turns to Will. "Fancy a shave?"

Will peers up from his blade, rubbing his thumb and forefinger over the ever-growing stubble on his chin. "I think I'll let mine grow a little longer. Thanks, though."

"I'll take one." Lewis shows up out of nowhere, his voice forcibly low.

Tilly laughs. Out loud.

"What? I've got stubble." He rubs his chin, the edge of his jaw, as if the "stubble" is really getting to him.

"Do you now? All right, let's have a look then."

Lewis walks over and lies on the ground where Jude was.

Tilly winks at us, then leans in close to Lewis's face. "Oh my, you do have quite the beard!"

Bug giggles.

Lewis searches all our faces. "Forget it." He starts to get up.

Tilly pushes him back down. "Wait, you little gnat. I do see a bit that could be trimmed off."

"See?"

"Mmm," she says, getting to work. On what, I'm not sure. Not looking up, Tilly adds, "Breakfast is next to the fire."

Bug pulls me by the hand, and she and I grab two of the three bowls left atop the rocks around the fire pit. "Where's Charlie?" Bug asks, staring at Will who's sticking his blade in the fire every few minutes, then sliding a large rock across one edge.

"Still sleeping. He had a long night, but I guess you already know that?"

Bug nods, looking up at me whose bed she ran to when she couldn't take Charlie's sleep terrors any longer.

Will nods, going back to his blade.

Bug and I sit.

"Sleep well?" Will asks, not looking up.

"Yeah," I answer, Bug's mouth full of fish and banana. "So, where did you ever find knives out here?"

Will glances up for a second. "Not found, brought. One with me—every red-blooded teenage guy in the sixties owned a switch blade. The other"—he motions to Tilly and Lewis—"came with Jude."

I take a few bites. The combination of fish and bananas

tastes like feet, but as hungry as I am, I eat it. I figure after a while I won't even notice and will make all sorts of yummy noises like Bug does. As I chew, the stringiness of the fish and the smoosh of the ripe banana swishing around my mouth, something occurs to me. "Hey, Will?"

"Hmm?"

"You don't talk like you're from the sixties." He stops mid-stroke, cocking his head at me. "I mean, not how I imagined people spoke back then."

"You mean like on *Leave it to Beaver*? *I Love Lucy*?" he asks, cocking an eyebrow upward, still searching my face in a way that sends that spring in my stomach haywire. Stupid stomach.

My neck goes warm and itchy because that's exactly what I'm thinking, all "Gee whiz, Mister" and "Aw, shucks" and pearls and perfection and poodle skirts. "Well, kind of, I guess."

He laughs, still under his breath, this time, more like, *silly girl*. "Those are cheesy television shows. I mean, sure, some of the slang is right, but mostly, people spoke normally."

"Makes sense."

I take another bite of fish-banana-mush, but a noise interrupts me mid-chew. It's the sound of a horn or pipe or one of those shells they used to announce the start of the luau we went to on our vacation to Hawaii when I was eleven. It's a long, flowing, *pha-ooh*.

Tilly freezes, knife raised.

Lewis sits up on his elbows.

Will peers up at the ceiling as if he can see through it. The rest of us follow his eyes. The noise is loud, but far away. Like from a sharp mountain top...

Charlie rushes in, half his hair stuck to his flushed-from-sleep face.

Another *pha-ooh* sounds as if a cry for help, the eerie call wailing from a cliff high above.

Jude also runs in, arms full of firewood and coconuts, face

still raw, but less red. He drops the load on the floor.

Another *pha-ooh* cries out.

Charlie shuffles across the room, skidding on his knees to Tilly. She puts her arm around him.

"What is it?" Bug shouts, hands over her ears.

Will's eyes are still frozen toward the ceiling. "It's the call of the King of the island."

We all look at one another like Will's lost his mind, hoping someone will confirm it isn't so.

"Huh? What the heck does that mean?" Bug says in a way only she can get away with around here.

Will glances at her, smiles, puts his blade in his pocket, and stands. He paces the room several times.

"I've never shared this because it didn't seem necessary." He shakes his head. "I apologize for that. I should have told you." Will pauses, his eyes on mine. My stomach tilts. He takes a deep breath. "When Duke and I arrived on the island, as you know, we split. I'm not sure how much time passed before Bug and then the twins arrived, but at some point—when it was only the two of us—I heard that same sound. Curious and desperate for human contact—even in the form of Duke and a possible fight—I went after the noise. I climbed up the mountain and into its sharp crests until I found him sitting at the mouth of a cave. He was blowing an old brass horn. I asked him where the hell he'd gotten it, but all he said was that he'd found it on the beach. Then we stared at each other for a while. Longer than a while. Forever. Finally, Duke stood and I could see in his eyes, he was torn. Just as lonely and miserable as I was, he couldn't decide whether to hug me or push me off the cliff. He didn't do either. Instead, he widened his eyes like a madman, dug his fingers into the soot of his fire and marked two lines under each of his eyes.

"Duke told me, 'I am King of the island. And this' —he held up the horn— 'is my call.' Then he spit into the fire and declared we were at war, that he, 'the king,' declared this island his and his alone. 'When you hear my call,' he said, 'beware.

The king and his army are comin' for you.'" Will shakes his head faster now. "I left, not looking back. That was the last I saw of him and the last I heard that horn. Eight? Nine years ago?"

I notice Tilly open her mouth to give him a correct number, but she decides against it.

Will walks toward the fire. "I never thought... He was unstable. *Is* unstable. Even after the bombs started, I never believed he'd ever come down from that mountain to face me — us. And he probably won't. But..."

"Do you think the kid died?" Jude cuts in with his deep not-a-care-in-the-word tone.

"Yes," Will answers.

I gasp.

All eyes zip toward me.

Bug hops into my lap. "Are they coming for Olive? Is the King of the island coming for her?" I watch her round peach lips, the words as they leave, floating along her sweet little voice.

I killed the wildling.

My head goes light as wildling calls, horns, and dying birds whistling, ring through it.

But the whistling isn't only in my head.

Everyone runs for cover. Will jumps at Bug and me, hurling us to the ground.

My eyes meet Bug's, then Jude's across the room, then toward the ceiling, waiting, wondering...is this one going to hit?

The whistling stops.

Pure silence, the bird is dead.

Then the now familiar *ka-boom* of a coconut bomb blasts the world around us like lightning striking the very ground we huddle against.

Chapter Sixteen

Bombs

The first blast is the loudest and closest, but it doesn't hit. We breathe a collective sigh of relief.

Two more bombs rain down, farther away, with less of an aftershock.

Silence coats our surroundings in a thick blanket. All of the usual sounds cease. Not even the birds chirp, and it seems the waves have stopped rolling in.

One by one, we get up, brushing off the dirt and sand, assessing the damage.

"Everyone all right?" Will asks.

We all nod, except Charlie, who runs to his room. The unmistakable sound of his body hitting the floor and sobs flowing follows.

"I'm on it." Jude strides after him. A few minutes pass, and we soon hear Charlie's sobs replaced by the gentle lull of singing. Perhaps Jude isn't all hard edges and scorn. Aside from the secretive smile stretched across Tilly's face, no one seems to stop and take notice. Daily life around here, I remind myself.

Other than a few pots having fallen off the makeshift shelf, the smoke filter above the fire askew, and things generally shaken and shifted—us included—the cave-tree, its inhabitants, we're all okay.

Tilly enlists Bug and Lewis in the clean-up effort, leaving Will and me in an awkward silence.

Will does that thing where he breathes out his nose. "I'm gonna head out to check the damage, make sure nothing's on fire. The last thing we need is for the entire island to go up in flames. Tell the others?"

"I'm going with you," I say, tossing my hair around, trying to get more sand out.

I brace myself for an argument, but miracle of miracles, he agrees.

"Let's go." He motions toward the next room where our shoes are. "Tilly?" he shouts.

"Yes?" she calls back.

"Olive and I will be back—just going to check things out."

"Very well; be careful!"

Once outside, we're hit by the woodsy burning of leaves and trees. Just under that is a sweet yet charred odor like someone's roasted their marshmallow way too long.

Will and I walk along the forest, side-by-side though he somehow leads the way. Not far along, smoke bellows toward us, the burned mixture in the air growing stronger.

Then we see it: a black crater in the ground the size of a Mini Cooper, trees split in half, bowing outward in splintered, cindered pieces. The fire is dying down, but plants still crackle and pop in cinders.

"Holy mother of…" Will trails off.

My thoughts exactly.

I stare in awe at the destruction. What if it had hit the cave-tree? We'd be crackling cinders, too, right now.

And I know Will's thinking a similar thought because

he clears his throat, rubs his forehead, then rakes his fingers through his hair. "Too close. Way too close." Stepping toward the crater, he searches the ground. "One—" He walks a few more feet, pointing. "Two—" Then he moves to the other side of the crater. "Three, maybe four." He stares across the space at me. I'm confused. "They're tying the bombs together for more power. There are too many pieces here for this to be only one. Damn it!" He hits one of the sad trees. It cracks in response.

I take timid steps to where Will stands. His head is down and his hand rests against the injured tree.

I lift my arm so my palm hovers over his shoulder where warmth radiates off him like heat from an oven. I let it fall. First, the tips of my fingers graze him, but slowly the rest follows until my entire hand makes contact. He shivers under my touch, glancing at me.

"I'm sorry," is all I get out.

"No. It has nothing to do with you."

"Well, I'm pretty sure I'm partially to blame." Again, my stomach wrenches.

"We don't know he's dead," Will says, his voice barely above a whisper.

I shake my head, dropping it toward the burned ground.

He sighs. "All right, if I'm being honest, he's probably dead."

I remove my hand. My legs instant Jell-O, I sit right there at the edge of the explosion.

Will sits across from me. "Hey, you did what you had to do." He picks up my hand and caresses my palm, leaving tiny sparks of static with each touch.

Still staring at the ground, tracing shapes in the sooty sand with my free hand, first the knot comes, then the stinging, then the tears. Despite my defying them, they plunk down my chin and into my lap. If I wipe my face, he'll notice. If I don't do anything, he'll notice. But does it matter? I've killed a boy. Taken a life. Oh my God. In doing such a horribly, terrible thing, am I no better than the Trio? I can name a number of times their stunts could have gone wrong and ended me.

More tears. There's also a whimpering waiting in my throat that I refuse to release.

"Olive?" I don't look up but keep making spirals with my finger. "I want you to listen to me. If you hadn't defended yourself, both you and Bug would be dead. I'm sure of it." It's true. At least, I think it is. Or I need to believe it is. "They'd been watching us. Taunting us. Those *wildlings* had been sent to either capture or kill any of us, and it was going to be you and Bug that day." He drops my hand back into my lap then lifts my chin with his thumb and forefinger, forcing my eyes to his. "I'm sure of it."

I have no choice but to stare through blurry tears. Will's beautiful, with his one mysteriously wonderful sage eye, the way his hair is ridiculously messy but also, somehow, so very tantalizing. I barely know anything of him except that he means to take care of everyone in that cave-tree, me included, with all he has. Tears fall more quickly, surely trailing hideous streaks down my dirty face. I'm more a mess than ever, yet more alive. The wrenching in my stomach turns to a flutter.

I decide to tell him. Because, honesty, right? And maybe if I give him something from my soul, he'll return the favor.

Maybe.

"While we're being honest—" I sniff, wiping my eyes. He removes his hand from my chin, an intrigued look on his face. "I was running from something, someone." Will raises his eyebrows, leaning back onto his hands in the ash. "I was running from my stupid life and one of three girls who have tortured me the past six years." My fingers go to the side of my head, above my ear.

"They did that," he states, matter of fact because he already knew.

I nod. "And so much more." The little sob escapes my throat.

He shakes his head. "Why? I can't see any reason—"

"My name. It all started with my ridiculous name."

"What's wrong with Olive?"

And the way he says it, so innocently, as if it's a good

name, a pretty name, and not a disgusting disgrace, several more tears fall from my eyes, each one a horrible memory I've been holding down.

"Well, it's not just my first name. My full name... My full name is..." Somehow I've avoided saying it out loud since standing in front of my new fifth-grade class the year we moved to Texas. "Olive... Maxi... Gagmuehler." With more tears comes a last sob, a long sob, the one that's been clenched around my gut for so long it's become a part of me.

Will stares at me, brow knit, my hurt reflecting in his face, his expression. "Olive?"

I raise my eyebrows in response, still reveling in what I've done, what I've said, and shocked I don't feel ashamed or embarrassed over it. Shocked I haven't run away yet.

"It's a great name—unique—and who doesn't love olives?" He smiles a crooked smile— it was a risky joke. "But it is only a name. You're so much more." His eyes meet mine and my cheeks prickle with heat.

And that's it, isn't it? So simple. So plain to see sitting in soot and surrounded by broken burning trees. It's only a name. Three words I answer to. One of them, Olive, which apparently, *everyone loves.*

Now I'm smiling a crooked smile, too, a small laugh replacing the place those sobs were dwelling, new tears— tears of relief—slipping down my cheeks.

Actions beyond my control, I lean over and wrap my arms around his neck, like Bug would. "Thank you," I whisper in his ear.

I feel his arms around my waist, warm, strong, holding me. He releases a long sigh as if he's been craving this embrace for ages.

Pulling back so I can see his face, it's glaringly apparent how close we are.

Will glances away, then back. Leaning forward, his breath still hinting of mint, our lips linger a fraction of a second apart before he kisses me.

Somehow, I gasp and kiss him back at the same time.

My heart beats into my neck, my ears, I memorize everything about the moment: the mixed smell of burned earth and mint leaves, Will's nose barely against mine, the way his eye patch grazes my forehead, the dizziness in my mind, his lips, slightly dry, how they scratch against mine in a pleasingly delightful way.

Abruptly, like a cold splash of water to the face, he pulls away. Too quickly. Too cold. As if an animal fleeing danger, Will scurries several feet away from me.

"I'm sorry. I shouldn't have. There's a rule. My rule," he says, head shaking *no*.

"Rule?"

"After Jude and Annabel, I promised myself, if ever, I mean, I'd never allow…"

Seeing him so frazzled is unnerving. I think I get what he's saying, but it's coming out in fragments, and I'm having trouble filling in the holes. I open my mouth to plead he slow down when a horrible noise steals my words with a long, drawn-out, ear-piercing, *pha-ooh*.

And it doesn't stop with one billow. The King's howling horn is set on repeat. Growing louder. Nearer.

Will stands, squinting in the direction of the sound. "Too close."

Chapter Seventeen

The King of the Island

I hold my breath. I don't mean to, but my lungs refuse to let go of that last stitch of air.

Will's lunged forward so he's in front of me, and my head is buried between his shoulder blades. He reaches his arm behind and around my side, protective—or more likely, worried—I'll do something stupid like run, which I was ready to do before he jumped in my way. "Just be quiet. Still. Whatever happens, do not go home." He speaks in a screechy whisper through his teeth.

I nod my head into his back and his shirt smells of the smoky forest.

It's then I hear footsteps shuffling the sand and ground plants.

Will's arm tightens around me.

He reaches in his pocket and pulls out his blade. It clicks.

The footsteps get louder until one final *pha-ooh* sounds, causing birds and other small creatures to flee the trees.

Then, silence. Total silence, and I wonder if the sound of

the horn, the blasts, have stricken me deaf. I can't even hear Will breathing, but feel his back moving up and down.

Barely, so slowly it's painful, I peek around Will. One, two, three guys stand in a sort of arrow formation on the other side of the crater. The shirtless one in front grips the horn: Duke. He has two black lines smudged under each eye, and his hair is light, cut close to his scalp. He laughs. It's a high-pitched cackle, like a hyena. The hyena arches his back but doesn't take his eyes off Will.

Will urges me back behind him.

I finally breathe. Slow, long breaths squeak up my throat and out my mouth, narrowly avoiding hyperventilation.

"Well?" Will shouts. My entire body jumps.

The hyena laughter is joined by a couple of lower, approving chuckles. I peek around to the other side of Will, to get a closer look. The two boys flanking the hyena are strong, steady. They almost seem to hold Duke up. One has black hair and a soft, surprisingly trustworthy face. The other is blond with a defined jaw, his face showing harder lines.

This can't be good in any way possible.

I'm pushed back again.

Duke stops laughing. "William. *William Matheson*. Long time no *see*. Pun intended."

Will's body stiffens. "What do you want, Duke? Or, since we're being so proper, *David Nathaniel Alperstein, the third*."

And I thought my name was a mouthful.

I peek around just in time to see Duke sigh out his nose. And we make eye contact. "Whatcha hiding? New recruit?" He sneers.

But the expression disappears when the guy to the hyena's right—the one with the trustworthy face and tan skin—smiles, deep dimples showing in his cheeks, then leans over, whispering something in Duke's ear.

"Ha! Boy, did we luck out!"

"Enough! Why are you here and what's with the bombs? The horn?" Will's slowly backing us away, but with each step, the Panthers close in to compensate, trailing the edge of the Mini Cooper hole.

I stumble over my feet, trying to keep an eye on Duke and not fall into the burned crater. He's still watching me, not Will, and I notice he has a scar on his chest loosely resembling the letter P.

"We're just here to get what's rightfully ours. Eye for an eye and all." Duke laughs, shaking his head. "I'd expected more of you, old friend, or don't you remember? I warned you about the horn, what would happen. I thought you'd be more prepared."

"Prepared for what?" We're moving faster now and I think Will's trying to keep Duke talking while we find a way out of this.

"War—the ultimate war over this island. The King and his army of Panthers are coming for you."

"Oh yeah, that. So this is your great army?"

Jesus, what is he doing?

Duke sneers again. "No. This is your one warning and, like I said, we've come to retrieve something that belongs to us."

The talking works, in that nothing's happened, but we aren't getting any farther away. With every few steps we take, they only close farther in on us.

"And what's that?" Will asks, and I swear the weirdo's smiling.

More steps back.

"Oh, come off it. Don't act stupid. We want the girl, of course. She killed Jack!"

A sharp gasp gets stuck in my throat.

"Not a chance."

More steps.

"Come now! Don't tell me you've gone soft on her?" Duke takes in a heaving breath. "How's this… You give her up without a fight, and we'll give you one week to prepare for battle."

Three more steps. I swear I hear water in the distance.

"How's this… I give her up"—Will squeezes my side with

his hand—"and you tell me how you're making the bombs."

Duke's quiet, considering the offer. Then he spits at the ground. "No deal!"

His bodyguards pull out what must be smaller versions of the coconut bombs, balls of packed mud with wicks sticking out of the tops like large, brown cherries.

We take one large step back.

I feel the edge of something under my heels. Glancing over my shoulder, I nearly scream. We're standing on a cliff hanging over a wide pool of water, a series of falls showering far below. If I let go, I fall.

To my death.

With cat-like claws, I wrap both my arms around Will's waist. I catch Duke's eyes widen then narrow.

"Now!" Duke yells.

Dimples and Strong Jaw Guy light their makeshift grenades.

Will turns and faces me. "Hold on, I've got you."

He shoves his body weight into mine.

The mud cherries, all ablaze, fly toward us as we jump over the side.

We fall like anchors or feathers, I'm not sure which because the sensation is so utterly foreign.

I hear someone scream above us.

And I want to scream.

But I can't breathe.

And I don't want to die.

But all I do is hold on to the body falling with me.

Two loud pops go off.

We hit.

As one, wrapped around each other, straight like pencils, Will and I enter the water with a loud clap and a splash. My skin is on fire as if I've gone through a window. All I want is to keep falling deep down into the cool pool until the burn goes away. But Will's got his arm around my chest, pulling me to the surface.

We rise out of the water and gasp for air, spitting and coughing. I kick my legs and Will pulls me toward the bank and solid ground. With my eyes set on the sky, the silhouettes of three blurry figures lean over the cliff.

Then, in a blink, they're gone. Working to get to the side of the pool takes forever. The faster I kick my legs, the farther away the rocks and sand seem.

Finally, my hands grip slippery stone. Will gets out first, then helps me up. We collapse in a heap. Flat on our backs, we pant from exhaustion, sucking in air and coughing out water. "You…all right?" he asks.

I nod, unable to speak. Several deep breaths later it hits me. I sit up, lightheaded. "They'll find us. We have to get out of here!" I mean to shout it, but it comes out in a huskier version of my voice, my throat raw from coughing.

"Shhh. It's okay, they've gone back. If I know anything about Duke, he's not going to risk running into more of us without his full army."

As if on cue, the King's horn sounds from a distance away.

"See? Already headed back up their mountain but had to get the final word in." Will raises up onto one elbow, his body facing mine. He raises his eyebrows, his jaw soft, giving a convincing and comforting look.

I glance away. Aside from the shock my body's still in and the welts and bruises forming beneath my soaked clothes, my head is on fire. Begging to boil over, about to explode like a homemade mud-cherry grenade, my mind roils on information overload: explosions, confessions, tears, kisses, rules, King's, horns, cliff dives.

I take a deep breath. Because, what now? I listen. In this moment, it's quiet as if nothing's happened, as if we've been lying here in the sand for hours, enjoying the shade of the trees, the breeze off the water, one another's company.

But reality hits me, jerking me out of the small daydream I'd allowed myself.

This is no leisurely afternoon. There's a cave-tree full of

kids who are probably freaking out, bombs raining down on us without warning, and the bullies want me as a consolation prize, or more, a sacrificial symbol.

Eye for an eye.

"What are you thinking about?" Will asks, studying my face. The way he stares, I swear he's trying to see my thoughts through my eyes.

I shake my head. "Too much."

"I understand." He looks at the falls, his jaw flexing, forehead creasing from the glint of the sun in his eye. "I used to come here. A lot. Back when I was alone. This was my place and that jump..." He looks up at the cliff.

"Yeah, about that... How did you know you weren't plunging us to our deaths?"

He cracks a slight smile but turns back to serious like it had been an accident. "The water's deep. Though I'll admit, the impact can give a good bite."

I rub the outsides of my arms, cringing.

Will glances down at me, features uncharacteristically soft, apologetic. "Sorry about that. But it was our only out. I've jumped from that same spot more times than I can recall. I knew, without a doubt, it was safe."

Something in his sage eye, the tiny flecks of gold and darker, deeper moss green, staring down on me like constellations, lets me know this is Will being honest. But...

"Why?" I ask. I can't imagine anyone voluntarily making that jump. Ever.

Setting his sight back up toward the cliff, he trails the falls down to the pool. "A story for another time."

Oh no. He's not getting away with that. Not after what I confessed earlier. I turn my body into his, leaning up onto my elbow, squeezing my face to hold back the cries of pain bubbling in my chest because my skin must literally be on fire. "Hey. I shared. Your turn." I strain to get the words out, putting on my best *I'm fine* face as he glances a suspicious eye down at me.

"We should get you back. Plus, the others must be in hysterics wondering what's going on."

"I'm-al-right." I breathe the words out in one string. "And I'm sure Jude and Tilly have everyone under control." I raise my eyebrows, waiting, refusing to let him off the hook. If I have to lie here all day, I'll do it. It's not like I have someplace to be.

"Fine, but I'm giving you the short version and then we've gotta get back." He snips the end of his sentence off.

I nod, satisfied I've worn him down.

Will inhales deeply. He looks away again. "You have to put yourself in my shoes. I'd been here so long, lost my eye, on my own aside from the person who took it from me. I was starving. Soaked from weeks of nonstop rain. I was hopeless, Olive. Dying emotionally, physically. I was halfway gone and quickly unraveling.

"I awoke beneath the same trees I'd been sleeping under each night, but they'd long stopped providing cover. The rain had gotten too heavy and the large flat leaves that had acted as shelter were water-logged and limp, doing nothing for me. I sat up and looked at my palms. My skin was translucent, saturated, and beginning to tear away. I took off my shoes and my feet were the same, nothing but sad, pruned skin. In that moment, at the sight of my feet, I decided I wasn't going to be here anymore. I stood up and walked away. I had no idea where to go, but I walked until my feet bled and I ended up there." He motions to the cliff with his head. "The ledge was slippery, the earth breaking off in clumps, falling down into the pool below. It was perfect. With my toes sinking into the muddy edge, barely hanging on, I said three words... *Please help me.* To whom or what, I'll never know. Maybe to the sun—I'd been cursing her for days for not showing face. Then, I fell forward." He shifts his sight over at me, then back at the water. "I hit the water at a bad angle, not perfectly straight like we did, but sideways. The impact should have killed me. And I thought it had. I sank like a rock, deep into that never-ending pool. I gave myself up, let go, but something pulled me to the surface.

"The sun. She was out. Finally. I looked to the endlessness below me. It was dark, as black as night. When I looked up, I was blinded by yellow, fiery light. I chose up." Again, he looks down at me, a tear building in the corner of his eye. This time, he doesn't look away.

"I never believed in much. My childhood, my life in general… Well, to say it wasn't ideal is an understatement. I wasn't the person I could have been, should have been." Will shakes his head. "But that day, that short moment, I was given something to believe in. I can't explain it, or give it a name, or tell you exactly how it felt, except that it was like being touched by the sun.

"Bug arrived three days later. It hasn't rained like that since." Brushing his eye with his fist, Will then clears his throat. "I've never told anyone that story."

I don't know what to say. There are no words to counter or compare with what I've just heard, just been given. So I scoot closer and dig my head into his chest. His shirt is wet, cool against my face. With a definite hesitation, he pulls me in, breathing onto the top of my head.

My entire body flips on the inside.

And I'm scared out of my mind.

Boys just aren't my forte. Yeah, I've had the stereotypical high-school boyfriend here and there. But it's been a while and I honestly wasn't into it. But Will? He's not your typical high-school boy. Far from it. And he's not someone I can ogle, not from a distance anyway. Plus, he has secrets. I know it. There are plenty more constellations hiding within that moss-green night sky I've yet to discover.

My heart aches for Tawny because she'd know exactly what to do.

Will lets go much quicker than I'd like.

I glance up and he's staring down, giving me a sympathetic smile.

"The rules?" I whisper.

He nods.

"Care to explain?"

He narrows his eye and cocks his mouth to one side. "I'm still working them out myself, but ever since the whole Jude-Annabel tragedy, getting *this* close" —he waves his hand between our bodies— "is dangerous. It's hard enough caring for everyone like family. But *this*" —he does it again. I scowl— "complicates things for everyone. Because when lines get crossed, people do stupid things. They don't think straight. It's just safer. Sorry, I shouldn't have." He sits up and backs away. When he's far enough away that I can't touch him he stands and haphazardly swats the sand off his clothes.

I pull myself up off my elbow, straighten my shoulders, and bite back the ever-present burning of my skin, which doesn't seem to be affecting Will.

"I understand," I say with an oh-so-nonchalant shrug. And I do understand. But something inside of me doesn't want to.

Chapter Eighteen

Eye for an Eye

We're back in the cave-tree.

I'm lying on my stomach, naked save for my underwear. We can't have privacy because Tilly needs to keep her mystery medicine warm next to the fire. I suppose everyone else could move to another room, but they're too enthralled in Will's account of what happened to notice what's going on by the fire.

All except Lewis. And Will. Lewis's eyes keep finding their way to me. Then Will's, following Lewis's, clearing his throat each time, catching Lewis in the act.

I gasp. A whine strings away as a hiss between my lips.

"Ooh, I know, I know. Just a bit more," Tilly apologizes, but keeps on, covering me with the mossy, mushy stuff.

There are cuts and bruises and I don't want to know what else. Gradually, I become a sea monster, draped in greens and browns and gunk.

But it's cool and soothing against my skin.

I close my eyes, listening to the fire crackle, the voices I now know so well.

"So you jumped? You just fucking jumped off that cliff and took Olive with you?" Jude says, running his hands through his hair, half laughing, half shocked.

"We didn't have much choice," Will answers, his voice serious though I can tell there's a proud smirk gracing his mouth.

"You're a badass, Olive!" Jude shouts.

"Psst! She's resting, you oaf!" Tilly calls over in a whisper, adding, "And watch your language."

Bug giggles.

Tilly sighs.

Jude laughs.

I creak one eye open. Tilly's smoldering, her china doll cheeks blotched of pink, but I'm pretty sure it isn't from the heat of the fire. She reaches into the pot and grabs a handful of goop. For a second, I swear she's going to throw it at Jude. Instead, she slops it onto my hip with more force than necessary.

I wince.

"Ooh, so sorry!" she says, catching herself.

I shut my eyes again, breathing deep.

"All right, what's the plan?" Jude asks, popping his knuckles.

"I say we push the bastards off their own cliff," Lewis weighs in.

"Lewis!" Tilly shouts.

I open my eyes.

Lewis shrugs. Jude's nostrils are flared, his chest heaving.

Will's shaking his head, walking toward Jude. He makes to put his hand on Jude's bare shoulder, the one with the large, menacing black widow tattoo on it, but the spider shrinks away before Will's hand lands.

Bug's playing with my hair.

Charlie's in his corner, watching everything like I am.

Our eyes meet.

He looks away.

"Okay" — Will breathes — "everyone calm down. Let's focus on what we know." He walks away from Jude and sits on a stump. Everyone else seems to soften, even Jude though he stays standing. "We know Jack is dead." Will stares at me. My chest folds. I shut my eyes, closing them all out. This is my fault. I've put them in danger. Done the unthinkable… unimaginable…

"Thank you, Olive," Bug whispers in my ear.

Tears heat my eyes.

"For what?" I whisper back.

"You saved my life."

Even so, if it wasn't for me, a boy would be alive, and the King of Vile wouldn't be waging war. But I don't say that. I just nod and smile, keeping my eyes closed.

"Duke's going to send his guys down to take Olive. I know him. He's thinking they'll get their revenge and it'll give us a reason to fight."

"Damn right," Jude cuts in.

"But we're not going to let that happen. We're going to get to them first."

"What?" "How?" "When?" "But…" Several voices blend together with questions all at once.

I open my eyes, those tears having receded.

Charlie sobs and runs into the other room, sending sand flying against the walls in the process.

Bug jumps up, runs toward Will, and kneels on the floor next to him. She wraps her arms around his knees until she's nothing but a brown tuft of hair.

Tilly's now joined in. Her, Lewis, and Jude surround Will with questions while I lie feet away, a paralyzed sea monster, beached, guilty for causing all of this, for putting everyone, and their one safe place on the island, in danger.

"Enough!" he shouts. "Enough." He exhales. Everyone hushes. "I'm not going to have us rush the mountain like a bunch of idiots. I've got a plan. First off, a couple of us are going to find out how they're making those bombs and get a better idea of what's going on up there. We can't continue to sit here and do nothing while we wait for the one that finally hits this tree. It'll be dangerous, but—"

"I'll go!" Lewis blurts, eyes darting to me, then back to Will.

"Yeah, I'm in," Jude agrees.

"Perfect. Exactly what I was thinking. So—"

"No!" I hear myself shout. And before I can think on it, I'm standing, grabbing my shirt off the floor and holding it over my chest. Lewis looks like he's about to pass out. Jude punches him in the shoulder. All of the guys avert their eyes to the ground.

Tilly runs and grabs one of the furs, wrapping it around me. "What are you doing?" she whispers.

I have no idea.

I take a deep breath. "I'm going." I try to sound strong, confident. I think I pull it off, but my damn hands are shaking, mirroring my insides.

"Like hell you are!" Jude yells, peeking over at me, making sure I'm covered before he continues. "Haven't you gotten us into enough trouble?" His words pierce my heart so it both bleeds and wants to shoot back in defense.

"Hey!" Will shouts, jumping up and shoving his face right in Jude's. "You, of all people, know this has been building for years. Maybe she sped up the inevitable, but it was always going to happen." Will's face turns toward me. He shakes his head, brow pinched into a *V*. "Why you?"

Don't cry, Olive. Don't. Cry.

"Because, Jude's right. If it wasn't for me, we wouldn't be in this mess. Not now anyway. I don't care how inevitable it was. And, they won't expect me. And..." I squeeze my fingers into fists to calm the shaking. "It's just something I need to do." My eyes are intent on Will. Despite how the tremors in my hands have found their way to my voice, the words are truer than anything I've ever spoken. I'm going to fix this.

Somehow. Or, at least, I hope I'm strong enough to.

With everyone now staring at me, I realize how ridiculous I must look: half naked with green goop smeared all over my body. I tug the fur a little tighter, not breaking the connection Will and I have.

Will stares, anger and respect lacing his expression. "Fine," he says, nodding. His eyes linger on me a second longer than they should until he must realize he's staring and then turns away.

"No!" Bug follows Charlie's path and runs out of the room.

I can't deny there's a part of me that wants to follow.

The rest are silent, their eyes glazed over. Will doesn't need a horn to reign over this place—his is always the final word.

"Olive. Wake up, Olive." Tilly's shaking me, her accent making the words so much prettier, softer than they are. "We've got to get you washed off before the medicine dries and sticks to your wounds."

That wakes me.

With Tilly's help, I stand. My body is stiff, the glop having hardened into a sort of clay.

Following her strawberry curls through the trapdoor, she carries the coconut "soap," a couple of scrub cloths, and my shirt and pants. Wrapped in the fur mat, I climb on my hands and knees, which proves tricky, and when I come out the other door, I've given up on using the fur as cover. But it's dark. And we're both girls.

Under the moonlight, we walk down the path to the springs.

We pass through a pocket in the trees, and the pools lay before us like a scene from a painting: moonlight glistening off the water, a billion stars reflecting in the sky. I can't help but stop and stare.

Several steps ahead of me, Tilly's stopped, too. She gazes back at me, spiraled hair framing her face. "Lovely, isn't it?"

"It is… God, this place is such a messed-up contradiction."

"How so?"

"Well…" I pause, thinking out my answer, biting the inside of my cheek. "I mean, we're all so tortured by being here, taken away from our families, worried over this impending war, yet it's like this island knows better. It just keeps being beautiful."

"Hmm. Yes. It is something." We stand in silence for a few seconds, admiring the deceit that is the beauty of our surroundings. "Shall we?"

I nod, walking forward, stepping into the warm water in my underwear, dragging the fur with me so I can wash it.

As I drape the mat out on a rock, I catch Tilly's eye.

"Mind if I join you? I could use a wash," she asks.

"Not at all," I say, moving deeper into the pool.

She's still fully clothed, so I keep my back to her, allowing for some privacy. Before I know it she's feet away, wearing a white slip I can tell has been mended several times over.

Tilly hands me one of the scrubby things and I get to work, gently washing off the medicine. The warm water is just as soothing as the cool moss had been.

Working around her slip, Tilly's doing the same. "It hasn't always been torture, you know." I glance over at her. "We've had several good moments here over the years. That is until…" She pulls her eyebrows together, staring at me like she's measuring me up. Seeing if she can trust me.

I venture a smile, lips closed, not sure what to say.

"Until," she continues, "Annabel. Cursed number thirteen. That's when it all went sour. Before her arrival, we weren't living like royalty by any means, but things were stable. There was a content routine about us. We stayed busy, still tried to figure a way home, but the air was lighter, less dense. Then *she* tumbled into our lives." Tilly stops, glaring up at the moon.

"What was so horrible about her?"

She sighs. "Oh, nothing. She was quite lovely, really. But she brought darkness with her. Days after Jude found her, the bombs began."

"So, Jude found her?" Now I see.

She nods. "He'd only been here a year or so and had finally begun to settle. At last, we'd started to—" Tilly shakes her head, inhaling a deep breath. "Then he found her, *Annabel*." The way Tilly says her name, I can feel her hurt, her anger. "Jude didn't leave her side. She'd been injured on the way in—like you." She glances at me, questions in her eyes, the silver light of the moon making them glimmer like glass. "They were inseparable. The one time they were apart was the day she was taken and killed. She'd gone to get fruit, and he'd stayed back to tend to Charlie, who was in a fit. She never returned and Jude hasn't been the same since."

"You like him," I say, going out on a limb I'm sure is pretty sturdy.

Tilly stares straight into my eyes. "I love him." She sighs. "But, enough of that." Tilly splashes water in her face, then dunks her head under. When she resurfaces, her hair is saturated but instantly springs back into loose curls.

We finish washing in silence, dry ourselves as well as we can in the night breeze, then get dressed. My old clothes feel dingy next to my freshly washed skin and the stiff material rubs at my cuts and bruises with each scratchy movement of my body.

Headed back to the cave-tree, Tilly stops me by putting her hand on my shoulder. "Olive?" I look back at her in response. "What I told you… You won't say anything, will you?"

"Never."

"Thank you." She smiles. "And, I didn't mean to imply you're bad luck."

"No, I know. It's okay."

"Good." She hugs me. "You'll do well going to spy. I just know it," Tilly whispers in my ear before letting go. The confidence in her voice makes my stomach hurt because I can't help but feel I'm completely ill-equipped. Not to mention the burning fear growing deep within me that I've shrouded my castaway family with a curse.

Olive Maxi Gagmuehler, unlucky number thirteen.

Chapter Nineteen

JUST BE

It's late. Midnight, maybe? I have no way of knowing and I don't ask even though the others have learned how to tell time by the sun and moon after so many days and nights stuck here.

When we return, Will's tending the fire and having a hushed conversation with Jude. Everyone else seems to have retreated to their respective areas of the cave-tree. Jude's eyes glare up at me when I enter the room. I stop mid-stride, returning his forceful stare.

"Thanks for the chat," Tilly says.

I break the eye contact. "No, thank you for helping me with my back."

"'Course. Well, 'night." She allows her eyes to wander over to Jude for a split second, then leaves.

"I'm going to bed, too," Jude breathes through his teeth, but he doesn't move.

Will clears his throat. "I'm going to grab some wood from outside." Looking from Jude to me, Will stands and walks away.

Jude gets up, raising his eyebrows and pushing his mouth to the side like, *See? No one wants to be around you.* He turns, starting toward the doorway.

"I know you basically hate me, and I know I can't change that, but do you have to be such a jerk?" I kind of regret it the second the words leave my lips, but it needed to be said.

Jude stops and heaves a breath. Then, cracking his neck from side to side, he disappears through the door.

Great. So much for talking it out.

When Will returns, I'm sitting next to the fire, breaking a stick and throwing the pieces in. He sits, too, but doesn't look at me.

Will readjusts the logs with a stick, throwing sparks in the air. "How's your back?"

"Better." It's mostly a lie.

He stares down on me, his dark hair a bit more careless, more mussed after the day we've had. I wonder what it'd feel like to run my fingers through it. Maybe graze his ear with my thumb. "Honestly?" he asks.

I shake my head, incapable of lying when he's staring at me that way, so deeply, entire galaxies just waiting to be found.

He laughs his airy laugh. "Sorry. It'll get better. That nasty stuff Tilly makes soaks into your body and somehow keeps working even after it's washed off."

"Good to hear." It comes out less enthusiastic than I mean it to.

He raises his eyebrows, and again, I'm tempted by what dwells beneath that eye patch of his. Turning more serious, his stare piercing deeper, Will moves down to the floor next to me, not taking his eye from mine. "Can I ask you a question?"

"Yes," I whisper and swallow hard because he's close. I can feel the heat of his body radiating along my right side and he's still staring. My God, does he ever blink?

"How did you feel? Back home, I mean, when those girls

were treating you so horribly? What…" He glances away, then back. "How…" He sighs, breaking our eye contact and speaking into the fire. "How did it make you feel?"

I think for a minute, twisting my wet hair into a knot over my shoulder, opening my mouth a couple of times to speak, but closing it because the words aren't right. My eyes follow his toward the fire, and I talk into the flames.

"No one's ever asked me, so I'm not sure how to answer. Mostly, I felt broken, like each time they hurt me, they took a piece of me with them. I felt helpless. Hopeless. Powerless." My voice breaks and my eyelids sting. "I couldn't be me. I didn't know who I was anymore or if I ever was anyone at all… If that makes sense." I shake my head at myself, sniffing, bottling the tears begging to drop. "But more than anything, I just wanted… To be. Just *be*." I look at Will and wipe my eyes with the heel of my hand. "Sounds stupid, I know."

He turns toward me. "No. It doesn't at all." He shakes his head, brows tugged together, his eye patch pinched. "I'm so sorry." Will's eye glistens, the constellations blurring. Running his hands over his face and into his hair, somehow, he makes his tears disappear. Had I imagined it?

"Well, thanks, but it's not like you had anything to do with it."

To that, he gives me an odd half smile, half frown and pulls me by the waist into him, his face nestled within my hair, his warm breath on my neck.

I swear I stop breathing because this is definitely against the "rules."

As Will pulls away, taking with him the scents of saltwater and earth with mint leaf undertones, I allow myself to exhale slowly out my lips.

"Sorry," he mumbles into the fire.

I tilt my face toward his, trying to catch his eye. "Don't be sorry, it's—"

"Forget it—"

Like a sharp wind, Will's lips are on mine, and we're falling back to the floor in slow motion, and nothing matters in the world but Will's perfect mouth, his salty skin, the firelight. Everything outside this little womb of a tree could explode and I'd be fine with that.

When he lifts his mouth from mine, I feel cheated. *Too soon.* But then I open my eyes and see how he's staring at me: deep, thoughtful, beautiful. Forehead lined, he raises his hand to my hair, the spot above my left ear now nearing a half an inch in length, and holds his hand there, palm down, as if to heal it. Something about it, his deliberate touch, the look in his eye, is more intimate than anything I've ever experienced.

And that eye patch, the firelight casting shadows across the black leather, calls to me, whispering to me to lift it, see what pain, what secrets, what other celestial worlds dwell there.

With Will's hand still warm above my ear, I push my head into it, desperate to feel more warmth. He brushes his thumb across my cheek. My eyes still locked in the intensity, the intimacy of the moment, I reach my fingers up toward his face, to the patch. His chest rises, shoulders tense, but he doesn't stop me. First, I trace the outline of the patch with my pinky. So slow. So slight, my finger a petal, the patch a delicate shell.

Then Will sits up, guiding me with him.

Now facing one another, our knees touching, he brings my hand to his injured eye and together, we lift the patch onto his forehead. He presses his lips together into a stern line and looks away.

I want to gasp and smile and cry all at once because the truths whirling beneath his eye patch aren't anything I'd imagined. They're secrets in the form of pain, hurt, and tiny swirling scars, like vines of unruly seaweed growing along the ocean floor. If his good eye is the night sky, this is its polar twin. Beneath the black, worn leather lies the deepest depths of the sea. Like those constellations, it too swims of unknowns and dark secrets. But, unlike the night sky, these truths are sealed off. Protected. Scarred over.

Unsure, hesitant, hoping to heal it like he did my source of pain, I place my fingertips over the ocean bed, keeping my touch light as if barely grazing a sea star.

Will's shoulders shudder and his chest rises and falls.

Then, he looks at me with his one perfectly green eye, yet another constellation showing through. It occurs to me I should name them. But not now.

As we settle within one another's arms next to the fire, the combination of the warmth, the lulling rhythm of Will's breath, how his chest rises then falls, sleep calls to me. Just when I close my eyes, he brings his lips to my ear and whispers, "I've waited all my life for you."

I'm not sure if he knows I'm awake or means for me to hear it or not, but I don't move. I barely breathe. I work as hard as I can to memorize this space in time.

Because in this moment, right here, right now...

We just are.

Chapter Twenty

CHARLIE

Will and I fell asleep in front of the fire, but I wake up in the morning in mine and Tilly's room. I rub my eyes, hoping—praying—last night wasn't a dream. When I finally open them, I find Charlie sitting cross-legged an arm's length away. But he isn't looking at me. He's staring at something above my head, blond curls dangling over his forehead, blue eyes glowing against his tan skin.

I tilt my neck back, straining my eyes to look up, scooting down my mat, terrified it's going to be a mammoth jungle bug.

There is something hanging above my head. A necklace. *My* necklace. But something's different. I sit up and remove it from the knob of wood it's hanging from. Without a doubt, it's my long-lost silver pendant, except strung alongside it is the carnival doubloon I'd had in my back pocket when I arrived. The chain's been replaced with a piece of leather, the strip, a similar brown to that of my jacket.

Once I pull it over my head, it rests perfectly at my chest, the silver pendant having turned over to reveal a carving that wasn't there before: *Just Be.* Two simple words that hold the weight of the world. I smile to myself, then remember Charlie's sitting in front of me, still staring at the necklace.

I try to make eye contact and notice there's a bit of sand stuck to his cheek. "Morning, Charlie."

His eyes flicker but don't move from my necklace.

Then something happens. Charlie points at his raggedy, torn and faded Castaway Carnival shirt, then motions to the doubloon hanging from my neck.

"Oh, you recognize this?" I pull the coin forward for him to see.

He nods and it's the first we've communicated. My heart warms and I'm terrified I'm going to say or do something wrong that will push him away.

"Do you want to see it closer?" I ask, taking the necklace off my neck and holding it out to him.

The kid glances up at me, one eyebrow cocked, as he considers my offer. He nods.

I push the necklace closer and like a bird pecking for a worm, he picks it from my palm, holding the doubloon close to his chest, rubbing the sides with his fingers.

"Hoh-m," he mumbles so I barely hear it. Aside from his night terrors, which are all screams and yelling, as slight as it is, it's the first time I've heard his normal voice. It's hoarse but high—a child's voice—like Lucky's. "Ho-me," he repeats more clearly, louder, and I'm freaking out but trying to stay calm.

"Home?"

He nods his head once, eyes knowing, the blue beyond his years. This kid can talk, something's just been keeping him from doing it.

"Home," he says plain as day.

Holy shit! I want to yell and scream for everyone to come, but I'm too stunned and too afraid I'll terrify the poor kid. Instead, I try to keep the conversation, such as it is, going. "Do you recognize this from home, buddy?"

He nods, glancing up from the doubloon with longing, tear-filled eyes.

"Would you like to have it?"

He nods his head ferociously. A definite yes.

I attempt taking the necklace back with care, but end up having to yank it from his grip when he won't quite let go. "Don't worry, you'll get it back. I just have to—"

"Home!"

"Yes, yes, home. I'm working on it. Shh…"

But he doesn't *shh*, he wails as I fumble to remove the coin from the leather cord, dropping the damn thing twice.

One by one our family descends on us: first Will comes sliding in, then Jude, followed up by Lewis and Tilly, Bug at their heels, when finally, *finally*, I get the doubloon off and all but throw it at Charlie.

He cradles the thing like a baby, holding it in his palm against his cheek. Charlie chants, "Home, home, home, home…"

Five heads peer around the doorway like turtles stretching their necks out of their shells. They exhale in a combination of gasps and cheers. To which Charlie swivels one-eighty on his butt, holds up the coin, and exclaims, "Home!" His first word in over a year.

"Home!" they all repeat, wide-eyed and googly-smiled as if cooing a puppy. But it's much more. We all know. Charlie even knows it. With his first word comes hope. Hope in the form of a bad replica and the hoarse, unused voice of a nine-year-old.

From the day Charlie says "home," he refuses to leave my side during waking hours and some sleeping hours, despite Bug's very vocal displeasure with that arrangement. But she loves him and relents, eventually conceding to share me.

And, if that isn't enough, the kid is speaking more now, trying to communicate, and giving my little Bed Bug a run for her money. Sure, his speech is pretty rusty, but he's trying, even using gestures when the words don't surface. It's all in there, he just has to remember how to put it to use. Because of that, he's easily frustrated. For some reason, he usually comes straight to me for consoling, which, after many repetitions, I've grown accustomed to.

Will's theory is that Charlie now associates me with home. I'm his security blanket. A place where he feels safe to use his voice after keeping it locked away for so long. It makes sense and is a big responsibility, but one I've taken on for better or worse.

Besides, I have a feeling once he finds that key and gets comfortable, we won't be able to shut the kid up.

Chapter Twenty-One

"Olive? You asleep?"

"Yes."

"Hey! Are not!"

"Well, *you* should be—and you know you're not supposed to be in here. If Tilly wakes—"

"I know, I know. I've…I've been thinkin'…" Charlie sighs.

"And?"

He nudges up to me like Lucky would. "And… I wanna go with you."

Before I can say an adamant *no*, Will enters the room, his silhouette unmistakable in the faint light of the coconut oil candle on the floor next to the doorway.

"Hey, bud," he whispers. "You sleepwalking again?"

Charlie's body stiffens. He sits up, stands, then walks, head down, back to his room.

Will sits next to me, not saying a word.

It's been like this with us for eleven days. Since our "moment," my necklace, and Charlie's first words, which opened some treasure box in his brain where the rest of his speech had been sleeping, yet still listening. While he's ever the quiet, observant Charlie we all know, the kid talks like any nine-year-old, but similar to Bug, there's this way about him that's far beyond his years. The transformation has been miraculous. And all because of that silly doubloon which Will quickly fashioned into a bracelet for Charlie.

Will lies down beside me, staring up into the tree ceiling. We stay silent for a while, listening to each other's breathing.

Then, the now familiar *pha-ooh* rains down from the mountain like clockwork.

We stare at each other.

It sounds again.

We wait.

Silence.

Will and I exhale at the same time.

The King's horn has been sounding each night since our encounter at the cliff over the waterfall. It's always late at night, always two blows, twice in a row. No bombs. No more appearances. It's as if he's taunting us, messing with our heads, so when he does strike we won't be expecting it. That's Will's theory, anyway.

He turns and faces me. "Charlie can't go with you. It needs to be Jude—*has* to be Jude. Everyone else is too weak."

"I know…"

"But?"

"But… What if they attack while we're gone? You'll need Jude more than I will." He sighs—because I'm right. "If not Charlie, who? Lewis?"

"Yeah right. Lewis alone with you for who knows how many days? He'll lose his mind. You'd be better off taking Charlie." He glances over at me and I can just make out his half smile. "Though getting rid of the lovesick, mopey stooge for a while would be nice, I'm not gonna lie." He laughs airily.

Lewis has been in a horrible mood since the day Will gave me the necklace. Apparently Lewis had found it next to me that first day I arrived and taken it, for, uh, safekeeping. Not only was he embarrassed, but probably now suspects Will and I have feelings for one another. And we do. What exactly those feelings are, I'm as unsure as Lewis must be.

I half smile back. "So? Who, then? I mean, I could go by my—"

"You're not going alone." He looks away. "Tilly needs to stay for Bug, I need Jude in the case of attack, and Lewis, well, Lewis can't."

"Charlie it is then?"

He heaves a long sigh. "Charlie it is."

Chapter Twenty-Two

THE KING'S MOUNTAIN

Duke's mountain is something straight out of Narnia—the White Witch's castle minus the snow and ice. It's barren. Tall peaks of rock scratch at the sky, trying to score and scar its perfect blue. Each sharp finger points toward several above it.

According to Will, to scale it, we need to find the perfect route. And there are several skinny pathways winding up the cliffs. Some find you higher, many lead to dead ends. Each day for the past two, Charlie and I have been following Will, slowly making our way here, memorizing the hike, where to camp if need be, and talking over what we'll do once we reach the cave, tirelessly speculating the outcome. The more I learn, the more I wonder why I volunteered for this death sentence.

Oh yeah, to fix things. Mend relations between the two sides and end this war, because if it hasn't happened in ten years, these two groups clearly know nothing about making peace. Not that I'm skilled in such matters, but there's this nagging in my gut that tells me I can do it. I can do this.

I hope.

Maybe.

Will, Charlie, and I stand at the base of the sharp hills, hiding behind thick ground plants and boulders as we gaze up into endless mountain and cloudy sky.

"You see that path? There, between those two huge rocks?" Will asks through his teeth and under his breath.

Charlie and I nod in unison, staring at what could be the gateway to Hell; two sharp boulders parallel one another marking two different lands. Where we crouch, it's green, alive, the forest reaching up toward the mountain, only to recoil at the gate, the other side dry. Barren. Dead.

"That's the way up to reach the cave. You'll know it when you see it. Its mouth is huge, a gaping hole in the mountain like a black, bullet wound," Will speaks toward the mountain and at that wound, wherever it is.

"Then what?" Charlie whispers, voice shaking. He grabs my hand and squeezes. I give him a look of reassurance, nodding.

"Just like we talked about, you'll camp out in a smaller nearby cave, there are hundreds up there. Stay as long as you can, get any information you're able—especially about the bombs—then come back down. Anything you get will be helpful, buddy—even if it's what they eat for breakfast." He winks at Charlie, giving me a more cautionary glance once Charlie looks away.

We hike back, retracing our steps, but at an expedited speed, reaching the cave-tree in half the time.

Bug's tiny calf muscles flex with each step as I follow her into the woods. Single-file, she leads, then me, then Jude, who wasn't shy about displaying his displeasure over being sent on the task with us—me.

Since I'm the newbie, Bug's to show me some survival skills and Jude was sent as protection in the form of an irritable tag-along. Collecting a variety of items in her bag,

Bug stops every few paces to pick something from a plant or dig into the ground.

When we reach a small clearing in the forest, she finally stops, settling herself atop a small green patch of moss. I crouch right across from her. Jude stays a good distance away and sits on the ground. He pulls out his knife then starts carving into a nearby stump.

I glance back at Bug who's laid out her hoard along lines of leaves.

"What's this?" I'm ready to be schooled in how-not-to-die-in-the-forest 101.

"You'll see," says the little sneak, narrowing her eyes up at me, cocking a sideways grin. The look reminds me of Lucky— one he's given me a thousand times. If it's possible, my heart shrinks a bit more. As if Jude senses it, he coughs, somehow, in a smug way. I want to throw one of Bug's specimens at him.

"Ready!" Bug whisper-shouts in my face. I snap out of the fantasy where I'm plucking the strings from Jude's guitar one by one. Before me is an assortment of nature, small pieces of the forest equally spread out like chess pieces.

She points a stick at a set of very similar plants. "First, roots. Ginger. Dandelion. Cattail. You can eat them straight from the ground or boil them. They're less sour boiled."

I nod.

"These are the ones we find all the time. They grow all over."

"Got it." Not so hard. I know these, we eat them daily.

"Next"—she points with the stick—"plants." From top to bottom she identifies the twigs and leaves: wild asparagus, amaranth, sugar cane, plantain leaves, and, of course, dried seaweed and kelp she must have brought with her from the cave-tree because we haven't passed by any water. She explains where to find each and how to best eat them.

"And this…" She picks up white flowers with yellow centers. "Wood sorrel. Well, that's what Lewis calls them. We called it 'tsee-nah.'" I take a deep breath, and she swishes her mouth from side to side. "It kind of means 'a flower you drink,' because it'll help if you're thirsty."

I nod again.

She furrows her barely-there eyebrows. "Are you getting all this?"

"I am, yes. Wood sorrel, cattails, amaranth. I've got it." But really I'm so distracted. Distracted by my shrinking heart, by memories of sweltering Texas summers and Tawny's bedroom and Mom's lasagna, the way Dad's always pushing his glasses up his nose, Lucky... All things Lucky. And then there are the present distractions. Little Bug's focus, her patient insistence on helping me. Jude's incessant chip-chipping away of the stump. The birds chirping. Waves rolling. Leaves jingling.

Next, we go over poisonous plants. "Keep away from plants with milky sap, thorns, or any with clumps of three leaves." She instructs me on how to collect water in a coconut shell or worst case scenario, a large leaf if we lose our drinking containers. And, finally, the little nature guru shows me how to build a fire.

She'd have won a fortune on a reality show.

By the time we get back home, I'm mentally and physically exhausted and so is Bug. With a yawn, she crawls into the cave-tree, no doubt to cuddle up atop her rug for a nap.

Jude was silent the entire walk back. When he makes to enter the door after Bug, he pauses, searching his pocket for something. He then turns to face me, handing over several crudely carved, sharp pieces of wood bound together and a sort of slingshot-type tool. With caution, like I'm not sure if he means for me to take them or not, I reach over. He places them in my hand.

"You already know how to use them, but you'll find the sling-shot's more effective. Just thought some protection was called for."

I'm speechless. So this is what all of his obnoxious chip-chipping was about? "Um, thanks," I finally spit out.

"Yeah, well, hopefully, you won't need them to defend

yourself, and you can use them to hunt if you need to."

"Okay," I say. "Thank you. Really."

Jude inhales through his nose, widening his eyes and nodding his head. He turns to go through the hidden door, but again, he stops.

"I don't hate you," he mumbles.

I barely hear it. But I do. Head down, he speaks to the door. "I hate this fucking island. It takes everything I love, chews it up, and shits it out." He sighs. "But I never hated you."

I swear he sniffs as he ducks into the tunnel and before I can say anything in return.

Chapter Twenty-Three

Maps

I lie on my stomach atop my mat, studying. Tomorrow is the big day. Across from me is Lewis, also on his stomach, our foreheads inches apart, his eyes darting away from mine each time I answer a question about the maps between us.

Tilly brought books with her. Her parents had sent her to live with her aunt and uncle to get away from the bombs. They were killed three days later.

The day she showed up on the island, she'd been walking home from school but stopped to watch a puppet show put on by a band of street performers. They'd been going around, cheering up children, many of whom were in similar situations as Tilly. Mid-show, the bomb sirens sounded. Everyone scattered. Tilly ran home, planning to duck into her cellar, when the horrible whirling airplane engines charged overhead. No time to think, she bolted into an alleyway. Then another. Twisting and turning, she came upon a loosely boarded manhole. She climbed in to find a series of tunnels. Her knees scraped and shredded into bits as she crawled along the cold, damp stone in the dark, clutching hold of the leather strap of her books. The sirens and engines grew fainter, replaced by ground-shaking booms. Tilly picked up the pace, eventually escaping up through what she thought was the way out.

Once through, she was on the island.

Over the years, she's refused her books be used for anything. They're *her* books, her connection to home and protested having them used as kindling. I can understand that. Once she let Bug and Charlie draw on a few pages with charcoal. Mostly, she reads from them to the kids before bed—fortunately, one is a literature book, though I can assume they'd take anything if it was distraction enough.

Another is a history book with a section on maps and map-making, several pages blank canvases. Lucky for Charlie and I, for our impending mission, Lewis is an excellent artist. He's created the most detailed maps for us to follow, spending days in the forest, recording each major landmark, body of water, and food source. And he's taken full advantage of playing mapmaker — being sure to school me nightly.

Tonight is no exception.

"Where's the first place you'll find water safe for drinking?" he asks, leaning up on his elbows, chin resting in his hands.

"About nine miles northeast of the cave-tree. There." I point at the small spring, thinking of Charlie and dragging the kid so many miles for water. I look at Lewis.

He whips his gaze down at the map so I don't see he's been watching me. Glancing up, his cheeks are stippled of red. He exhales like he's been holding his breath.

"Correct. And…" He searches for another question, knowing we'd exhausted the need for this several nights ago. Still… "Ah, are these plants here edible?"

I instantly recognize the spiked tongue-like stalks from Bug's lesson a couple days before. "Bluetongue shoots? No, they'll make our throats swell and kill us."

"Good… Good…" He nods, again searching, flipping to the next map, dark hair falling over his eyes. He sits up and brushes it aside, wrists and forearms thin, delicate, not that of a boy's, but not near that of a man's. Lewis holds up the second map so I can't see it, peering over the top, his brown eyes innocent yet so wise. "And—"

"Knock, knock," Will cuts in, striding into the room and crouching down next to us. Lewis drops the map and his face falls, those bright eyes of his switching from hopeful to tired and incensed. Will smiles. Not a half smile, but a rare full smile. "Studying again, are we?" he asks.

"Well, we want to be sure she's prepared, her and Charlie." Lewis straightens his shoulders.

"Yes, for her *and* Charlie." Will's grin widens.

They stare at one another. Each waiting for the other to leave.

Stalemate.

Lewis concedes. "I suppose if you don't know it all by now…" He breathes in. "You'll do fine Olive, I know you will." He picks up the map and stacks it on the pile. Then he stands, shoulders slumped, like he's saying good-bye.

I sit up on my knees and grab his hand. "Hey, thank you."

Lewis stares at our hands. "Sure," he says. "My pleasure." He peers down at me, smiling, his lips closed, more pressed into a line.

"I'll say good-bye before we leave."

He nods, turns and leaves, and doesn't glance back.

"Poor kid," Will says, shaking his head.

"Well, you're not being much help." I glare at him.

"What's that supposed to mean?" He's still grinning, smaller, but it's there, twitching at the corners of his mouth.

"Will, you embarrassed him."

He scoots closer, smile gone. With a deep breath, he says, "You're right." One of Will's hands rests on his leg. He squeezes it into a fist and closes his eye. "I'm a jerk." He opens his eye. "I'll give him some time, but I'll talk to him;

apologize." And it's as if he's genuinely surprised at himself—
like that other guy was an alternate version of Will.

"I'm sure he'll be fine, but talking to him would probably
help. He looks up to you."

"I will, I will…" His voice trails off, face serious, lines
stretched across his forehead. "How are you feeling?"

I pull my shoulders forward and drop my head. Something
inside of me shrinks because I have no idea what I'm doing.

Will moves closer, sitting cross-legged in front of me, his
bare feet blurring behind the tears burning and pooling in my
eyes.

"Hey." He bends down, leaning in closer, trying to catch
my sight. "You don't have to do this. No one's forcing you."
I shake my head, the motion freeing a couple of tears. They
drop to my knees. I take a deep breath because *I do* have to
do this. "If you don't mind me asking, why'd you request—
well, *demand*—to go?"

I stare up at him, the blurry version of him. I'm fighting
the tears, painfully managing to suck them back. They don't
fall, but are collecting and pooling. Before they spill over,
I wipe my eyes with my arm, trying to pretend they never
were. "Why?" I repeat his question. Will nods, not blinking. "I
just know it's something I have to do. Being here, getting to
know all of you, being accepted into your family… I have this
overwhelming need to protect what's important and prove to
myself I can fight back. I finally feel like I have something to
offer, something to fight for. But…with Charlie coming along,
I'm not so sure anymore. What if I fail? What if something
goes wrong? If it were only me, that'd be one thing. But
Charlie…" I bite my lip, trying hard to hold back the crying
fit that's knotted in my chest, but it's slipping, ready to fling
up and out of my mouth any second. "I'm… I'm…" And I
can't finish the sentence because the knot breaks. Instead, a
horrible quake leaves my mouth as Will scoops me up and
into his lap.

Curled up like a child, I weep into his chest, his arms

clasped around me as he whispers in my ear, "You can do this, Olive."

The King's horn wails.

I gaze up at Will and silently promise myself that if I make it up the mountain I'm bringing that damn horn back with me.

Another *pha-ooh* sounds as if in answer to my challenge. It's the loudest yet.

Chapter Twenty-Four

IT'S TIME

Jude busts through the door, a mix of concern and dread sending lines branching away from his eyes.

"It was close," Will says, pulling away from me.

Jude, that dragon tattoo on his neck eying me, nods. "If you and Charlie plan to leave, you'd better get going now."

Now or never.

Will stands and proceeds to walk in circles, hands pressed into his forehead.

I jump up so fast I get light-headed and have to bend forward, taking deep breaths and resting my hands on my knees. Okay… Okay…

We'd planned to take our time. Prepare. Check and double check and then breathe and then triple check we were ready just to be sure.

Once my head stops swimming, I stand upright to find Will marching toward me. He crashes into my body, taking my breath away and holds me so tight I'm back to light-headed.

"It's going to be all right. I promise." His voice is soft,

concerned yet strong. I nod, my face once again pressed against his chest. He pulls away, looking down on me. "I'm getting Charlie up." He kisses my forehead and leaves. The sensation lingers, tingling even once he's gone.

Everyone's been dragged awake and gathered around the trapdoor to the cave-tree. Bug's eyes are half open, swollen from sleep, her hair an impressive ball of static. Next to her is Tilly, stress lines etched across her forehead, two long braids framing her face. Jude and Lewis stand to their right. Jude, unreadable. Lewis, someplace between crying and livid. Will stands between Charlie and I as we stare down at the door.

Charlie and I are bid several "be safe's" and "see you soon's." No good-byes.

Everything is rushed. Set on fast-forward. I'm not ready.

I get a quick embrace from Tilly. A baby bear-hug from Bug. A nod and approving half grin from Jude—which is more than I expected.

I'm not ready.

With an awkward side-hug, Lewis slips me a flat, dark green stone with a dip in the middle. A worry rock.

But I'm not ready.

"Time to go," Will announces, those three words sending any sliver of confidence I have running out the door.

With one last fleeting look at each one of my new family, Will, Charlie, and me descend one by one into the door, crawl through the tunnel, then emerge out the other side of our Lion's den.

The plan had been to leave mid-morning. Instead, it's mid-night. The air is fresh, the breeze cool, that familiar forest scent of rusty dirt and green sweetness floods my senses. It's the same air I'll be breathing in for I don't know how long.

The thought terrifies me.

Will must be picking up on my emotions because he's lost his composure. Charlie and I stare as Will stands still, his face in his hands.

He paces.

He tells us to leave and then stops us.

Twice.

Finally, with a sigh that somehow spans time and space, he says, "I'm going. Charlie get back inside."

"No," Charlie says, shaking his head.

"I'm sorry, but it's best this way." Will leaves no room for Charlie to argue. Instead, the poor kid just glances away, bottom lip quivering.

Oh jeez. I put my hand on Charlie's sad, slumped shoulder. "Why don't you wait over there. Give us a minute?"

Without a word, he walks out of earshot, sitting on a large rock.

I lean into Will, speaking just above a whisper. "What the hell are you doing? We don't have time for this!"

He glances at Charlie then back at me. "I thought I could let you go, but it's too dangerous."

I drop my bag to the ground. "Are you freaking kidding me? You can't do this, Will. We're ready. And we're going."

Jaw tight, Will tugs at his bottom lip with his teeth, looking over at Charlie again. My eyes follow. Charlie's picking at the moss on the rock, blond waves covering the top half of his face. We hear him sniff.

I gaze back at Will, his eye patch is slick like ink in the moonlight and the green of his right eye is more silvery, like a gemstone. "He needs this as much as I do. Maybe more."

Pha-ooh!

My eyes go wide because it's even closer now.

Will kicks at the dirt and stares up at the sky, puffing a breath out his nose as if cursing the stars. "Fine. You're right. I'm sorry." He rakes his hands through his hair so it sticks up in all directions. "Go." He motions to Charlie but doesn't take his eye off me. "You're up, bud."

Charlie runs over, smile stretched across his face.

Will scruffs Charlie's hair. "Sorry, buddy. You've got this."

Digging into his back pocket, Will produces his blade and hands it to me. I shake my head no, but he nudges it at me. "I want you—need you—to take it."

I nod, taking the blade, and put it in my pocket.

Will steps closer, resting his forehead against mine. "You're more a Lion than you know, Olive Maxi Gagmuehler."

I flinch. He steps back, nodding to himself, shoving his hands into his pockets. Will then turns his head to Charlie, who's picking at the bark of a tree. In a motion so quick it doesn't register, Will yanks his hands from his pockets, grabs me by the waist, and jerks me into him, tight, like he's never going to let go. Breath heavy and warm in my ear, he kisses my earlobe then speaks.

"Be safe. And come back so you can force me to rethink my rules." His words are as weightless as snowflakes and my heart thumps into his chest where, I find, there's a similar rhythm, his heart racing, working to keep up with mine.

"I promise," I say.

With one last squeeze, he moves away, slowly, grazing his face along my cheek, stalling where our noses touch and our lips are nothing but a breath, a gasp, a sigh, away from each other. And there's that hint of mint. Does he always have it in his mouth? Because it's there, his breath sweet with it and I'm spinning. Closing my eyes, I can almost taste the mint.

"Take care, little Lion," he says, pushing his forehead into mine, bringing one hand up to that place above my left ear, holding it there, then letting go of me.

I nod, trying not to cry, begging myself to be strong in this moment when I'm terrified out of my mind. Why was this so important again?

Pha-ooh. The King's horn sounds as if in answer.

Now or never.

Will pulls me even closer. "Watch out for the sheep" —

he whispers into my lips— "they're assholes." He steps away. "Go."

But I'm not ready.

But now or never.

We leave.

I want to look back, but I don't. I can't. Because I know how much he's dying to run after us, and I might just let him.

Chapter Twenty-Five

Olive and Charlie

Our gear, haphazardly thrown together in a rush, consists of a bag each, short spears shoved into the sides and water bottles made from the shells of gourd-like plants hanging from a loop of braided twine (another one of Lewis's inventions). My pack is slung over my shoulder. Tilly stitched it together from my leather jacket, and really, for what it is, it's beautiful. Charlie's is crafted from an old sheep skin. We carry the bare minimum, because we'll mostly be living off the island.

We've been moving for hours, making as little noise as possible, choosing our steps carefully so we don't run into whoever was blowing that horn so closely.

It's still dark, but an ever-expanding lip of orange sunlight is inching its way across the horizon.

Based on Lewis's map, Charlie and I are headed northeast, toward the first source of fresh water along our route. Before our test run to the mountain, the longest I'd ever traveled on foot was a 5K Tawny had talked me into running with her. And I did run. I sprinted the first mile to keep up wither her, threw up my bagel from breakfast, then walked the rest of the way. Tawny, being sweet Tawny, insisted she walk with me, but she'd have rather run it out.

Between my non-skills and a nine-year-old's short stride, we've got our work cut out for us. It'll take the better part of the day and drain us dry of the drinking water we've brought from the cave-tree to make our intended mark by nightfall.

I lead the way, taking calculated yet quick steps, switching off glancing at the ground before me and searching for the landmarks Lewis had me memorize. This place is so unpredictable, one misstep and I could hurl us over a cliff or into a pack of Panthers.

All night, I've been aware of Charlie's footsteps behind me, but now I can hear his breath wheezing. A sound I know all too well. I glance over my shoulder. "You all right?" I whisper.

He nods, but his curls are soaked with sweat and, with the sun rising quickly, I can see his face is red, his eyes puffy. I stop. "Let's take a break. Reward all this walking with a snack."

"Okay," is his breathy reply.

I know we shouldn't stop. That whoever was attached to that horn is out here somewhere. But, what else can I do? The kid's gotta rest and, honestly, sitting down sounds like the best thing ever right about now.

We settle beneath a group of broad-leaved trees and I pull out the fish flakes Tilly dried and cured with saltwater along with a handful of coconut chunks that we've already dug into a couple of times while walking. I separate the food sparingly, giving us each two bits of coconut and a small handful of the fish.

We sit in silence, listening to the sounds of the island and each other chewing. Charlie takes a long swig of water, wiping his forehead with the back of his hand. "It's so hot already." With a sniff, he turns his gourd upside-down. It's empty except for the few drops trickling out.

"Oh my God!" I hiss, trying to keep quiet but freaking

out. "Did you drink it all?"

"I didn't mean to," he whispers back. "I was thirsty." The kid gives me a set of blue puppy dog eyes that damn near breaks me.

"Listen, bud. You know we don't have much water with us. You've got to pace yourself, just a few sips here and there. You can't gulp it down like that."

"Okay. Sorry."

"We can share mine, but small sips."

Charlie nods, shoving his last piece of coconut into his mouth, making a grossed-out face as he swallows it. "I hate coconut."

I laugh. "Bad luck for you, eh?"

He flashes a wide grin. "Don't tell Tilly, but I give all mine to Lewis." He takes a deep breath.

"Are you all right to go on? It isn't too late to turn around. This is rough. It's hot, and we still have a long way to go," I say.

"No. I don't want to turn around. Please don't make me go back," he blurts out, spewing small shreds of coconut at me.

"Shh! It's okay." I pat his back. "But we've gotta be quiet and keep moving."

Something in my gut nudges me to turn back. I ignore the urge. "Ready?"

"Yeah." Charlie wipes his nose with his shirt, hopping to his feet like a peppy puppy.

By the time we reach our halfway point, Charlie's lost his pep and we're down to a few sips of water at best. We're behind schedule and stopped so he can rest and catch his breath—

Pha-ooh. That damn horn.

I gasp.

Charlie's eyes go wide.

It's close. Like, around the corner close.

I pull myself and Charlie back behind a tree.

We're ducked in the brush, squeezed side-by-side as if our lives depend on how close we can get, and still the trunk barely covers us.

"Do you think they're coming— " Charlie whispers in my ear, stopping short. He hears something. The same something I hear: quick footsteps.

My eyes dart from tree to tree, plant to plant, searching for a better place to hide. But there's nothing. No cave-trees, not even a ditch. We stay put. Unmoving. Barely breathing. As the footsteps grow louder, closer, Charlie hides his face in my shoulder, clutching his fingernails into my back, his breath whistling through my shirt sleeve.

I wrap my arm around him, pat his back, hoping to calm the kid.

But he stiffens. Then I stiffen. Because the kicking of ground brush is about to pass right in front of us.

"Olive?" Charlie whines as air into my shoulder.

I rub his back harder, hoping he'll hush, hoping no one heard.

The running feet slow. Then stop.

"Why the hell did you stop?" a girl snaps.

"You hear that?" a boy says, his voice cracking in a screech.

"What?" a gruffer, older boy asks.

"I'm not sure…" Screechy voice moves closer. "Something. A whisper." Wait. That voice. I know its screeches. The Wildling twin. My stomach twists and I swallow the gasp caught in my throat.

With both his arms clamped around me, Charlie tries as he might to keep his wheezing under control. I stop breathing altogether.

"I didn't hear anything," the girl says.

"Me neither. Probably an animal. Let's keep going," Gruff voice says.

"But— " Wildling twin tries to argue.

"We have a deadline, man!" Gruff voice bites back.

"Come off it, guys! Henry's right. It was probably just an animal. Let's keep going. Duke wants results *today*," the girl cuts them both off and they're on the move again, footsteps now running away from us.

Charlie and I exhale simultaneously but don't dare move until we can't hear so much as a distant shuffling.

Charlie's first to break the silence. "What are they doing?"

"I don't know, buddy. The girl said Duke expects results, so I can't help but wonder if they're searching for me." His face crumples. "It's fine. Don't worry."

I stand, brush myself off, and look up at the sky. "We better keep walking toward the water. We won't make it today, but let's get as close as we can. If we're lucky, we can find some coconuts and drink from them."

"Mm'kay," is Charlie's tired reply as he, too, gets up, not bothering to brush off. Gathering our gear, re-packing our bags, we move on—in the opposite direction of the small group of Panthers who are headed straight for our cave-tree.

Our cave-tree.

Neither of us speaks it, but I know we're both thinking it.

Finding a place to camp proves difficult. More difficult than Lewis made it out to be. *"Just locate a cove, or cave, or large tree and set up camp,"* he'd said. Well, there are no coves, or caves, or large enough trees to hide behind or under or in. Not here anyway.

Charlie and I settle on a small area surrounded by thick plants—a dead-end just off our route. It'll hide us, but also trap us. Not the best, but we're exhausted, and while Charlie's not wheezing anymore, he's off. This will have to do.

As the sun falls behind the mountains, casting the island in shadows and dim purple light, there's a smoky, nostalgic campfire smell filling the air.

The Panthers are far enough away that we can't hear them or see their fire, yet close enough that its odor surrounds us.

This is cause alone to avoid building a fire ourselves, and once again, we must eat from our rations and promise to replenish our stash tomorrow. We're a good hour walk from the small spring, then two, maybe three more hours to the base of the mountain.

We work quietly to pierce a couple of coconuts while Charlie whispers about why he hates anything coconut flavored because he once threw up a macaroon.

"My dad always keeps a tin of them in his desk drawer. When I was four, I snuck in and stuffed a bunch in my mouth. I think I ate almost all of them. When my mom called for me, I jumped up from the chair, and—barfed. All over the floor." He shakes off a shiver. "It's my arch enemy." Charlie lets out an airy laugh under his breath, reminding me of Will. "It was gross." He scrunches his forehead and makes a sad sound like a puppy whimpering. "Anything you hate to eat, Olive?"

"Oh, definitely. I actually hate seafood. It reminds me of giant bugs. So creepy. But, I guess I'm outta luck there with that." I wink at him.

He smiles. "Yeah…" Charlie's blade pops through the coconut skin, jarring his upper body forward. He jerks the knife out, wide grin visible through the shadows, and all I can think is how I'd never let Lucky use a knife like that. I force a smile back.

"Nice work," I say.

Charlie keeps smiling, sucking the milk from the ripe coconut like a sippy-cup. He lies down on his bag when he's nursed it dry.

I go back to work on mine, turning the rough thing over in my hands, searching with my fingers to find the three eyes like Bug showed me. I pierce one. Then another. With the third, I shove the knife in, pull it out, turn it, and shove it in again, making an X, then swivel the blade in a circle. I put my knife away, bring the coconut to my lips, tip my head back, and pour. My mouth is so dry it instantly absorbs the water. After going the last half of the day without anything, it tastes like heaven.

When I'm finished gulping, I remove the small fur blanket from my bag, lay it over Charlie, then untie the woven mat from his pack and cover myself with it.

I close my eyes, but can't fall asleep. Instead, I listen to Charlie's breathing, how the wheezing is coming back. Worried as I am, I'm also more tired than I've ever been, and the soft whooshing lulls me to sleep.

I awaken to the horrible and unmistakable sound and stink of barfing. Charlie is on all fours, puking into the plants beside us.

"Shh… It's okay." One part concerned for Charlie's health and two parts terrified he'll give us away, I try to quiet the kid while consoling him by rubbing his back. He makes more gagging noises. "Shh…" He sits up and wipes his mouth with his hand, spreading the froth across his cheek. "Use your shirt," I whisper. "We'll rinse it tomorrow."

He nods, pulling up the bottom of his shirt, mopping his mouth and chin.

I reach for my coconut from earlier. I'd saved a few drinks for the morning, but offer it to him now.

"Thanks. Sorry." He takes the coconut and drinks.

"No biggie, buddy." He stares at me with heavy eyes. "Do you think you're sick?"

"I don't know. Maybe. I feel a little better now. When I woke up my stomach was hurting so bad. But… Oh no, not again. It's getter…worse…er— " He folds his arms around his waist. More puke.

"Worse," I correct his grammar in a whisper only I can hear, because what does he care? He's throwing up the only food and drink he's had all day. We're already failing and haven't even begun.

Shits.

Chapter Twenty-Six

CAN'T ESCAPE THE MONSTER

I awaken mid-wheeze. "Hhhh…huh. Hhhh…huh—" I sit straight up, clutching my throat. "Hhh…huh. Hh…huh… huuuhh—"

I tuck my legs underneath me. Curl into the fetal position. Shove my head between knees.

"Hhhh! Huuh…hhh…hhhuuhh—" Breathe, Olive. *Breathe.* Through the nose. Out the mouth.

There's shuffling in the background.

"Olive? You okay?" Fear shakes Charlie's whiny words.

I nod my head—still shoved between my knees.

"Hhh…hhuh…hhh…hhuh…" I swallow, the fit settling.

Head still down, I stretch my arms straight out in front of me, opening up my ribs, my lungs, breathing in the dirt below me.

"I'm—huh—o—hhh—kay…" I say between quick breaths. This is how I do it. How I've been doing it since that first time the Trio struck. *Calming the storm.* Or better, *killing the monster.* I've learned to slay the physical and mental mind blow before it takes me down its hellish spiral. I've never fallen all the way down. But the threat is always one breath away.

Eyes watering, nose running, I've created a not-so-cute mud puddle in the dirt below me. I lift my head, wipe the sludge from my face, and sit up in slow motion. I'm still breathing heavily but am passed the storm.

"Sorry," I say.

Charlie's frozen, horror mixed with concern contorting his face. A breeze picks up the leaves in the trees above us, urging me to look into the branched sky.

"Is that normal?" he asks.

"For me? Yes." But I've never had one this big without the Trio to get it started.

"Does it happen a lot?"

I meet his eyes. "No. It's fine. Nothing to—" I'm about to say "worry about," but I see the kid for the first time this morning and I'm shocked. His eyes are swollen, puffy, black against chalky skin. And bloodshot. "Your eyes!" I shout, then slap my hand over my mouth. "Your eyes," I whisper through my fingers.

"What? Oh. Yeah. Do I have the circles?"

I nod.

"And the pillows?"

I nod again. How does he know?

"It's allergies." He sniffs. "I used to get them at home a lot. Peanuts and dairy mostly. Sometimes wheat, though, depends what it is. It hasn't been so bad here. Until now." He wipes his nose across his forearm.

Great. Perfect timing. "Is that normal?"

"Kinda. Mom used to tell me my allergies were like a big cup: my body was okay until it filled up, but if it spilled over the side, I was in trouble. Worst thing is the itchy eyes."

Charlie's last word is taken over by a loud, long *pha-ooh*.

No.

It's loud.

Near.

Before I can say anything, another horn sounds. It's the same *pha-ooh*, but this one calls from a distance, answering the first.

What the hell? Do they have two horns? Are they communicating?

No, no, no chants in my head as Charlie and I scatter in circles like mice, collecting gear, stuffing our bags, clearing any evidence we were ever here.

The stampede of feet drums toward us.

We drop to the ground, landing flat like snakes, half put-together packs falling from our backs.

"Hurry!" The girl from last night shouts.

"Hey! I'd like to see you run with a hundred pounds on your back!" Gruff boy yells after her.

Wildling laughter.

"Ha. Ha. You finished? Now, come on, less bitching, more running!" the girl shouts, drill-sergeant style.

Neither argues and their footsteps quicken.

But wait…

A hundred pounds. Of what? Of *who*?

Still lying on our bellies, I stick my face in Charlie's ear. "Can you run?"

He nods and I ignore the hesitation in his nine-year-old eyes. Because he isn't your typical nine-year-old boy. He's stronger. Wiser. At least that's what I tell myself as I hoist him up by the armpits and pull him along after me—after the Panthers, who have something and are running it back up their mountain.

An offering for their leader? Wild animals with fresh kill?

But lions eat panthers.

Or so I've been told…

Sweat beads on my upper lip and I can taste the salt in my mouth. We've been tip-toeing as well as anyone could ever possibly tip-toe through a forest for hours and without a cloud in sight. Even here, under the trees, the heat and humidity is getting the best of the island.

We've gone off course. Off the map Lewis worked so hard to perfect.

We've gone without drink or food for far too long.

We've fallen farther behind, quickly losing the Panthers. The only indication we're going the right direction is an occasional swear or demand shouted by one of them.

Charlie and I don't dare speak. We barely make a sound save for our breathing and an occasional, unavoidable branch under foot.

He's not well. The kid is pasty and wheezing. So far, the low, whistling breath streaming out his mouth and nose isn't horribly loud. But if it continues and worsens, I'm worried he's going to make the Panthers turn around for us.

With the image of them bagging us up and adding two more mounds to their backs, two more kills to present to the King of the island, my body is forced around by a horrible retching behind me.

Charlie's doubled over, arms hugging his gut, and dry heaving into the forest air. His bracelet has fallen off and lays on the ground in front of him. I backtrack to where he is, pick up the doubloon, and shove it into my pocket. He doesn't even notice.

I place my arm around the kid's shoulders and open my mouth to ask him what's going on, to plead with him, for the love of God, to be quieter, when I hear the trickling of water.

The beautiful, wonderful, amazing, lovely, sweet trickling of water.

He stares up at me. I didn't believe it possible, but his eyes are in worse shape than this morning: darker, puffier, screaming red veins webbed behind the bright blue of his irises. "Water," he wheezes.

"Yes, okay." *I'm so sorry.* What was I thinking dragging a sick, dehydrated nine-year-old through the forest in this heat?

"Come on. This way." I grab his hand and it's clammy, listless, barely able to grasp back. His head bobs with each step we take toward the sound until we reach the spring.

Flopping down onto a rock next to the pool, Charlie holds his head in his hands while I fill his gourd. When I hand it off to him, he pours it into his mouth, spilling half in the process.

"Slow down, buddy. Too much and you'll puke it all up."

He nods but continues pouring.

I head back to the edge of the water and fill my own gourd, barely resisting the urge to stick my face in and drink straight from the spring. And then I understand. It's hard to drink slowly when your mouth is so dry it's as slick as rubber. The water slips and slides down and I choke a bit because it's so fast.

Now we're both coughing, but it's a joyous sort of coughing—it's wet. We stare at each other and laughter sets in. I think we're delirious.

Eventually, the delirium settles after we've soaked our heads in the pool, and I realize we've lost our one-way ticket to the mountain. It's about the same time Charlie's stomach realizes how much water he's tossed down his throat. We both lie back in the grass, me moaning internally over my stupid half thought-out choice to avert our plan, and Charlie moaning over the pains in his belly.

"This is bad. This is really bad," he says between moans at the spring like it's the water's fault.

I turn my head toward him. "What can I do? You probably need food. I'll go search."

He nods, rolling onto his side and curling into a ball.

I stand and am instantly dizzy, my head all kinds of floaty and buzzy. Breathing deeply, I pull the map from my back pocket and try to orient myself to our location. We're at one of two springs: the one we were en route to find or another, diagonal from our course but closer to the mountain. I hope it's the second one.

I wander the forest, searching the trees and plants, not

veering far from Charlie. I pick some dandelion roots, a couple fallen coconuts, and three almost ripe avocados.

When I return, Charlie is in the same position I left him—unmoving, eyes closed. Tip-toeing my way to him, I have an irrational—but maybe not so irrational—fear he could be...

"Buddy?" I nudge him gently with my foot, my arms full of the bounty I've collected.

"Mmmm..." he moans.

"Okay. Good." I set down the food. Then, digging Will's knife from my pocket, I get to work.

I wash, cut, chop, and core for what feels like a short while, but when I finally take a break, rubbing my eyes and stealing a glance around, it's clear the sun has begun its descent. Where did the day go? The shade of trees casts down on Charlie's exhausted form as shadows scream at me how ill-prepared I was for this task. I can't even keep the time, much less keep my small companion well.

Atop large palm leaves as plates, I split the food, carrying it to where Charlie still lies. He hasn't moved, but every once in a while, I called his name and received a moan in reply. It's been enough to satisfy me and I'm hopeful some food and a good night's rest are the answer.

I sit next to his small body. "Charlie?"

"Hmm?"

"I've got food."

"Mmm 'kay." He lifts his neck, eyes straining to open into slits. His head falls back to the ground. "'Mmsootrrrd."

"I know, buddy. You can sleep soon, but first you have to eat."

He doesn't respond, so I fumble around for something to prop his head up, grabbing my pack. Gently lifting his neck, I stick my bag beneath it.

"I'm going to put some avocado in your mouth, okay?"

He barely nods.

My hand shakes as I bring the firm light green square to his lips. The color reminds me of sage and my heart sinks a bit.

"Open your mouth, bud."

He barely does it and I pop the avocado in.

I wait.

He doesn't chew.

All Charlie does is roll the thing around his mouth until it eventually slips out the side and slides down his chin.

Oh God. This isn't working. I'm going to have to soften it, cook it for him, which means making a fire, which means possibly exposing ourselves. And I'm not even sure food is what he needs. But what's my alternative? I can't carry him home. I can't just sit here and do nothing and watch him get worse.

I pluck the spongy piece of avocado off his chin and place it back on the leaf. Waste not, and all of that.

"You rest, buddy. I'm going to make yours into a soup so you can drink it."

He grants me another barely there nod.

While attempting to collect my thoughts, I wrap my food up to eat later after I've taken care of Charlie. When I stand, I do a quick scan of the area.

The Panthers seem to be long gone—probably back up their mountain by now—so I hope it's safe enough to build a fire. I gather materials and find most of what I need right here, just as Lewis said I would. *"Building a fire is easy. The forest is a pyromaniac's playground."* Thankful it's still light enough to see, the sun not yet behind the mountain, I begin the process Bug and Lewis made look so simple just a few days ago.

"All right," I say to myself, search my bag for the square plank and bow that are waiting to help me make fire. My chore is to find moss, anything dried out enough to burn, and a rock with one flat side to place on top because, *"Lugging rocks in your pack isn't a wise choice"* and *"The forest is filled with them,"* Lewis had reminded me in *duh* fashion as I dropped the large-ish rock I'd been practicing with into my bag. After further consideration, I left it behind.

As sun rays shine low through the trees and sparkle off the spring, for a fraction of a second, I take in the beauty of this place, the contradiction of its magnificence and our horrid situation. So much natural beauty housing so much pain, confusion, and anger. The corners of my eyes sting, and I wish I'd let Will convince me to leave Charlie behind. Had it been Will and me, we'd probably be at the base of the mountain. Or we'd have intercepted the Panthers before they stole whatever they're hiding in that bag of theirs. Or...

"Olive?" Charlie calls with little energy and plenty of pain.

I run to him, swallowing my *or's* and *what-if's*, forcing my stinging eyes to cool.

Kneeling next to him, pushing the dirty straw hair from his forehead, I swipe my hand back in shock. He's hot. Burning hot like a furnace.

No.

"How you doing, buddy?" My voice shakes along with the words.

"I'm so hot and my stoma-ugh!" Charlie doubles over, hugging his belly like he's keeping it from exploding, coughing like he needs to vomit, but there's nothing left to come up.

Nothing in that tiny belly of his.

He dry heaves.

I rub his back. "It's okay. It's going to be okay, bud." The fear in my voice is so heavy, even I doubt my words. Still, I refuse to give in to the island's dark side. It's not an option.

I jump up, pull out my knife, and cut a strip of fabric from the bottom of my shirt. I run to the pool, dunking it in the water, then return to Charlie.

"Here, keep this on your head while I build a fire and get you something to eat." I drape the dripping rag across his forehead and it practically evaporates from the red-hot heat coming off his skin. I dunk it again, then cut another piece of my shirt and do the same but pile it behind his neck. Again, the rag is hot within seconds. I continue dunking and draping the rags until they're finally staying cool enough for me to feel comfortable walking away.

"I'll be right back; just going to find fire-building stuff. Okay?" He doesn't respond. "Charlie?"

"'Kay." He barely utters the sound.

I'll take it.

I turn in a helpless circle and search the area. The sunlight's been reduced to a sheer, golden sheen as it sets behind the mountain. I have minutes, at best, to find what I need and do what I have to do.

I scavenge the ground like a rodent and soon find being near the water, most everything here is damp. The moss, the sticks, the leaves, they're all teeming with life and moisture. A quick squint back at Charlie shows he's shivering, the fever breaking—or, at least, I hope that's what's happening—my diagnosis based on several movies, books, and a vague recollection from my freshman health class with Coach Nelson.

"I'll be right back, bud. Just gotta find some dry wood," I call through cupped hands, no time to run to his ear.

He nods his head with a slight nudge, curling into a tighter ball.

I mentally give myself five minutes—a generous estimate for how much longer I'll have light and the amount of time I feel comfortable leaving Charlie alone.

With no way to time myself, I'm forced to rely on my gut and instincts, two things I haven't quite figured how to gauge in my sixteen years, though, like it or not, this island is forcing me to tap into it.

"Moss, sticks, bark, leaves, where the hell are you?" I ask myself. Another quirk I've picked up on this island. I'll be hearing voices next, for sure.

I walk, bend, stand on tiptoes, and search in this "pyromaniac's playground," which isn't such. Everything in this part of the forest is green and blooming.

Careful not to lose my way, I take calculated steps along a sort of natural path between the trees. The path forks and I veer to the right, not thinking, just going. I take a curve, stepping around the corner, and it's as if the climate changes with it. Leaves crunch underfoot. The scents change from fresh, ripe aloe, to crisp, bitter oak. Yes.

I drop to my knees and crawl along the dry forest floor, Lewis's voice like that of a ghost in my head reminding me, *"Can't find what you're searching for? Turn a corner. There are five different climate zones on the island. Well, five I know of—so far."* Then he had looked at me, blushed, pushed the dark hair from his eyes, and glanced away.

My heart warms and longs for my family. Both my families.

"Thanks, Lewis," I whisper.

My shirt doubles as a hammock as I lift it up and away from my stomach, gathering handfuls of dried moss from a grouping of boulders, fallen leaves, and several bunches of sticks. My once-white shirt is now dusky brown and stretched to capacity as I hold the bundle like an infant across my chest.

I make my way back, unsure if my estimate was wrong or if I've taken longer than I'd intended, but it's dark, the light of the moon and stars, despite their brilliance here, barely illuminating the path.

But it isn't the night sky that finds me back to the spring.

It's the sound of laughter.

Screechy, Wildling laughter.

Chapter Twenty-Seven

THE OTHER WILDLING

My hands fall.

I drop everything I've worked so hard to gather. All of it tumbles to the ground, leaves crunching, sticks clapping, the rock pelting the forest floor with a thump.

The Wildling cackles again. It's a scratchy, whistley, *whee-hee-hee!*

I run toward the laughter. Toward Charlie.

The night is not my friend as roots and fallen branches, plants, and stones trip me up.

I stumble, skinning my knees.

No more than twenty strides later I fall again, scraping my palms.

Another *wee-hee-hee* pierces the night air. It's louder. Closer. The laughter trails off followed by chattering and a girl's voice demanding, "Where is she?!"

A moaning Charlie responds.

Then I'm there. Just behind a line of trees.

And they're there, three Panthers: the girl, the other twin, and Dimples von Trustworthy. Damn, what is it about his face?

Charlie lies as I left him, on his side in the fetal position, the girl and Wildling standing over him as Dimples digs his bear claws through our packs.

I peek around further, but can't see any sign of the one-hundred-pound bag we heard Dimples complaining about carrying this morning. Is it possible they made it up the mountain, deposited their prize, and hiked back to us already?

"Where. Is. She?" the girl shouts right into Charlie's face.

He flinches, squeezing his body into a tighter ball.

"God. What a useless little shit." She lifts her leg over his stomach and nudges him with her boot. Hard.

Charlie bellows then coughs.

I squeeze my hands into fists. Unsure. Still not ready.

The girl laughs as Charlie continues sputtering.

I crack.

My feet move before my brain can agree with the action and I sprint straight for her back. Hands out, I push all my weight into her and she flies, feet off the ground, head first into the spring with a splash.

"Hey!" yells Dimples.

"Yes!" Wildling twin hisses through his teeth, leering at me like I'm prey.

All the while, the girl makes quick work out of the water, screaming a slew of four-letter bombs my way, the rate of which make Tawny sound like a Girl Scout.

I search from one to the other and then down at Charlie who's whimpering into the dirt. They all appear as stunned as I feel. All but the girl, who's coming straight for me. For the first time, I get a good look at her; her long black hair swings side to side like a slick, inky pendulum as she trudges and slips over rocks, bloodying her knee but not taking her furious dark eyes off me.

No time to think, I lunge to the ground and try scooping Charlie up, but he's so limp it's like lifting a sixty-five-pound bag of jelly. I get him maybe an inch off the ground and tumble back onto the dirt with him.

"Get her, Henry!" the girl shrieks.

Two large hands pinch my shoulders and warm breath pants against the back of my head.

"Nice try," Henry says, his voice laced with a smile, that dimple surely showing in all its conflicting glory.

The Wildling lets out a long *whee-hee-hee*.

The Wildling's squeal still rings in my ears as I'm lifted off the ground, thrown onto my stomach, and bound with rope like an animal—tied wrist to wrist, ankle to ankle. Henry does the same to Charlie, though I don't see why. The kid's in bad shape, his body listless, skin clammy and pale. *Really* bad shape.

"He needs food. He's sick. Please, untie him?"

My answer comes as a cold sneer from the girl. She's still wet, having braided her hair into two long black ropes, the tips dripping onto her once yellow blouse.

Next to me, Charlie breathes into the ground like he's in a deep sleep, but his eyes are open as slits, staring right through me and into nothingness.

"Buddy? You okay?" The fear clings to my words and scares me. We're out of options and it's my fault. Why didn't I stick to the plan? Follow the map? But, no. I had to chase after the Panthers, running Charlie ragged instead. This is bad. *Bad*, bad.

I stare back at Charlie's empty eyes, the blue clouded, my own eyes beginning to prick.

I'm sorry, I mouth because the words won't come. They're stuck behind the knot in my throat.

Tears poke like hot needles from my eyes, streaming down my face onto the forest floor, and I swear they smell like coconut. It's been my main source of food and drink since we left, and now it's secreting from my pores.

Charlie begins to shake.

"Charlie!" I shout.

"Oh, for God's sake. Here, pour this down the kid's throat! We don't need him dying on us before we get back to Duke," the girl says, and I can just make out the blur of her tossing a coconut to Dimples—er, Henry—over Charlie's shivering body.

In swift motions, he pierces the coconut with Will's knife, which I'd idiotically left by the food. Then he flips Charlie onto his back, shoves my pack beneath his head, and proceeds pouring the coconut juice down his throat as instructed.

"Thank you," I whisper. Catching his dark eyes, I swear I see a flash of Grandma Olive's dimpled smile. And there's my connection. That trust I sense in his face? It's in his dimples. They remind me of her, so much so it's unsettling.

He clears his throat, opening his mouth to say something, when Charlie lurches his body to the side, vomiting all over Henry's feet.

"Aw, man! Come on!" Our moment over, he strides to the spring and rinses off.

Charlie lies his head back onto my bag and continues coughing, gagging, and shaking. I can't escape the fear, the guilt, the coconut tears that follow. And I'm angered and sickened over how everything at this moment is coconut. The spilled coconut juice at my right shoulder. Remnants of the coconut I ate earlier lingering in my mouth and throat. Charlie's puke.

A memory floods into my mind. The story of Charlie throwing up a macaroon, his puffy eyes, the allergies. The kid's words go off in my head like a siren. *Mom used to tell me my allergies were like a big cup—that my body was okay until it filled up, but if it spilled over the side, I was in trouble. "*

"He's spilling over," I scream, trying to lift my head. "He's spilling over!" Charlie winces at my shrieking nonsense in his ear.

Footsteps approach and I crane my eyes to the sides in time to see all three of them crowded around, staring down at me.

Chapter Twenty-Eight

His Cup Spilleth Over

"Hey Shiloh, you have any idea what she's talking about?" Henry asks the girl, the gravel of his voice part confused, part…concerned?

"Ugh, who knows. Hey!" She kicks me in the back. "What the hell are you saying?"

"Charlie must be allergic to the coconut! It's killing him!" I shout into the dirt.

"Turn her over," demands Shiloh.

I'm flipped from my stomach to my back, tied hands crushed under my own weight. Henry towers over me, dimples concealed, then takes a couple steps back.

Shiloh bends down, meeting my tear-filled eyes with her emotionless, cold and murky brown-green ones. It's a color I've never seen, like muddy moss.

"All right now. Why's he shaking like that? He's dying?" She smirks, shaking her head in disbelief. Tommy lets loose a nervous cackle. Henry just stares.

I spit the words out as fast as I can. "He has allergies. One of them must be coconut. He didn't know. I didn't know until just now." I take a breath. "It's the coconut." I say the last part under my breath, so damn angry I didn't figure it out earlier.

"And why should we believe you—*murderer?*" She cocks her head, pressing her lips together and narrowing those muddy eyes.

"No. I… I didn't mean to. They were attacking us. It was an accident. I… I'm—"

She kicks me again, this time in the stomach. My breath sucked dry, I ball into myself as Charlie did. "An accident? Did you hear that, Tommy?" She laughs under her breath. "Oh no, I *accidentally* slipped and the sharp rock went into his head. Oops!" Wildling Tommy and Henry glare at me. Can't say I blame them. "Accidents don't matter where death is concerned." She shoves me again with the toe of her boot. "We might get to find that out with your friend here."

Coconut tears of guilt, sorrow, exhaustion, and fear streak down the sides of my face.

"I get it. I'm sorry. I know that doesn't bring him back, but I am." I glance over at Charlie. His eyes are shut, face scrunched in pain. "Just please, give him water. Let him go. I'll do anything."

Shiloh, still squatting next to me, softens her expression, smiling, a small space separating her two top teeth. Her skin, a deep tan, reflects the oranges and yellows of the fire, lathering her with a golden sheen. I can see she'd be beautiful if she wasn't completely evil. "Anything?"

Charlie's body shifts. "No," his small voice whimpers. In all his agony, he's listening to us.

"Anything." With that word, I'm forced to put my mission on hold. I'm also pretty sure I've made a deal with the devil.

The three Panthers sit around the fire, murmuring beneath the sounds of popping wood.

They've given Charlie some water and cooked a bit of

the avocado down for him to eat, probably to shut me up. Whatever the reason, I'll take it.

He's sleeping on his side, his back to me. I've managed to wiggle onto my side, back to him, and am holding his hand as best I can.

"It's okay, you're going to be okay," I repeat the words in a whisper over and over until the sounds blur together with my breath and begin to lose meaning.

Heavy footsteps break my endless plea.

The trio of Panthers once again stands over us.

Shiloh speaks down at me. "All right, we've — wait — what's your name?"

"Olive. My name is Olive."

She laughs under her breath.

My blood boils.

But the all-too-familiar shame and embarrassment creeps up, too, blending with my anger. Setting fire to it and shrinking me to ashes at once.

"Olive? That's a food, not a name."

Even here, so far away, I can't escape it.

The desire to sweep my feet under hers, knocking her on her ass is almost beyond me. Instead, I breathe and remind myself I need their help.

Shiloh clears her throat. "So, *Olive*, we've come to an agreement. We will let your coconut barfing friend here go. The last thing we need is to take some freaky illness back to our base."

"Thank you." My entire body softens. It's slight, but I swear I feel Charlie squeeze my hand.

"No, thank *you*. Because here's the catch…" Shiloh raises one eyebrow and shoots me her own version of the Lesley sneer. "We'll escort you both to your little tree — " My eyes go wide. "What? Of course, we know where you've been hiding."

I shake my head in disbelief, thinking of the hundred-pound bag. "How do you know?"

She considers my question, biting her lip and rolling her

eyes toward the sky. "A little glasses-wearing friend of yours told me."

"Lewis? You have Lewis? Where is he?" I shout, fighting the ropes around my limbs as if I'll be able to save him if I can get away.

"Calm. Down." She stares daggers into my eyes. "If you keep your end of the bargain, you'll be reunited." She punctuates it with a smirk. "Anyway, once there, we'll drop the kid off so he can get your group sick, not ours. I mean, allergies? Really?" She pauses for dramatic effect.

"It's true! He's never eaten the coconut until now. Until I made him." I mumble the last part. My shoulders fall.

Shiloh grins. "You really are quite the catch, Olive! First Jack and now one of your own?" She pauses for dramatic effect. "All the more reason for you to tell them you're jumping ship and joining our cause. Not only do you owe us for killing Jack, but you've decided after hearing us out, we're the stronger, more capable side to be on. It'll seem like you came willingly. We'll deliver you to Duke. And they won't think twice about coming for you. Or, better, they'll be so pissed you jumped ship, they will, and they'll bring a fight along with them. Win, win."

"They'll never believe it."

"Oh, they'll believe it. Why else would you betray them by taking us to your base and leading us to…Lewis? Is that his name?"

All I can do is shake my head. What have I done?

She continues, smirk widening. "It'll be lovely. They finally send one of you to get us and you flip sides." She leans in closer. "And if either of you try anything, we'll give the signal to Duke, and he'll blow your Lion's den to dust." She turns her head. "Tommy?" Tommy flashes a crooked smile, runs to their bags, and pulls out the second horn. They do have two. This other one is smaller, less grand. And I wonder, if at some point, an entire band washed up here when Shiloh moves to my face, her eyes narrowed. "It'll only take one blow and…"

She lowers her voice. "BOOM!"

I jump under my skin.

"They won't be there. If they suspect their location's been compromised, they're long gone."

"Guess we'll see. But, if no one's there, deal's off. I blow the horn, and you and barf-boy both come back with us." She looks down, straightening her filthy yellow shirt as if it matters. "We leave before sunrise."

The only thing keeping me from shoving her back into the spring is the lone idea whirling around the back of my head: *you wanted to get closer to the enemy.*

Chapter Twenty-Nine

How to Stab a Lion in the Back

Henry's heavy footsteps send waves across the forest floor and island animals fleeing for their lives. Birds flail from branches, lizards zip up trees, even one of the asshole sheep dashes into the bushes. We avoid the trails, stomping over fallen trees, tall prickly grass, and climbing up clumps of rock. Henry leads the way, a limp Charlie slumped over his shoulder.

The poor kid had a rough night, or what was left of it once we all attempted sleep. He kept calling out for his mother, nightmaring his way through what I assume is part allergy-induced illness and part dehydration from throwing everything up. After hours of his outbursts, Henry snuck over, dimples deep with something resembling sympathy or pity, and untied one of my hands—retying the other to the loop in my jeans—so I could give Charlie water and "shut him up." He curled into me like a kitten, staying quiet until we were kicked awake by Shiloh in the wee hours of morning. The girl likes to use her boots as weapons every chance she can.

The sun now shines down on us in early morning pinks

and oranges. We're getting too close to our home, our family, and all I can think about is each of their faces—how they'll hurt with pain and anger once I tell them my lies. The only thing keeping me from turning and running the opposite direction is Charlie and the hope my Lion family sees through the deception instead of shunning me for straying.

"Hey, Olive?" Shiloh pushes me from behind, shoving the handle of Will's blade between my shoulders. "Are you enjoying our shortcuts? This is how you get around the island—avoid the trails and stomp right through the overgrowth." She laughs as if the growing scratches and bug bites on her legs tickle her. "You should be able to take it from here. Recognize anything yet?"

I've been keeping my mouth shut, hoping they'd get lost. But there's no denying how gut-wrenchingly familiar it is.

I nod and walk around Henry, pulling Lewis's map from my pocket, in part to stall, but a tiny piece of me doubts our location. I grip onto that piece with all I have because this spot seems especially familiar—everything does. It's like going in constant circles, all green and leaves and stones. For all I know, we're on the opposite side of the island.

I glance at the map.

According to Lewis's drawings and the large grouping of boulders coming up on our right, the cave-tree is half a mile away.

The long and silent minutes that follow are like death. Then things turn so recognizable it's like I'm walking the plank, mere paces separating me and a fatal plunge.

I take five slow steps, with each one, I remind myself this is all for the greater good. This could work to my advantage. I'm closer to the enemy. Closer to peace. Yet another contradiction.

I stop.

The secret door to the cave-tree is only yards from my feet.

I look up.

Time freezes.

There stands Will. He's bent over, packing things into a bag.

Charlie moans.

Tommy flashes the horn as one last reminder.

Will stands still, moving only his head. His good eye sets on me. It wavers then moves to the trio of Panthers behind me, then to Charlie, who is still moaning as Henry lays him on the ground.

"Olive?" says Will.

"Charlie's really sick." My voice breaks with *sick,* and I motion to the lump on the ground that is Charlie, biting back the urge I have to run straight into Will's arms. "I had to bring him back or—" I swallow and glance away. *Damn it, Olive. Be strong, or you're going to get everyone you love killed.* I straighten my shoulders, swallowing the sob in my throat. "Or he might die." Despite my attempts, several hot tears break free and silently stream down my face.

"But... What happened? Why are *they* with you? Are you hurt? We were leaving to find Lewis." He steps forward, hand on his hip and grasping the spear slung through his belt. "Where is Lewis?" His voice lowers as he glares toward the Panthers behind me.

Shiloh steps forward.

"Olive!" Bug bounds in long, quick strides at me from the spring, several gourd bottles slung over her shoulder and sloshing against her small body. I fight the urge to smile at my little Bed Bug. As she runs toward me, Will throws his arm out and stops her mid-stride.

"Hey!" she shouts, forehead scrunched. But then she sees what's happening. Who I'm with. Charlie lying on the ground. Her eyes go wider than I've ever seen, the whites glowing like coconut pulp. "Jude! Tilly!" she screams like an alarm.

The others come running from the same direction. When they see us, they stop dead. Jude pulls a knife from his boot.

"What the fuck is this? Where's Lewis?" he asks Will, looking back and forth between the two sides.

"We were just getting to that." Will motions toward Shiloh.

"So glad we're all here now." She smirks. "Henry, Tommy, and I came across Olive and Charlie days ago. We were getting to know each other when the kid got sick. Coconut allergy. I'm not so convinced, but that's what Olive thinks, right?" She nudges me in the arm like we're old buddies. I nod. "Whatever it is, he's in bad shape and the last thing we need is to bring disease back to our base. So, he's all yours."

Henry picks Charlie up and lays him before my fellow Lions' feet.

"Will?" Charlie groans.

"It's all right, buddy." Will glances over his shoulder. "Tilly, take him to the spring, get him washed off." He squeezes Bug's shoulder. "Go with her."

"But, Olive — "

"Go with her, Bug," Will snaps.

Tilly jumps into action, eying me, and shaking her head like, *what's happening?* I want to run and hug her, get lost in those strawberry blond curls and tell her all about the last few days more than I've ever wanted anything. But I can't react. I can't show her I love her. I can't step over to the side where I belong, because if I do, they'll blow that horn. I swallow back another sob.

She picks Charlie up like a baby and marches toward the spring in slow motion. Bug follows, walking backward, not taking those dark chestnut eyes off mine.

Jude shifts from foot to foot, ready to pounce at any minute. "Where. The. Fuck. Is. Lewis?" he says through his teeth.

"Funny story," Shiloh says. Tommy laughs his wildling laugh. Bug, nearly out of sight, cringes and runs to catch up with Tilly. "Would you like to tell it, Olive? Or should I?"

I can't speak. Literally. I open my mouth, but nothing comes out. Not a word or a whimper. I try again. Nothing. Because I know if I do the truth will come spilling out and... I squeeze my fingers so tightly into fists my nails pierce my skin, the warmth of blood and pinch of pain is a welcome distraction. Anything to keep my mouth shut. Just a few more minutes. To keep them safe.

"All right. You'll probably get it all mixed up anyway. She's always mixing up details—like when she told us how to get here—"

"What?!" Will shouts.

"I knew it! I fucking knew it!" Jude screams.

"Oh, oops, I probably wasn't supposed to say that. Sorry Olive, that was your part. Oh well, it's all out in the open now. So, Olive told us how to get here using her map, and on our way, we ran into Lewis. He wasn't nearly as cooperative as this one" —she swats me on the back— "so we had to take him back to the mountain."

I've never wanted to pit someone's eyeballs like cherries until now.

Jude jumps forward, knife up and at the ready.

Henry and Tommy pull weapons out, too: a short, sharp stake and one of the mini bombs.

"Stop!" I scream before someone gets blown up. "It's true. I did it. And I'm going back with them."

Jude turns the knife at me. "I knew we never should have trusted you!" He leans forward. "If anything happens to Lewis, you're dead." And I believe him. My throat pricks.

I open and close my fists harder. I bite my tongue so the tang of metal webs my mouth. Just a few more minutes. *Please, let me get through this.*

Will walks up to me. Jude follows, staying a step behind.

"At ease," he says to Henry and Tommy, who lower their weapons, but don't move. Will's at my face, so close I can smell the coconut soap he probably used this morning. "Is it true?" He peers through me with that gentle sage. I teeter on the verge of losing it. The thorns in my throat catch and make my eyes itch. But then I think of Charlie, of all of them. The vision of our cave-tree engulfed in flames steels me.

"Yes," I say.

Inside, I wail.

Jude runs toward me. He shouts in my face, so close spit lands on my cheeks and in my hair, but I can't hear anything he says. It's all white noise and static beneath the sorrow and regret and fear inside of me, surrounding me like I'm the eye of the storm.

Despite Will's unwavering stare, he manages to pull Jude away, but the screaming doesn't stop. I envision the noise flowing away from Jude's mouth — it's black smoke and sparks and floats up in gusts, bouncing away along the tops of the trees.

Then I'm pulled. At first, my feet don't move, but I remember Charlie, our deal, the bombs, and the Panthers' horn signal for Duke. *"It'll only take one blow and... Boom!"*

I shudder under my skin.

My feet move in a forced walk as I'm yanked along by the hand. Looking back over my shoulder, I catch Will's back.

He's turned away.

Given up.

All I want in the world at that moment is to break free, to run back and wrap my arms around that cave-tree and all of those inside it and never, ever let go.

Will! I scream on the inside. *Don't give up on me!*

Without so much as a glance back, he disappears behind the trees.

He leaves me, because I've left him.

Chapter Thirty

THE KING'S CAVE

I refuse to take my eyes off the cave-tree and the ghost of Will until they disappear from my line of sight. Shiloh's death grip on my wrist turns my hand cold, but all I can focus on is how, before he turned his back, Will had stared me down. Confused and hurt and angry. And then he was gone. Nothing left but my memory of him.

One minute, I'm gazing back at our home, watching it all get smaller and smaller; the next, I'm scaling a mountain.

The route to the King's cave is rocky, always a cliff on one side or the other, sometimes both, as we tiptoe along narrow passes. Another one of Shiloh's great shortcuts.

I'm numb and dazed after the pain I just caused, but I can't avoid envisioning myself falling off the side of this thing every time my eyes deceive my judgment by glancing down. I can't imagine why they'd choose such a horrible, barren, dangerous place to be their home. Then again, I'm not totally shocked, either.

Shiloh finally releases my arm as the trail narrows and I

shake it and rub it to regain feeling. Rounding a corner, as I hug a particularly sharp edge, she turns her head back at me. "Being on the highest point of the island gives us the best advantage." She answers the question I never asked out loud.

"But aren't you afraid you'll fall?"

"No. But you should be," Tommy says with a wildling laugh. "We've been here a while. You learn how to get around without sliding off the side." I can tell he's smiling and it's creepy as hell.

I stay quiet, concentrating on not slipping and falling to a gruesome, horrid death.

We turn another jagged corner, single-file, to find Shiloh standing, arm's raised, at the opening of a large cave.

"Here we are. Home sweet home," she announces.

It's an enormous black hole, sharp rock shards hanging down like the cave's mouth is open, baring its spiked teeth.

"You should feel privileged, Olive. You're the first enemy to arrive by choice, not force." She winks.

I ignore her. My only hope is that they'll take me to Lewis and he and I will be able to figure out how to escape.

And then I hear him.

The hyena.

Duke materializes from the dark cave's mouth like a ghost. His head is tilted back as a high-pitched cackle tumbles out of his throat, his Adam's apple bobbing with each *whoop*.

When he catches a glimpse of me, he stops, seriousness overtaking his face, the black war paint under his eyes relaxing from the force of his laughter. He walks toward me, each step causing his stomach to flex in response. His muscles twitch, the "P" scar on his chest a skin colored sheen in the sun.

"Ha! Well done!" he says, looking me up and down from only feet away.

Duke walks closer, giving Shiloh an approving nod and smile. She smiles back. There's something there, but I'm not sure what. Moving along, Duke slaps both Tommy and Henry on the backs in a show of masculine solidarity. Laughter and excitement ensue.

Tommy *whees*.

Duke *whoops*.

Henry's dimples deepen into shadows, that trustworthy face contorting into something more sinister. Something not so Grandma Maxine-ish. He's a predator now. A panther stalking its prey.

I'm in the mountain exhibit at the zoo.

The laughter at my capture dies down just as a large figure emerges from the cave behind Duke. It's the guy with the strong, square jaw.

"Nice work, Panthers!" he shouts, stepping into the crowd.

Strong Jaw and Henry fist-bump.

Duke joins in. "Two down, four to go," he says, then sets his dark eyes on me. "And tell me... Why is it you've come so willingly... What's her name?" He looks to Shiloh.

"Olive. My name is Olive." Duke's eyes glaze over.

He glances down, laughing a little under his breath. It oddly reminds me of Will. Then, staring back at me, Duke raises his eyebrows and sneers. "So, Olive, why weren't you tied up and dragged here like the others?"

"We made a deal for Charlie. He was—"

"What? What deal? We don't make deals!" Duke shouts at everyone.

Shiloh scoots closer to him and puts her hand on his shoulder. "Calm down. Please, just listen." She pulls him away so all I can hear are murmurs.

They quietly go back and forth until Duke yells, "Fine! Take her and tie her up with the boy." He rubs his temples and strides back into the cave.

I'm picked up by the armpits. Henry and Strong Jaw not-so-gently carry me away toward the boy I assume—hope—is Lewis.

Please, please let him be okay.

Like a rag-doll, I'm carried into the cave where darkness swallows me. It isn't until my eyes adjust that I see there are torches lighting a never-ending rock hallway that dips deep down into the mountain. I'm Alice descending on a crueler version of Wonderland, and this is one messed up rabbit's hole.

At the end of the tunnel, we enter a large cavern, a single fire in the middle, three more tunnels leading off the room.

I'm beginning to grasp the appeal of this place. It's like our cave-tree, but high up, out of reach from most animals and us, their enemies. Just as I'm thinking on the weather and wondering how cold it gets way up in the clouds at night, something on the far wall catches my eye. Written in chicken scratch on the stone is a large list. The letters are red.

Lifeblood
1. Loyalty—Panthers who stray are left behind.
2. Superiority—This island is ours and ours alone.
3. Revenge—Those deserving will meet their punishment.

My eyes linger on number three, then I'm dropped to the ground. They tie me to a huge rock next to a quiet lump that must be Lewis.

Tweedledee and Tweedledum leave—no doubt going to consult with the Mad Hatter, the Queen of Hearts, and one of those wildling flying monkeys who's escaped from Oz to join the effort.

Does Alice lose her mind in Wonderland? There are probably entire books on that subject.

Once their footsteps have dissolved into the rock walls, I nudge at Lewis. "Hey," I whisper. "Lewis, can you hear me?"

Silence.

"Lewis?" It comes out as a fearful whine and I kick some part of his body harder than I should.

"Ow," I hear.

"Damn it, Lewis. You scared me." I kick him again.

"Ow, quit it." His forehead and squinting eyes peek up out of the shadows. "Are they gone?" he asks, his voice barely registering, muffled beneath a scrap of material over him. "They think I've passed out or something."

"Yes, they're gone."

Lewis exhales as if he's been holding his breath for days. "Good." His hands tied at his waist, he leans up onto his elbows, coming out from under the fabric like a turtle poking out of its shell. He's still squinting and I notice he looks different.

"Your glasses—"

"Broken. Figure it was about time, I mean, it's a miracle they ever lasted this long."

"Can you see?"

"It isn't so bad." But he strains his eyes to see me. "The dark doesn't help." Lewis takes a good, most likely blurry, look around the room, then rounds back at me, shaking his head. "What happened? How'd you end up here? Where's Charlie? The others?"

Ugh, where do I start? My stomach instantly aches.

"So much has happened. We're in trouble." He scoots closer, clears his throat, and stares at me, waiting for the explanation I can't find the words to articulate. "Charlie got sick. He's allergic to coconut—"

"No kidding?"

"Yeah. He's really sick and when I left him to search for fire-building stuff, the Panthers found him, then me." I drop my head toward the floor. "I didn't have a choice. They were going to throw him off a cliff because he was dead weight, so I made a deal." I swallow, keeping my head down because I can't look at him for the next part. "It was me they wanted— payback for Jack. Plus, they already knew where the cave-tree was, and—"

"Wait. How did they know where the cave-tree was?"

I glance up. "Because you told them. I mean, no one blames you, you had no—"

"Olive, I didn't tell them. They kicked me around, broke

my glasses, and eventually hit me over the head and brought me here, but I never told them."

There's silence between us as I realize what's happened. What I've done.

"Olive?"

No.

My stomach no longer aches, it whirls.

I'm spinning.

The entire cave tosses in circles around me, and all I can do is shake my head as hot tears I can't begin to hold back pop from the corners of my eyes.

"It's all my fault," I say, staring up at the ceiling.

"What's your fault?" Lewis asks from some far-off place.

The spinning stops with a jolt like someone pulled the safety lever on a nightmare of a carnival ride.

"*What's* your fault?" he repeats, louder, closer.

"I led them right to our front door." I stare into his eyes because I can't escape the truth, not now. "Shiloh told me you showed her where the cave-tree was, that they already knew. But… God damn it!" I kick my feet against the rock floor. "Once we'd gotten to where they found you, she had me lead the way as part of the deal. I was supposed to act like I was leaving the Lions, switching sides. If I did that, they'd let Charlie go back to the cave-tree so Tilly could take care of him."

"And you did it?"

I nod. "If I didn't go along with it, they said they'd blow our home up." I kick my heels into the floor again. "Of course, that was a lie, too. They didn't know where our home was… But they do now."

And that's when we hear it.

A dying bird shrieks across the sky.

A sharp crackle pops in the distance like a firework, tearing a wound down the center of my heart.

The crackling is followed by the *ka-boom* of an exploding coconut bomb.

Celebration ensues: laughter, cheering, running footsteps.

Chapter Thirty-One

PUNISHMENT

It's been days since the explosion that may or may not have destroyed our cave-tree and everyone in it. I seesaw back and forth between numb robot and emotional basket-case.

Worse, I can't escape the horrible images of Bug and Charlie, Will, Jude and Tilly all sprawled out along the forest, blown to pieces…

The dreams are worse—so real—when the cave is still and the island sleeps. It's the same scene each time: from high on a cliff, I see my family, their bodies bloodied and broken, but I'm unharmed. Then an arm wraps around my shoulders and Duke cackles in my ear. "We did it," he says, then sneers.

I wake in a cold sweat on the verge of hyperventilation, sit up, take in my surroundings, and remember where I am. All of that, only to fall back asleep to the same nightmare. It plays on repeat like a bad movie marathon. I fear my wounded heart can't take it any longer. Each night it tears a little deeper. Bleeds a little faster.

The only Panther who's acknowledged us thus far is

Strong Jaw Guy—Noah, we figured out was his name after hearing Shiloh argue with him over the fire. I've tried talking to him each time he brings us food. But all he grants me in return is dried mystery meat and silence.

Lewis and I live in eternal darkness, unknowing of the time of day, whether it's cloudy or if there's a full moon. I miss the sun, the stars, the breeze, the smell of ocean mixed with forest. This place smells like sulfur, dirt, and death.

His mouth open in a wide yawn, Lewis stretches his body out into a long plank and begins exercising. It's his wake-up ritual, so it must be morning. Or, so he thinks. Hands and feet tied, he attempts awkward sit-ups and leg lifts, convinced if we get out of this dark cave of despair, there will be a fight.

While Lewis pants, struggling to do backward push-ups with his wrists tied together behind his rear, we hear the familiar footsteps of Noah. For some reason, he barely lifts his feet from the ground, so his steps sweep and swoosh against the floor like a heavy broom.

As with the last two mornings, he brings us water and a small meal of unidentifiable meats and, of course, coconut, a reminder of Charlie and the horrible deal I made with people I should have known wouldn't keep to their end of the bargain.

"Either of you need to go?" Noah asks, dropping our breakfast on the floor before us.

We shake our heads in unison. Yes, they're feeding us, but it isn't much and water is even more scarce. Lewis says they're making a point, punishing us by depriving us, showing their power. And I believe him. From what I've observed, these Panthers, while royally messed up kids, are just that—kids. When stripped of their anger and tough exterior, I bet they're not much different than Lewis and me.

With his broom of a foot, Noah kicks our bowls closer to us, not doing much for the pounding I'm desperately fighting in my head. Then he nods and leaves us to eat without use of our hands, bending to the floor and slopping our food like animals.

"Aren't you going to eat?" Lewis asks, mouthful of slop in his cheek.

With the sweetness of coconut turning my stomach over, I answer by pushing my portion away with my foot, because right now, I'm in emotional basket-case mode with no end in sight.

"If you don't eat, you're going to die and then what?" He shrugs, eyes wide, waiting for the sad lump I've become to speak.

"We're all dying eventually, Lewis. Does it really matter?" It's harsh, but I can't get past this thick, desolate cage of misery I'm in. Unfortunately for him, he's stuck here with me.

"It matters to me," he murmurs under his breath. Turning away, I curl into myself, assuming the same position I've been in for far too long.

I appreciate his words but don't respond. I don't deserve any of it. Not coconut. Not the sun or stars. Not the breeze. Not Lewis's kind words.

But I don't get to make those choices.

What I do or don't deserve is in the hands of other people. People who hate me. People who think the only thing I'm deserving of is punishment. They want revenge. And it's coming.

I know it's coming.

Chapter Thirty-Two

HEROES AND BULLIES

"Shiloh's from some small town in Spain, ahead of your time—
" Lewis raises his eyebrows as if he can't fathom it. "She's
the one making the bombs, some sort of child genius. Also,
pretty brazen. She was with a group of girls who had snuck
out of their boarding school the night she got here. They were
chased, nearly caught, but managed to hop a train where they
met up with a group of guys one of them knew. No details
after that except they tried to get into a club, but instead, she
ended up on the island. She was the first of Duke's members."

We've been alone all day, and Lewis is ignoring my balled-
up body language, rambling on about what he overheard while
pretending to sleep. Each night, the Panthers gather around
the fire for a meeting. But since I arrived, and Lewis "woke
up," they've conducted the meetings in hushed whispers.

Before that, they mused over how they had ended up
here, trying to crack some code that would get them home. But
Lewis said it was bizarre, more like giving thanks and less like
brainstorming. And it gets weirder. They still perform their

closing ceremony and not at all quietly: they stand, closed into a tight circle, and recite their Lifeblood laws. We've entered into some bizarre teen cult. If they start passing out Kool-Aid, I'm tossing my own body over the cliff.

"Tommy is from Hawaii, closer to Will's time." Lewis goes on like he's checking off a mental list. Trying to puzzle things together. "He and Jack were runaways, but also pretty skilled at skateboarding and surfing." That sort of explains the jumping from tree to tree and gravity defying balance. Wildlings. "It's how they made money to get by. Doing tricks and entering competitions. Apparently, their next gig was going to be to ride a dangerously tall wave, hoping to make a name for themselves or prove something. They paddled out to sea, got cold feet once they saw how huge it was, and hightailed it back to shore. Except it wasn't the same shore. Duke found them washed up on the beach."

"And Henry?" I bite my lip, remembering I'm punishing myself and should be silent.

"Henry?" I can tell Lewis is smiling. He clears his throat. "Henry's from closer to my time and grew up in a rough neighborhood in New York City. According to conversations between him and Noah, they were friends and came here together—kind of like Will and Duke. They'd fallen into a gang, made the wrong people angry, and were running for their lives from a car full of guys shooting at them. They ducked into an alleyway and, well, you can guess what happened…"

"They ended up here." I open out of my ball slightly.

He nods, staring off toward the fire, thinking, squinting. "I swear we're closer to figuring it out, finding the common denominator that will get us home. But there's still something missing."

"What are you thinking?" I ask, giving up on being silent.

"Yes, please share. What *are* you thinking?" Shiloh cuts in. She hovers above us, long hair draped over one eye like a black curtain.

Lewis and I bite our tongues.

"Oh, come on, Olive. We're friends, remember?" The way she says it, all fake-sweet and high-toned, reminds me of Lesley and makes me want to kick her again. Something in me snaps.

I sit up. "We are not your friends and you know it. I kept my end of the deal and you totally broke yours!"

"You didn't see that coming?" She narrows those mossy eyes, flipping her hair off her shoulder.

"I should have… I should have told Will the truth. He'd have—"

"He'd have what?" Duke asks.

I gasp. Damn it.

Yet again, he's appeared out of nowhere. The ghost. Dark marks under his eyes, shadows over his face that gives him the appearance of a floating skull.

"Please, enlighten me. What would truthful, honest, good ol' Will have done? He does always do the right thing, doesn't he?" All I can do is stare, my heart in my throat because the guy scares the shit out of me. Duke smiles wildly back at me. He's up to something. "No? Well, that good boy act doesn't fool anyone, but I don't have to tell you, do I? I'm sure you both know all about our Will." Duke raises one eyebrow.

Our Will?

"He isn't who he claims to be, now is he?" Duke sits down next to us. I try to scoot away a bit. Then Shiloh leans down, whispers something in his ear, smirks at me, and leaves.

Lewis glares at her back.

"Huh, you two still seem confused. How about I remind you of the story in case you've forgotten. I'm sure he's shared it with his fellow Lions—Will, always one to be honest, and all." Duke takes a moment to stare at us. To breathe. To draw out this God-awful moment to be in his presence.

And to think I had the half-assed idea I could somehow get to know him. Make peace? As I stare back, I can't see how that would ever be on the table. Maybe defending ourselves, fighting back when necessary, is the only way. Though the idea feels gross against my mind.

Duke sits up straighter. "The night Will and I entered the island through the corn maze, I was running from him, not the other way around. You see, sweet, compassionate Will gave poor little David — or *Mule* as Will and his friends so lovingly called me — daily beatings."

Both Lewis and I yell in protest then Duke puts his hand up.

"Think about it!" he shouts. "Look at how much bigger, *stronger* Will is. Does he really have you all believing I want to rule this island and that's why I fight?" Duke lets out a long hyena laugh, raising his thin eyebrows so they nearly reach his hairline. "While, yes, the island would be much more pleasant without Will and his good-time gang, what I want is revenge. To rid this island of Will and anyone who follows his lies — something I didn't have the power to do back home. That's what I want — and what I'll eventually achieve."

"I refuse to believe it." I shake my head and scoot away.

Lewis stares from me to Duke and back.

With a burst of quick movement, Duke makes up the space I've put between us.

"You think this — THIS — stands for Panthers?" He shoves his chest and the "P" in my face. "Think again." He sits back, wrapping his arms around his middle and glares into the fire. "It's an old scar. One of many. This one just happens to show on my skin." Duke bows his head down to the floor. When he looks back up at us, I swear, the Mad Hatter has the shine of tears in his eyes. "*I* was running from Will, *his* bat, *his* beatings, that night in the maze."

I open my mouth to argue because he's a jerk and a liar but an image of Will fills my head and I can't see anything else. That day he took me over the cliff and the story he confided in me. The story of how he'd found the spot searching for a place to end his life, how his childhood wasn't ideal. Had he been trying to tell me something? He said he "wasn't the person he could have been." Though, isn't that true for everyone?

Couldn't we all do better?

Duke swipes the undersides of his eyes with his knuckles, smearing the black war paint across his cheeks so they look like ink blots. He stands.

"Don't count on good ol' Will coming to your rescue." His mouth sets in a thin-lipped sneer. "You're the last two Lions left. Time to join forces. Think about it." He smacks the rock a couple of times with his palm then walks away, but stops, not glancing back. "Oh, and Olive, your haircut is…unique. Did you do that yourself, or did you let a little Lion cut it for you?" He laughs in a sigh under his breath.

I tug my hand to place it over my head, but can't. It's tied behind my back.

Duke is gone as silently as he entered.

Lewis blows air out his nose and jerks himself into a straighter sitting position. "He's lying. They'd have left the tree as soon as you left with the Panthers. As soon as they knew our location was compromised."

"I hope so." My voice quivers.

We stay quiet, no sounds other than the wind whistling through the cave. It makes the fire flicker and reflect off the walls in orange and yellow waves that sway in a sad, grievous dance.

I break the silence, asking the question we both must be thinking. "Do you think it's true?"

Lewis shakes his head before he answers. "No. No way. I can't let myself believe it." He shakes his head faster. "Will is the most caring, loyal person I know. There's just no way."

I shrug, a sigh escaping me. "It *was* a long time ago. And it would explain Duke's hatred toward Will, toward us."

Lewis pushes himself up onto the rock, and I get a glimpse of the man-version, his face rigid, angry, his jaw hard. "You can't honestly be considering this. You believe him? After he's done nothing but try to kill us? Come on, Olive. I expected more of you."

Something inside my heart cramps up tight.

His face softens. "Sorry."

"No, you're right. It's all wrong and it's late... I think." I roll over, assuming my position of self-loathing.

I hear Lewis shuffle and he curls up closer but doesn't touch me. "I'm sorry, Olive," he whispers to my back.

"Me, too." I open my hand, and he nudges my palm with his knee. Before too long Lewis breathes the soft rhythms of sleep.

My eyes heavy, I can't stop thinking of my Will—gentle, stoically quiet, beautiful Will. Could he really be the male version of Lesley? The very thing I ran from the night I stepped onto this island?

I can't begin to wrap my mind around it, but I can't totally disregard it, either.

So, what does that say for making peace?

The more I learn, the more clearly this becomes a lost cause.

I'm falling.

Will's arms are around me, the waterfall streaming next to us. Everything moves in slow motion.

He kisses me, things speed up, and we drop like stones.

We hit the water with a thunderous clap.

Our arms tangled like pretzels, he holds me down under the water. I kick and hit him, shove his chest.

He disappears and I swim to the surface, catching my breath and climbing out of the water.

Time passes and I'm dry, sitting in the spot where we lay that day he told me his story. There's a mound of coconuts next to me. Shiloh sits before the pile, cutting each fruit into large white chunks.

"Here. Eat," she says, handing me a bowl of white flesh.

I eat it.

"Here. Eat." She hands me another.

I eat it.

"Here. Eat." She hands me another.

I eat it.

"Here. Eat." Another.

I eat.

"Is your cup spilling over yet?" she asks, smirking, narrowing those mossy eyes of hers.

"No!" I yell.

"Here. Eat." And she hands me a bowl the size of a tree stump overflowing with coconut meat. It's the wooden water container from the cave-tree.

"Where did you get this?" I ask.

"What? They don't need it anymore." She laughs. "Eat."

I eat. Somehow I stuff in every last chunk.

Then my cup spills over, and I puke and cough and puke some more. It's all white and soon it takes over like someone's poured paint on everything. The grass. The water. The trees and the sky. All white. Even Shiloh turns white and disappears into the background.

I glance down at myself. The white has taken me, too. I'm bleached out, and can't see my own outline. I've blurred into the nothingness. I no longer exist, but continue coughing and puking, filling in the last cracks with white. And I can't breathe.

I wake up in full-on hyperventilation. "Hhhhh…huh. Hhhh…huh. HUHHH." I gasp for breath. I try to sit up. I try to clutch my throat, but I can't because my hands are tied. "Hh…huh…huh…huuh!"

I roll over onto my stomach.

The wind sings a sad song.

"Olive?" Lewis's hands are on my back.

I scoot my legs up and tuck them underneath me, my head on the cold stone floor.

I can't stop wheezing in *huhs*.

"It's okay. You were dreaming," he whispers in my ear. "Shhh…"

"Hhhhh! Huuuh…hhh…HHHH!" *Breathe*, Olive. Through the nose, out the mouth, slowly.

"Shhh," Lewis says.

"Whooh. Whooh," the wind sings.

"Hhh. Huh." I breathe. "I'm…hhh…okay…huh."

Lewis's hands are still on my back and it occurs to me they shouldn't be. His hands should be tied behind him at his waist like mine are.

I pull my head up. "Your...huh...hands?"

"I worked all night." He begins untying mine.

"But... How?" I ask, my breathing almost back to normal.

"Sharp spot on the rock. Doesn't matter. Are you all right?"

"Whooh. Whooh," the wind sings again.

"I'm okay. What's that noise?" Like magic, my hands are free. I pull them in front of me and stretch. It feels amazing. "Thank you."

He nods. "We've gotta find a way out of here."

I quickly work to untie my feet.

"Whooh. Whooh."

"That sound, Lewis. What is it?"

My feet are free.

We both stand.

"Whooh. Whooh."

He stares into my eyes, pushing a dark pelt of hair off his forehead. "It's the conch shell."

Chapter Thirty-Three

THE WIND'S SONG

"What conch shell?" I ask, but Lewis pulls me by the hand, jerking me out into the main cavern, searching from side to side. "What shell?"

"Shhh!" he whisper-shouts at me, yanking me back against the wall. "I'll explain when we get out of here," he barely says, voice shaking.

I decide to leave it, to assume it's nothing but a song on the wind, except I don't want to because the pit in my stomach tells me otherwise.

Lewis and I scoot along the wall like shadows, just a couple of flames reflecting off the fire. Soon we reach mystery tunnel number three, one we've never seen anyone enter or exit from.

We have a choice: dash for the main tunnel and risk trying the cave entrance or gamble on the mystery cave right next to us.

Lewis glances over at me, but before I can say anything, we hear Noah's swooshing footsteps headed toward us from outside—he's bringing our breakfast.

Without a word, we duck into the mystery cave. But I stop dead because something brass catches my eye. On the edge of the stones surrounding the fire is one of the horns. I turn around and run full sprint toward the fire.

"Olive!" Lewis hisses.

I skid on the balls of my feet, grab it, then turn and run back just as Noah's shadow comes shuffling down the main tunnel.

"What the hell?" Lewis again hisses.

I lift the horn to his face.

He smiles but mixes it with a stern glare.

We take off.

The cave twists and turns and snags and dips and at one point we hear a faint and low, "They're gone!"

We run faster.

Far behind, but still too close, the sounds of footsteps stomping, the soles of shoes heavily swooshing, follow us.

We pick up the pace even more.

There's a pinhole of light far ahead of us.

We sprint toward it, slipping on loose gravel, tripping over our own feet. The pinhole gets bigger and bigger until it's the size of an egg.

A beach ball.

A boulder.

Then, blinding sun. It's the white flash of light from my dream all over again.

I squint, forcing my eyelids open. Keeping my sights on the ground, I take several steps forward then stop with a lurch when the ground drops away into nothing.

Lewis flings his arm against my chest like Mom does in the car when she slams on the brakes. My toes push dirt and rock over the edge of the hanging. I nearly drop the horn but manage to salvage my grip on it as I lunge my body back, taking tentative steps away from the cliff.

"Shit, Lewis. What do we do?" Horn hugged to my chest,

I look from the drop-off to him, back to the drop-off, then to the rocks and mountain above us—all around us.

"We climb," he says, a new confidence behind those timid, dark eyes.

I shake my head, hyperventilation churning in my lungs, closing in on my chest, the brass horn now as heavy as an anchor, which won't do for this great feat before us. But I'm not climbing, so it's fine.

Lewis puts both his hands on my shoulders. "You can do this." He stares into me like Will has so many times, connecting to something deeper. "Don't look down. We're just playing around…like we're on the beach…climbing rocks." He shrugs, his tone all nonchalant and breezy.

"On the beach," I repeat, surveying the jagged crags jutting up behind us.

He makes to take the horn from me, but I snatch it back, slipping the thinner end, mouthpiece first, down the back of my shirt and tying the flowy bottom of my tunic into a knot so it doesn't slip out.

Lewis's eyes are wide, and he glances from the knot in my shirt to the horn-shaped bump on my back, and back up to my face.

"Yes, a simple day at the beach." He grabs my hand. "Shall we?" And he smiles as if we really are playing around on the beach.

I nod, the hyperventilation monster in my throat, waiting to make its move.

We turn and face the mountain.

The Panthers' shouts grow louder, closer.

"Follow me. Put your feet and hands where I put mine."

I nod again, my voice paralyzed.

Lewis scales rock after rock.

I follow.

One hand here.

One foot there.

Up. Up. And up even higher.

Don't look down. Don't look down.

Of course, I look down.

And freeze.

Everything is suddenly below us and all the world's water surrounds us. I get lightheaded. Dizzy. I was never one for heights. Or water.

The horn in my shirt is five times its normal size when hanging off a cliff and I regret my decision of not leaving it behind. My fingers dig into the side of the mountain so my nails break against the rock. I'm on the side of an effing mountain!

Short bursts of breath leak out my mouth in wheezes. The monster.

No.

"Huh. Hhhh. Huh."

No.

"You okay?" Lewis calls down to me.

"Hhh. Huh. No, I can't do it!" Tears burn and prick my eyes.

"Yes, you can! The beach, remember?"

The beach. Just the beach.

"Okay. Hhh. Okay." I start moving again, the jagged stone before me blurring from the water in my eyes, helping my imagination along. *Rocks on the beach...*

"We're almost to a flatter area. Then we'll climb down the other side. Just hold on. You can do this," Lewis coaxes.

"You can do this, Olive," a nasty voice mocks. "Oh my God. Total déjà vu!" Shiloh shouts. "This is how Annabel fell!" She laughs. I listen but continue climbing. "Don't slip, Lions."

God, I hate her so much.

My foot skids, raining rocky dust down onto them.

"Whoa, careful there," she taunts me. "You're on the top of a mountain. One bad step and you're fish food. Just like your friend."

"Shut up! You pushed her off!" Lewis yells down.

"Don't listen to her, Lewis. She's messing with us," I say.

"Oh, come on. We aren't that cruel. Annabel tried to escape. Sadly, she wasn't successful. We aren't monsters."

Monsters…

"You *are* liars," Lewis says from the top where a sort of valley in the rocks forms.

I'm almost there. Almost to him. Shiloh, as much as I hate her, seems to have distracted me and pulled me out of my panic.

Lewis reaches his hand out to grab mine.

"Whooh. Whooh." The song. It sounds from the other side of the mountain. So close.

Far below, Panther footsteps skid and take off back through the tunnel.

Lewis takes my hand. I stare into his dark eyes. "What's the shell mean?" My voice hitches with the last word.

He sighs and helps heave me up over the side. We both breathe heavily. Him, a normal heavy. Me, a part-hyperventilating heavy.

Lewis clutches my hands, his expression part strong, part terrified. "The last time I heard the shell was after we found Annabel's body."

"No…" The word sneaks out of my mouth, along with a gasp and a whimper.

Charlie.

Chapter Thirty-Four

LIONS VS. PANTHERS

It can't be Charlie.

No.

It just can't.

I won't allow it.

I clutch my necklace.

Because I know it is.

As much as I want to roll back down the mountain, I force myself to walk. One foot after the other.

Climb over that rock.

Squeeze through those huge boulders.

Duck under the rock that looks like a sharp knife on its side.

The farther we go, the louder the yelling gets.

We speed up.

The jagged indent along the ridge of the mountain descends until we hit the spot where we'll have to climb back down.

It's a total drop-off. Right over the entrance to the cave we just fled. And also, the location of all of the commotion.

Before I can gather my thoughts on how to get us out of this, a loud *boom* shakes the earth below us.

Lewis and I drop onto all fours.

We scoot to the edge of the cliff and peek over the side.

Near a line of boulders is a black circle singed into the ground, smoke coming off it.

The only Panthers I see are Duke and Shiloh, and I assume they're who set off the explosion. They stand to the side of the entrance and, based on the yelling and swearing, the others must be right inside the opening. Across the way, heads poke out from behind the large gathering of rocks.

Will.

Tilly and Bug.

And a curly blond mop of hair. Charlie. My chest creases in on itself in relief.

"Oh my God. Thank goodness," I whisper, glancing at Lewis from the corner of my eyes. They all wear war paint: black lines and symbols on their arms and faces.

Lewis stares ahead. "Where's Jude?"

Jude?

I forgot about Jude.

Jude's there.

Of course, he's there.

He'd never let them come up here…

No.

Not. Without. Him.

I shake my head.

"He'd be here," Lewis says. The finality in his words erases that relief in my chest, slicing the creases into sharp thorns.

Tears fill my eyes, immersing everything before me under water. The last Jude knew of me was what a traitor I was. Poor Bug and Charlie. Poor Tilly.

Lewis sniffs.

I wipe my eyes.

"This is over!" Will yells, stepping out from behind the rocks, spear at the ready. He's shirtless. Black charcoal marks his chest in the smeared outline of a lion's mane.

The hyena whoops. The Wildling joins in.

"They need us," Lewis says. He crawls to the side and is half gone before I realize he's climbing down. I look from Lewis to Will.

Will's face hardens. "Release Lewis and Olive."

"Or what?" Shiloh says. "Besides, Olive is with us now, remember?"

Will's eyes fall, but he shakes his head no.

Duke arches his back so his ribs show and whoops some more. He has red stripes under his eyes today. I don't want to know what he used to paint them. "Your Lions are defecting, Will. They know who's stronger. Anyone else want to join?"

Bug, Charlie, and Tilly stare daggers at him.

"Ah. You run a tight ship. Olive was smart to get out when she could."

"I did not join you!" I hear myself shout and I'm standing, leaning over the edge of the cliff, holding onto a rock.

Will's eyes widen.

The other Panthers come out of the cave and look up.

Tommy goes to light one of the mini bombs, but Henry grabs his wrist until he drops it.

"You'll blow the entrance in!"

Tommy curses.

I glance at Will.

His eye bounces from me to Duke, to Tommy and his mini bomb, to Lewis, who runs toward him. Once Lewis reaches them, he stands next to Will. Tilly hands him a spear. She holds one herself, black rings drawn up and down her bare arms. Then she eyes Bug and Charlie who duck behind the boulders.

I make my way to the place where Lewis climbed down.

You can do this, Olive. You can do this.

Your family needs you.

You climbed up. You can climb back down.

One foot and one hand at a time, I begin the descent, a

good thirty-foot drop.

I don't think about it. I think about Will. He's here. Charlie's here. Bug and Tilly.

But Jude's not.

No. My hand slips.

I gasp, hyperventilation bubbling up.

Charlie. Charlie's alive.

And Will… I've got the horn for him, just like I promised myself I would.

Though he's not who I thought he was. I don't think.

One foot. One hand.

Is he a bully? Did he brand that "P" on Duke's chest? Could he?

One foot. One hand.

P? Pathetic?

One foot. One hand.

Pariah?

One foot. One hand.

The ground closer, somehow between the top of the cliff and the bottom, I've gone from loathing Duke to torn. I'm not sure if I hate him or feel sorry for him. If it is true, he's a victim. A product of cruelty.

My feet hit the ground.

Everyone's yelling.

I run to Will, Tilly, and Lewis.

Tilly hands me what I recognize as Jude's small blade. My head goes fuzzy. I pull the horn from my shirt and set it on the ground. Tilly cocks her eyebrow, and the corner of her mouth tugs up, but she doesn't say a word.

"What do you want us to do?" Noah calls to Duke, bomb in hand.

Duke doesn't answer, his eyes set on Will.

"You use that bomb, you'll blow us all up!" Shiloh, arms out like she's ready to make a run for it, answers for Duke.

Noah lowers his arm.

Duke sighs. "This isn't how I saw it ending," he mutters to

himself, pacing. "I had a plan. A war. *They* weren't supposed to come here." He stops. "You weren't supposed to come here!" He screams at us. Birds fly from the trees. Then, silence. It's like a movie. We stare across at each other, waiting for someone to make a move.

If this is war, we're two clueless armies of children.

Will steps forward, lowering his spear. "It doesn't have to be this way." He takes another step.

Duke stops pacing.

"We can work together. Find our way home. Isn't that what we all want? To get home?"

Duke steps back. "Home?" His eyes narrow in on Will. "I'm nothing at home. Thanks to you and your friends, I have no home. I'm a disgrace. A P-P-P-Pussy." He points to the scar on his chest, eyes intensely dark, one corner of his mouth twitching up into a smile.

A stutter? And a capital *P* for Pussy. Bad combo for Duke; perfect combo to get made fun of.

"Do you remember that day, *William*? How I used to stutter my…" He pauses, swallowing. "My P's?" And I can't help notice when he says "P's" there's a definite hesitation, more an "H" sound to it than it should have.

"Look. I can't take any of that back. I wish I could. God, I wish I could. I'm so sorry!" Will's voice cracks. He steps closer.

"Let's tell everyone about that day." Duke steps toward the cave. "Gym class. Boy's locker room. Super glue in my underwear. You and your friends held me down. Torn skin. Blood."

The guys all cringe and suck air in through their teeth.

"'P-P-Pussy,' you yelled, pointing. Pussy!" Duke cries and whoops at once.

He bends forward, holding his stomach with both hands, laughing his hyena laugh louder so it echoes through the cave and beyond.

I stare at Tilly and Lewis, then at Will. He *was* like them. Locker room antics and all.

He lowers his head.

"Anyone need more details?" Duke says, wiping his eyes, smudging the red across his face like fresh wounds. No one responds. He nods, moving on. "But now? Here?" He surveys his mountain. "This is all mine. I did something here. I became a man. A king." He lunges toward Noah, grabs the coconut bomb away, and runs to the edge of the cliff.

We all stiffen, instantly on guard, watching him. Each one of us studies Duke, trying to read his body language, because surely, he wouldn't… He couldn't…

Will walks toward Duke in slow, calculated steps.

Duke pulls out a lighter. He clicks it, a small flame glowing next to the wick. "I wouldn't do that if I were you," he speaks through clenched teeth, warning Will.

Will jerks to a stop.

"Now this—*this* is how it ends. On my terms." Duke waves the flame around, eyes wildly wide.

Noah, Henry, and Tommy run into the cave for cover.

Shiloh backs toward us.

"Don't do it, man," Will says, shifting closer to Duke. "It isn't worth it."

Duke gazes out over the cliff. "Do you hear them? It's beautiful." He laughs. But not the hyena laugh, a real person laugh. A human laugh laced with all kinds of sadness.

"Hear what, old friend?" Will asks.

"The angels, they're singing. They've come to take me to my real castle."

"Well, they don't want you to go this way. Not by blowing everyone up. Just—drop the bomb. Please, David."

Duke grimaces at his name. He then glares at Will, evil grin stretched across his face. "If I can't have this island, no one will." Duke lights the bomb.

"Stop!" Will shouts.

Lewis pulls Tilly to the ground.

I run toward Duke.

No.

"No!" My thoughts spring to life as one loud word in

a guy's voice. I turn my head and see Jude running up the mountain path straight for us. He throws something on the ground and the smeared lion's face on his chest twists and roars as he sprints. Past Bug and Charlie behind the boulder. Past Tilly and Lewis.

"Jude, no!" Lewis yells.

Tilly screams, scrambles out of Lewis's grip, and follows Jude.

Will tries to grab Jude. He misses and falls, tumbling to the ground.

Jude comes straight at me, and with one long arm, shoves me so I roll back toward Lewis. Once I stop, I force my eyes to watch.

Tilly chases Jude.

Jude runs straight for Duke. The bomb. The cliff.

Duke's eyes go wide.

"No! Stop! Wait!" Several voices shout at once.

Lewis lunges, shielding me with his body.

With one eye peeking over Lewis's shoulder, what I see is most definitely a scene from a movie because it's in slow motion and cannot be real.

Jude slams into Duke, shoving him to the ground, then grabs the bomb.

He's about to take himself and the bomb over the cliff, but the bomb bobbles in his hand, and he nearly drops it. He doesn't see Tilly coming up behind him. She runs full force toward the bomb, wraps it in her arms, hugging it to her chest like an infant, and jumps.

The last I see is a gloriously beautiful mane of strawberry blond curls, the sun illuminating it like a golden halo.

Then, there's a *crack, ka-boom*.

The loudest yet.

It pierces clear through me like I've been sliced in two.

The mountain shakes.

Time stands still.

The wind sings a sad song. Or maybe it is an angel.

Chapter Thirty-Five

My ears ring like a locomotive. Or maybe it's a tornado. Don't they say they sound the same?

Beneath the ringing is moaning. Crying. Yelling.

I lift my head. Everything is gray smoke and ash. Lewis stares blankly toward the cliff.

Tommy and Noah sit on their knees, stunned, as Shiloh runs in and out of the cave with rags and water. I can't see his state, but Duke lies on the ground near the edge of the cliff, unmoving. Jude lies face down not an arm's reach from Duke. He's trying to lift his body up, but failing. And there's another body near them. But it isn't Tilly. Henry, holding his arm tightly to his chest, is sprawled on his back near Duke like he'd gone after him, too, but Jude and Tilly beat him to it.

Oh God, Tilly.

Sweet, sweet Tilly.

No, no, no!

Sour heat rises from my gut.

My breath shudders as I force myself to breathe.

How can this be real? That conch shell's song wasn't meant for Tilly.

Never for Tilly.

Quietly strong, mother to all, lovely Tilly. Memories flash like a film strip behind my eyelids: Tilly shaving Jude's face, her light eyes and bright smile, the freckles that stippled her nose, how she tended to Bug and Charlie like they were her own. She kept us all grounded and fed and clean. That knowing way she looked into my eyes the day I betrayed them. She knew, saw right past my forced act.

Oh God.

I glance around at the chaos, the smoke still lifting.

What is this cursed place? This nightmare?

Tears flee my eyes, blurring my vision, as I search for Will through dust and smoke, my body shaking and numb at once.

I don't see him.

I search from rock to rock, tree to tree, my heart stopping and starting up in spurts.

No.

Will?

He was close to the blast, too.

I sit up on my knees. "Lewis?" My voice sounds weird like I'm in a dream—no—a nightmare.

The dust finally settling, debris floats through the air like a million dark fairies. Lewis lifts himself off me but refuses to look toward the cliff.

"Where's Will?" I ask him.

Lewis glances around then nudges his head toward the rocks where Bug and Charlie were. I follow the direction with my eyes.

Will…

Thank you.

I'm not sure who I'm thanking. The angels? Maybe.

Of course, he'd go straight to the kids. Always looking out. Always protecting.

Will is on his knees, gash across his forehead, skin covered in dirt, and he holds Bug and Charlie into him. Bug's black puff and Charlie's yellow mop of curls burrow into Will's chest.

I can't stop staring at the scene when Will catches me. His eyebrows buckle and he closes his eye, tucking his face into Bug's hair. His shoulders shake and his body bows into them.

A piece of my heart splinters and a sliver chips away. I'll never forget this image. Ever.

I walk over. The ringing in my ears has lessened, but it's still there, a lingering, high-pitched tone. I swallow my sadness, the terror, Tilly's strawberry halo, erecting a wall between myself and all the horror for the kids.

"You guys all right?" I force out.

Bug and Charlie wriggle free and attack me with hugs. "Guess so," I say.

Their eyes are surprisingly, impossibly dry. I can't imagine how anyone's eyes aren't overflowing at a moment like this. But then I realize. They don't know. They didn't see any of it. Will made sure of it.

Will wipes his face, smearing dirt around.

Bug pulls away and stares at me with those June Bug eyes. "Oh, Olive, I missed you!"

"I missed you, too, Bed Bug." I pull her back into me and kiss her forehead. "And you…" I glance down at Charlie. "You scared the crap out of me." My voice slips, the knot in my throat creeping up, but I manage to push it back.

He smiles a cockeyed smile.

"No more coconut?" I ask.

"No more coconut," he confirms, "but Tilly is gonna have to figure out a new way to make soap for me." He squishes his mouth to one side.

My heart drops to the dirt-covered ground, puddling in a muddy heap.

But I nod, then pull him in, too. "We'll figure it out, buddy." My voice is a scratchy, quaky mess.

Charlie and Bug squeeze me back and let go at the same

time. Then the two little sneaks sit underneath a tree where Will's told them not to move an inch until he comes back. Obedient pups they are, they nod, then begin a game of I Spy. So innocent. So pure to the evils and cruelties of life.

I envy them.

When I turn to speak to Will, he's already several steps ahead, scoping out the scene. No doubt tallying who's where and in what state.

I catch up and grab his arm.

He pulls away. "This isn't over. I've gotta—"

"Gotta what?"

Without answering, he scans the cave. Still on guard. Always on guard. But when he sees what I see—the fight has stalled. Sides have been temporarily suspended in the chaos, in the unbelievable, horrible reality. His shoulders fall and his chest folds and shudders.

"What about you?" I whisper. "Will you figure it out?" The question is so loaded, full of so many possible meanings, I'm not sure I even understand it.

Will shakes his head, peering up at the cloudless blue sky.

I hug him and he melts into silent sobs at my neck.

Who is this complicated, beautiful, tortured creature, anyway? He isn't the Will I knew before. He's different now, but not. And I care so much for him. My head spins. I'm not sure what any of it means and I can't begin to dissect it right now.

Instead, I shove it aside and wrap my arms around his waist tighter. "Is it Tilly?" I ask.

He breathes into my neck. "Oh man." He sniffs. "This is all my fault. Tilly. Annabel. The cave-tree being bombed. Duke. Nearly getting us all blown to shreds. My. Fault." His voice is higher than normal, cracking with emotion.

I pull back, shaking my head. "No."

Will rubs his eye with more force than necessary then pulls his hands through his hair with a jerk. He nods meaningfully because he knows there's truth to his comment.

And I've got nothing to say to that. I want to find something. A group of words that will make everything all right, but they don't come. Because I haven't a clue what they are.

He pulls away, his expression soft, mournful.

"Can we get some help over here?" Shiloh calls.

Will jumps as if being awoken from sleep. He takes off and I'm left with an empty space and too much to grasp.

I turn and run after him, following the sound of voices up near the cliff.

Will runs toward Shiloh, Duke, and Henry, but Lewis leaps up from where he's tending to Jude and stands in front of him, forcing Will to stop or plow Lewis down. "Why should we help them?" Lewis shouts.

Will grabs Lewis's shoulder, turning him so they're face-to-face. "Lew—"

"No!"

"Lewis." Will squeezes.

"No! They killed Annabel! Jude's hurt. And they—" Lewis's eyes pool like great lakes as he looks to the cliff, then falls into Will. He punches Will in the chest with loose fists but soon melts into a shaking, sobbing boy. Just a kid. There's a burning in my stomach and my sobs catch at my chest because we all are, aren't we?

"I know, brother. I know," Will consoles Lewis, pulling him into a hug, breathing in the top of his head, and staring down on Duke and Henry. I swear the look in Will's eye is one of doubt, distrust. He can't get over this war. None of them can. They're all too close.

But I'm not.

I take off in a sprint, running back toward that spot where Tilly handed me the blade. I pick up the horn I'd left there and make my way back to the cave. In the mere minutes I'd been gone, the two groups have broken out into full-on shouting. Two sides divided. Always divided.

Damn it, why can't they just see?

I take a few steps forward so I'm in the middle of them all. My hand clenched in a fist around the horn, that sad, sickening heat I felt earlier in my gut has turned to a burning ball of fire. I lift the horn up and blow into it as hard as I can.

I expect the familiar and commanding, *pha-ooh*, but instead, it gives off a deep and severe *phoooo!*

The shouting stops and all goes quiet. Time stands still. All eyes are planted on me.

I drop the horn to the ground with a thud.

"This is shit!" I yell, the words resonating from deep down, so deep they sting on their way up. Everyone continues staring. "How many of us have to die before we open our eyes and see what's going on?" I ask, not expecting an answer, but taking in the silence, the dirty, tear-streaked faces staring back at me. I inhale through my nose, out my mouth. "A girl just died. She sacrificed her life for us. All of us." I glance around. "This has to stop. We've got to work together. For Tilly." My voice breaks and I swallow back the pain, determined to get the words out. "The last thing that's going to get any of us home is war." Drawing in a shaky breath, I run my hands through my hair, pausing a moment to gaze into the endless blue sky. It's so perfectly light blue, it could be paint on a canvas. Not a cloud or blemish upon it.

I bring my eyes, along with my thoughts, down from the blue and back to the present.

This starts with me.

A light breeze whips through the rocky valley and, I swear, a faint song rides along the wind.

Tilly.

Lump in my throat, but with my head held high, I walk past Will, who stares, and Lewis who averts his eyes from mine, over to Shiloh. She kneels between Duke and Henry, her hand resting on Duke's chest, where blood seeps under her fingers, running down his ribs like wax off a candle.

"How can I help?" I ask.

Shiloh stares up at me then back to Duke. His face is

covered in scratches, that gash across his chest extends to his abdomen, and he's fallen unconscious. I think.

"Is he…" The words seep from my mouth in a numb buzz. Please, no more death.

"He's breathing," Shiloh answers, and my shoulders fall as I remind myself to breathe, too. Long black hair a shield, she bends over Duke, her hands trembling and flailing, not sure where to begin. "Do you have anything that will help?" she asks, her tone desperate.

Footsteps come up from behind. Will and Lewis stand beside me. Lewis pulls his shirt from the back of his pants and hands it to Shiloh, who sponges Duke's blood.

On the other side of Henry, Will bends down. He's already torn his own shirt into a strip and is bandaging the cut on his forehead. "His arm looks broken," he says, fashioning a sling from what's left of his shirt, then helping Henry sit up.

Before I know it, there's a fuzzy, brown crown of hair right next to me. Bug has Tilly's small medicine pouch and digs for the ointment shell, holding it out, then setting it in my palm. We exchange a glance and I realize her and Charlie must have heard everything. Her eyes are swollen and red, but she doesn't say a word, just nods, going to Will and dumping the contents of the bag next to Henry.

Noah and Tommy race toward us from the tunnel, carrying large containers of water. They join the cause, jumping to action, and we're all accounted for. Well…most of us.

Glancing over my shoulder, Charlie is deep in an embrace with Jude, who's rocking the small boy in his lap, golden curls swaying just under Jude's chin, against the colorful tattoos on his neck.

I catch his eyes, and it's like they're open for the first time and he finally sees past all that anger and remorse masking his vision. With a slight nod, Jude squeezes his eyes shut. His face twisting in pure pain, he drops his head into Charlie's mane, Jude's broad, bare shoulders and back quaking. I can only imagine the expression gracing the smeared lion on his chest now, and briefly find myself caught up in whether lions weep.

Turning back to Shiloh and all the commotion—the backdrop to weeping lions and golden curls and singing angels—I kneel next to Duke. His chest quivers as Shiloh sops up blood and Tommy pours water over the wound. I scoop ointment from the shell, then slather the coconut oil-herb concoction onto a non-bloodied strip of cotton T-shirt and tenderly place it over Duke's wounds.

Shiloh and I share a look. It isn't one of friendship or forgiveness, defeat or hatred, but one of mutual understanding—differences aside, we've got to work together.

Her gaze set back on Duke, Shiloh's forehead is lined in concern. "Can you help us carry him inside?" she asks all of us and none of us in a far-off, un-Shiloh voice.

Jude stays outside with Bug and Charlie while the rest of us head to the cave.

With Shiloh leading the way, holding the bandages steady, Will, Lewis, Noah, and Tommy carry Duke into the cave.

They're careful, taking slow steps as Duke goes in and out of consciousness. Once inside, they settle him near the fire, wrapping his body in the makeshift blanket Lewis and I had been under for so many days. Shiloh settles next to Duke, and Henry lays flat on the ground near the fire. Tommy lifts Henry's head, making a pillow for him with a piece of clothing.

No one says a word, but all our minds toss like riptides, the questions and concerns palpable. Despite the silence, *what now?* fills the cave.

"I'm gonna check on Jude," Lewis breaks the stillness. Will gives him a manly pat on the back before he leaves.

Shiloh, Noah, and Tommy stare up at Will and me, and I can't help fall back into old habits. The sense we're invading their side of the island, their home, takes over and I instinctively back away.

But Will turns his head toward me, that wild, lively green of his eye reminding me things have changed.

Stepping forward, I make up the distance and then some. "Here's what I'm thinking," I say. "First, we need to allow our injured friends to heal and we..." I look to Will. "We need to tend to the kids, address Tilly's death properly. Have a ceremony. Something." I choke the last word out because it's not nearly enough.

Shiloh nods, her mossy eyes glazed over. "Okay," she whispers, staring back to Duke.

"Okay," I say back.

When Will and I leave the cave, we stumble upon a sweet and somber scene.

Jude lies on his back on the ground, forearm shading his eyes from the sun, one leg up, the other stretched out flat. Next to Jude is Lewis, who's wringing a wet piece of material over a cut in Jude's knee. Charlie's head rests on Jude's stomach, and Bug, doll tucked under her arm, is curled in a ball on the other side. They're like a pile of puppies.

But...

That doll. Bug didn't have it before. I glance to Will from the corner of my eyes. "Where'd the doll come from?" I whisper.

"Bug insisted on bringing it along but dropped it at some point. Jude had run back to get it right before... Well, before."

I nod, inhaling deeply, still in shock, everything in fast motion or stuck at a standstill on this messed-up island.

But as I take in the scene before me, the pile of puppies, Will nudging his way into the huddle, there's a tiny spark of hope fluttering at just the right pace.

Chapter Thirty-Six

The Conch and the Horn

Will blows the conch shell. *Whoo. Whoo.*

Shiloh blows the King's horn. *Pha-ooh. Pha-ooh.*

It's haunting and beautiful as the two sounds come together as one in tragedy.

There was no point in searching for Tilly's remains. It wasn't even discussed, the sheer thought too horrible. Too raw. Too much to bear. Besides, the side of the mountain had a hole in it. Tilly had turned to golden dust like the angelic being she was. At least, that's what we'd all collectively, though silently, agreed upon.

Two hollowed coconuts surrounded by flowers and torches are set like a centerpiece before us on the beach. Etched in one is an ornate "T," the other a strong, solid "D."

Duke is still alive, but barely. Shiloh filled us in when her, Tommy, Noah, and Henry surprised us by showing up on the beach, horn in hand. They told us this will be a remembrance of sorts, a prayer for their leader, their friend.

One by one, we approach.

Each of us stuffs a scrap of tree bark or leaf or whatever we could find to write a message on into Tilly's island-made shrine.

No one says a word.

I'm first to put a message in. I wrote five words across a leaf in charcoal. "Tilly: Nurturer. Loved. Too soon." They seem insignificant. Not nearly enough.

I walk up, drop to my knees, and cry for Tilly. Sweet, sweet Tilly who welcomed me with open arms from day one, confided in me, and believed in me when no one else did. She had the biggest of hearts. So big, that in the end, she sacrificed it for all of us. And I have a feeling she wouldn't change a thing.

A hand comes to rest on my shoulder. It's Will. He bends down, puts his piece of bark in, pauses, then stands, helping me up along the way.

Everyone else says their silent good-byes. Lewis and Jude go up one by one, setting their messages for Tilly in the coconut, taking a moment of silence. When Jude rises to walk away, he pauses, placing his hand on the coconut. He bows his head, mumbles something under his breath, and then, sniffing, wipes his face with his hands.

The little Lions are quiet, eyes down, drawing pictures in the sand with sticks. They get it, but they don't.

The Panthers' ritual is quieter. Quicker. Less emotional, though their sadness is evident. Shiloh lacks her usual sass. Tommy, Henry, and Noah stand tall and still. There are no *whoops*. No *whees*.

At one point, I notice Will watching them, eyes glistening, and I'd do anything to know what he's thinking. No one else cries for Duke, and that makes me cry. Because, damn it, the guy never had a chance. He's me in so many ways. So maybe I'm really crying for both of us.

Will and Shiloh cork the coconuts with makeshift stoppers so they'll float. Then they throw our symbolic friends out to sea.

We stand in a long line and watch until the coconuts are tiny brown dots.

I glance from side to side.

How did we get here? Just hours before we were at war. And now? It's like reality has finally set in. Like we've realized this thing, this island, is in control. And it's so much bigger than us kids—because that's all we are. Kids.

And we best stick together. Right?

"Let's take the rest of the day to regroup and meet up in the morning." I hear myself blurt out. Shiloh glances over at me from the corner of her eye.

"Sounds good," she says. "But you'll need to come to us, because of Duke, if he's still…"

"Of course," I answer and Will takes my hand, squeezing it. I'm still unsure as to which version of Will I know. Which is the truth? Am I holding the bully's hand or the hand of the boy I've come to trust?

I accept the warmth. The closeness. But eventually I let go.

When my Lion family fled our home, they found shelter within the cove of another cave-tree. It isn't nearly as grand as the original, but it's shelter and they brought most of our belongings and equipment. They left the minute after I'd shown up with the Panthers at their doorstep. Tilly had insisted.

"I kept telling her we needed to stay a few days in case you or Lewis came looking for us." Will huffs air out his nose. "The bomb hit that night." He pushes the wood around the fire with his spear. "That 'gut feeling' of hers was always right." Will does his airy laugh, but it's heavy with sadness, regret.

We're all there, gathered around a fire—together, but not truly—each of us lost in our own emotions and thoughts. Jude comically, yet sweetly, attempts taming Bug's hair for the night like he's grasping for a distraction while Charlie keeps pulling Bug's attention—and head—away in a game of tic-tac-toe on the sandy floor.

It's as if nothing's changed. But everything has. The grand cave-tree is gone. Our Tilly is gone. Will isn't the same person I thought he was.

How is it life does this? Right when you get comfortable with one thing, everything sweeps out from under you. You move across the country. Walk through a corn maze onto an island. A friend dies.

Life is brutal. A total asshole, like the sheep.

I miss Tawny. And Lucky. My parents. Sweet Tilly…

But I can't do this. Not now. I have a war to mend. An island to beat. It feels like an outrageously tall order—like I'm at the bottom of that craggy mountain again, staring up at it. God, how it towers over me. Just as tears collect in my eyes and my throat tightens, Will takes my hand.

"Can we talk?" he asks.

I sniff the tears back, clear my head, and nod.

Will leads me outside. It's a beautiful night, the moon close to the full circle it was when I arrived.

He sits on the ground against a tree. I stand in front of him, arms crossed. He pats the ground next to him and stares up at me with what I can only compare to Lucky's heart-shattering puppy-dog eyes.

Be strong, Olive.

I sit but keep my emotions on lock-down. Because I don't know this Will person, do I?

"I should have been honest—with everyone…" He breathes deeply. "But especially you."

I don't respond. Just stare. Waiting. Staying strong. Hoping there's more.

Will leans back against the tree. "I didn't know any different. It doesn't excuse or justify what I did, but it's the truth. My mother was young when she had me, and my father was one of a long line of men she'd been with. She couldn't handle her own life, much less a baby added to it. She left me with my grandmother one afternoon and never came back. My grandmother was a saint and did the best she could until she got sick. My grandfather had died years before."

There's truth and sadness to his words, but also a steely strength like he can't quite tear down that wall.

"Then I went to a great aunt who never wanted me. I stayed with her until I was thirteen and started getting into trouble. She shipped me off to her son, my uncle, in Dallas. He tried to beat me into obedience, but that only made me more rebellious. Angrier. Hateful and spiteful.

"One evening, he took me out for a long drive and a soda, then dropped me off on the doorstep of a children's home in Hillings. They were expecting me." His voice breaks from emotion. The first crack I've seen in that great iron barrier of his. I want to hear the rest, but also, I don't.

"Will, you don't have to—"

"No, I do. I owe it to you. To them." He motions to the cave-tree. "I owe you all so much more. More than I can ever give." He shakes his head and clears his throat. "From the children's home, I was shuffled from family to family. No one wanted me. No one could handle me. I don't blame them. I didn't want to be around myself." He stares up into the tree, thinking God knows what. "Pretty soon, I didn't care if anyone wanted me, and I started taking it out on Duke—David. A couple of guys used to tease him and before I knew it, I'd become the ring-leader, upping the ante each time. Poor kid never knew what hit him." He sighs and digs his fingers into the ground. "I was a monster. A torn-up, sad, mean, punk of a kid."

Will peers over at me with that green eye. It's filled with tears. The steel melting one drop at a time. "I'm not that kid anymore." A tear falls. It's silver in the moonlight. "Coming here? It was a blessing and a curse for me. Those first few years I spent here alone after losing my eye? They were hell and I deserved every minute of it. I found myself during that time, Olive." He looks at me. "I know it sounds stupid, but there's no other way to explain it. I settled my demons. I forgave my mother and father. My grandmother for dying. My uncle for abandoning me when I needed someone most." He sighs, gazes up at the stars, then back at me. "This island gave me new life. I got to start over here. I got to do better. Take care of people. Be good." He glances away into the forest. "All I ever wanted was to be good, to be loved. I just didn't know how."

What was once an iron fortress now has a tiny space carved out of it. And it's just big enough for me to squeeze through. I put my hand on his. Will laces his fingers in mine, then speaks to our hands. "Funny… David and I—we aren't so different after all. We both found ourselves on this island— found something to believe in. I hope I get the chance to tell him. I'd roam this island forever, making it up to him, and it still wouldn't be enough." He wipes his cheek with the backside of his hand. "I don't expect you to forgive me or trust me again, but I needed you to know."

Both our heads are down, staring at our hands. He's rubbing his thumb over mine, and I wonder if his vision is as blurred as mine. If our hands appear as one fleshy blob to him, too.

I squeeze, then let go and stand up. I walk away. Will doesn't say a word or move.

I'm not sure how long I walk or where I go, but at some point, it hits me and I see how connected we all are. Will, Duke, me, the Trio. God, like this island, it *is* so much bigger than us. We're just kids tripping our way through a really screwed-up world.

I find myself walking back up to where I left Will, but he's not there. He's coming out of the cave-tree, hands terrorizing his hair.

I stop.

He strides right up to me.

"I talked to them, told them everything," Will says, voice straining to get the words out.

"And?"

"And, it went better than I thought it would. Trust has definitely been broken, but I'm so lucky. I don't know how I found such amazing, forgiving people. I don't deserve it. None of it."

"Yes, you do. Everyone does."

He glances away, pain in his face.

"Will?"

He nods.

"I'm so sorry."

He whips his head back around to me, face wrecked with emotion, brow furrowed. "Why are you apologizing?"

"Don't you see?" I crouch to the ground, pulling him down with me. Knees to knees, we stare at one another. "You're a result of your situation, just like Duke was a result of the bullying. Just like we're all products of this cruel island."

Will reaches across and smooths the shaved side of my hair. "Products..." His voice is low, quiet.

"Yeah. It sucks," I say, a small, airy, Will-like laugh escaping me.

"It does suck." He smiles his crooked smile and puts his hand to my chin, urging my face toward his.

"But, the beauty is, we can change. I truly believe we can turn this all around. Make things right." His stare burns into me, part doubt, part intrigue. "Charlie went from a terrified kid to a fighter. Bug, a little girl who didn't speak a word of English to a precocious chatterbox. Tilly, running from bombs to heroically facing one head-on."

"And David went from a poor, frightened kid to a warmongering 'king,'" Will says, expression heavy with hopelessness.

"Yeah, well, he still has time. You changed."

"I did." He shakes his head like he still doesn't believe it. "And what of Olive Gagmuehler?" He turns the tables.

I glance away because it's my name. *That* name. "What of Olive Gagmuehler?" I repeat him, the dreaded two words sneaking out in a whisper, knot lodged in my throat, stomach squeezed into a tight ball.

"The girl who ran from her life through a maze, then stumbled onto an island, and into a pig trap. Olive Gagmuehler, who never smiles a real smile."

My eyes dart to his like I've been caught.

"She's changed," Will says.

"I suppose she has."

"Suppose? She definitely has. Her hair's grown out—you can hardly tell it was ever shaved. She's defended herself and her friends. She climbed a mountain. Kept a sick boy alive. Managed to get six strangers to fall in love with her. She's somehow brought two groups of kids who were set to blow each other up just yesterday, together. And that smile? I swear I've seen glimpses of it." He traces my lips with his finger.

My stomach stretches out of its ball and squirms up into my ribs. I blush. Thank God it's dark.

"You're well on your way, Olive Gagmuehler." Will takes my other hand and pulls me in, resting his forehead against mine. Those emotions I had on lock-down break free and I place my hands on the sides of his face, running my fingers across his jaw, down his neck. His nose brushes against mine, my eyelashes graze his eye patch, and our lips touch.

This kiss is different.

It's truth. No secrets. No expectations. It's pure and honest and warm and beautiful.

We lie back on the ground, Will on his back, me facing him. I stare at him, noticing how his eye color is more metallic in the moonlight. He plays with my hair. We kiss some more. I put my head on his chest and listen to his heartbeat, thinking on his silver-green moonlit eye.

"The moon is almost where it was when I showed up here that night—however long ago," I admit.

"Twenty-eight days."

I smile. It's almost real.

Chapter Thirty-Seven

Egg Hunt

The next morning, I'm up before the sun, determined to take on Tilly's duties. First order of business? Breakfast.

I leave a quiet, warm, and sleepy cave-tree to find the dawning day is cool, the sun just rising over the horizon. Now knowing what is safe to eat and what isn't, it's no trouble collecting roots and fruit. But I'd love to make something special. If I could only find a wild chicken. What I wouldn't do for scrambled eggs. They'd all go wild over it.

I look toward the budding sun and decide I've got some extra time to search. I've seen chickens before, but they're surprisingly quick and total jerks if you try picking them up. Eggs, though… Tilly had managed to snag some from time to time.

Stopping, closing my eyes, I say a sort of prayer requesting Tilly's guidance.

"Help me?" I whisper to the forest, and it's more than clear I'm not only asking for help to find eggs. Tears prickle behind my eyelids at the thought of Tilly, and I realize this is the first I've been alone in a long time. In the absence of prying eyes and questions of concern, I allow my tears to fall freely. I cry for Tilly and for Duke. For Will and Jude. For the little ones and Lewis. For poor Jack and Tommy. Noah and Henry. Even Shiloh. No one asked for this.

Finally, I cry for myself. For Olive Maxi Gagmuehler.

Step by step, I walk the forest aimlessly, sobbing, but keeping an ear out for any clucking.

When I'm all dried out and the crippling weight on my shoulders has lightened, I realize where I am. It's like I'm opening my eyes for the first time since arriving.

My boulder sits before me. The huge thing is still mossy. Still enormous. I walk up to it. Touch it. It's cold and fuzzy and hard as ever.

When I pull my hand back, cinching the hammock I've made with my shirt to hold my bounty, several nuts slip out, tumbling to the ground.

"Damn it," I swear under my breath, crouching to pick them up. As I crawl around the base of the boulder, gathering the nuts, this time putting them in my pocket instead of further overflowing the makeshift hammock, something catches my eye. There's a shimmering just on the other side of the large rock like heat waves rising above the Texas sidewalks in August. I squint, unsure if I'm seeing things when I'm hit with the unmistakable scent of popcorn. My mouth instantly waters.

Inching my way closer to the illusion, I crawl until I'm face-to-face with the bizarre and barely-there shimmering. The sun now up, from this angle, the reflection, image—whatever it is—glistens in lucent rainbows, pearly like a bubble.

Cautiously, in super slow motion, I poke at the iridescent waves with my forefinger, which disappears behind them. I yank it back.

Both my hands stretched out in front of me, forgoing all I've gathered for breakfast, allowing the items to fall out of my shirt and scatter to the ground, I reach toward the mysterious opal waves.

My hands disappear. But I don't pull them back this time. Instead, I get even closer, swallowing hard and, breath held, sticking my face right up to the surface.

Closer and closer I move until my chin is in. I don't feel any change in sensation, no pain, no alarm sounds off, I can still breathe. I figure it's safe to keep going, so I push my mouth and nose in, then my eyes, and lastly my forehead.

A cornstalk tunnel greets me.

I gasp and scramble in reverse, bumping back-first into the boulder.

Home.

That was *definitely* home.

I could return right now and, in a matter of seconds, be back in Hillings where beds and showers and French fries exist. Lucky and Tawny and Mom and Dad. And, oh my God, chocolate and movies and clean clothes.

But... The others.

Though, what if this is my only chance to get back? What happens if I leave and return and the shimmering disappears?

But I can't go.

Not now.

Not this way.

Shit.

Eggs and nuts and fruit forgotten, I sprint back to the cave-tree.

I arrive to Lewis, who stands outside our home like he was watching for me. I'm out of breath and can barely form the words, but manage, between breaths, to spit out a nonsensical sentence that includes, "heat waves" and "boulder" and "home" and "get the others."

Once Lewis deciphers and translates, everyone follows me back to the boulder. As we speed-walk, I don't stop talking, explaining my morning, the egg hunt, the nuts, and how I almost accidentally went home.

God, I nearly went home. My head spins at the thought.

The endless *what-ifs*.

When we get there, I'm out of breath again, hunched over, hands on my thighs, verging on hyperventilation.

"There," I say, pointing at the shimmer, thankful it hasn't vanished.

"Whoa!" Bug shouts, tip-toeing up to the wavy window like a cat stalking prey.

"Careful, Bug," I say, glancing over at Will, unsure of what might happen.

Will jumps in front of her.

"Hey!" she shouts.

He gives her a look that lays to rest any ideas she had of messing with the iridescent waves.

"Fine…" she mumbles, backing away.

Will moves forward, taking her place.

"So this is what it looks like?" Lewis says, following Will closer to the surface. He runs his hand in front of it as if checking for heat or static. "Fascinating."

"It's so subtle," Will adds. "I'd have never noticed it." His face is close as he studies the practically invisible door back to the corn maze. "Is that…popcorn?"

I nod.

Charlie, Bug, and Jude all step up to take a whiff. Their eyes widen at the magic that is freshly popped popcorn.

Out of nowhere, Jude shoves his hand into the waves.

"Jude—" Will begins, but his warning is useless because nothing happens. Jude's arm goes through the bubble as if it isn't there. He then takes a step right through it.

Nothing.

"Hmph," Jude grunts. "Damn it, I really want popcorn now."

"I wonder…" Will says, following suit. He encounters the same result.

Everyone has a go at the mysterious, shimmering pane, passing through it without ceremony until I'm the only person standing on the other side.

"Can you see it from over there?" I ask, gazing through the barely-there iridescence at all their faces.

"No, we only see you," Will answers. A slight tugging at his lips, he shoots me a crooked smile. "Try again," he urges.

Pulling my sight from his lips, I nod, pushing my hand into the waves. It disappears.

"No way!" Charlie shouts and I jerk my arm away.

"That thing's here for you and only you," Jude says.

I nod.

But what now?

We brainstorm the entire walk home, deciding to visit each of the places on the island where the others had arrived. With each one, we grow less and less hopeful. Lewis's, Jude's, and Bug's haven't opened. No heat waves. No shimmers. Charlie's and Will's were obviously closed.

Last, we visit Tilly's. She had shown up on the northern side of the island, near the largest, windiest section of beach.

Palm trees sway like a sad dance, as Jude leads the way. Once there, next to an overgrown prickly fruit bush, there, along with the strong breeze, shimmer the now familiar heat waves.

"Holy shit," Jude mumbles, his hand placed over his mouth.

Holy shit, indeed.

The irony and tragedy and sorrow is overwhelming.

No one says another word, and we walk back to the cave-tree in utter silence.

"Let's get this straight," Lewis says, tapping a stick of charcoal against the inside of the cave-tree wall where he's already jotted down all sorts of theories and ideas from the obvious to the completely unrealistic. "The boulder is a regular destination for us. We pick food there, gather firewood, trap pigs…" He glances at me and I playfully scowl. Lewis grins. "No one's ever seen anything like what's there now?"

We all shake our heads.

"So we can assume the window is new," he states to himself more than anything.

We rarely venture to the north end of the island, so it's hard to say how long Tilly's window has been there.

I glance at Jude. He sits in silence in a sort of hard daze, not saying a word since we arrived at Tilly's place. Damn it—poor, sweet Tilly. The echoes of that horrible bomb still ring in my ears. What a terrible way to leave the world and for such a gentle creature it's doubly tragic. Wrong. Then there's the irony… She'd arrived at the island running from bombs and left it with one hugged close to her chest.

Wait.

My body is taken over by goosebumps.

I stand.

I walk toward the wall where Lewis scribbles the charcoal down to nothing.

Everyone stares at me.

My arm thrust outward, palm up, I wait for Lewis to give me what's left of the charcoal, as my mind reels over and over, worried if I don't toss the idea endlessly, I'll forget. Lewis, albeit reluctantly, sets the black charred chunk of burned stick in my hand.

I write it as it appears in my brain:

Tilly + runs from bombs = the island
Tilly + faces bomb head-on = window home

Turning on my heels, I wait for a reaction—a round of applause, a series of gasps. What I get is shocked silence. But they're with me. And surely, they get it.

Just in case, I say, "What if…to get off the island, we have to somehow face what we were running from when we arrived?"

"Makes sense for Tilly, but what about your window?"

Jude breaks his silence to point out the flaw in my theory.

"Well... I don't know." I shake my head because I hadn't thought that far before I jumped up and started writing things in front of everyone. I lean against the wall and slide down it until I'm sitting, knees pulled into my chest, wracking my brain for answers, jotting down crazy equations in my head as Lewis drones on with speculations and lists.

Olive + runs from the Trio = arrival on the island
Olive + x = window home
$x = ?$

Tilly's equation was so clear.

Mine looks like a complete cluster of crap. Unsolvable.

But...

What if Tilly's equation wasn't so easy? I mean, I'm looking from the outside in. Of course, there's more to it. If we asked Tilly, she'd have a much different answer to "what were you running from," right?

And, if looking from the outside in, what would one see of me? My reasons for running?

The answer comes like a flash of lightning: *my name.*

Simple.

I'm so defined by that name.

And searching on the inside, that name has been the scale of which I've measured myself for so long.

So, was I running from myself?

Maybe.

If so, what about myself do I fear so much that I'd run from it?

I fear the unknown without a doubt. And I'd thought that by doing the bare minimum, by not fighting back, even as shitty as it was at school, at least, it wouldn't get worse. The Trio had become predictable in a way, and there was safety in that because it meant I wasn't bringing conflict onto myself.

Because I also fear conflict.

Instead of facing the Trio all these years, I'd run from them, hoping they'd go away or stop noticing me or move on without me. In doing that, I'd chosen avoidance over coping and confronting both the Trio and myself, my name.

But getting stuck here, thrown into everything, I'd had no choice but to confront my fears. The unknown? God, everything about this place, including its existence, is one big unknown.

And, Olive Maxi Gagmuehler? It's like I had to figure myself out to survive. Face bullies and friends and family and all the conflicts that came along with it. Realize my name is simply that—a name.

But all of that happened slowly over time. And the window appeared recently. I glance up at the wall, where I scribbled Tilly's equations. I think back the short distance to that day on the mountain. That seemingly defining moment when everything seemed lost and I blew everything I had into that damn horn.

I inhale a slow, heaping gasp and it's like I can finally breathe.

That hyperventilation that's always right on the surface clears, leaving nothing but a beautiful openness in a place previously in constant constriction.

With that act, stepping forward, blowing the King's horn, and taking charge, I'd faced all I'd run from head-on. Like Tilly and the bomb, but I'd been my own bomb.

x = confronting myself.

With a therapeutically deep breath, I stand and write:

Olive + running from confrontation = arrival on the island
Olive + confronting herself = window home

I explain my epiphany to the others and they accept it. They believe me, but it's also all we have to go on.

We spend hours in deep speculation and endless lists and equations until the wall is covered in math graffiti like a genius's—or madman's—chalkboard and all our hands are stained charcoal black.

Individually and together, we come up with an equation for each of us. They're full of question marks and speculation and missing components, but, more than anything, they're full of hope.

Chapter Thirty-Eight

Windows

On the way to the mountain, which is much closer from our new home, we decide not to divulge our findings to the Panthers. Not right away, anyway.

Shiloh waits outside for us when we reach the cave. She's sitting on a rock, riffling through the tangles in her long hair. When she sees us, she stands. "You came."

"We said we would," I say.

She nods, narrowing those deep green eyes of hers. "Follow me. Everyone's waiting inside."

"Everyone?" Will asks.

"Everyone."

Everyone.

Duke is still alive. My shoulders soften in relief, but at the same time, my stomach tightens with suspicion. God, this could be a trap. As much as I want to believe we've smoothed things over, I can't completely ignore the fact we were at war yesterday and for years before that.

"We'd prefer to meet out here. More neutral territory and

all."

Shiloh huffs but concedes. "I'll get the others." She disappears into the mouth of the cave.

No one says a word.

One by one, the other Panthers emerge. Tommy, shirtless as always, seems eager, but skeptical, and Henry, sling of knotted rags cradling his broken arm, flashes me a dimpled smile I can't help but return. Last is Noah who carefully carries Duke, still wrapped in the blanket, but conscious and so different from the Duke I've come to expect. He's boyish. Small. Frail. His eyes squint into slits at the burning sun, and Noah sets him just inside the entrance. Duke winces in pain, his head falling to one side. He's close enough so he can hear, but is out of the blinding sun. He keeps his eyes down.

Aside from Duke, we're in two lines staring across at one another. Two sides. Divided, yet connected by a common goal.

Bug grabs my hand.

Shiloh steps forward. "Truce?"

Will takes a step toward the Panthers' side but stops. Glancing over at me, he nods, then steps back in line.

This is my thing, isn't it? "Truce."

The Panthers then sit on the ground. We follow their lead.

Shiloh opens her mouth to speak.

"But first, there are just a couple things we" —I stare down the line— "need to know first," I say.

"Like?" Shiloh asks.

Lewis nudges me because he's dying to know about the bombs—how they made them, where they found the materials. But it isn't necessary. Not now. What's done is done and we need to keep things peaceful. But before he loses it and blurts the question out himself, I jump in.

"This war has gone on for years. We know why *we're* willing to come together now, but we…" I glance at my family. "We need to know why, after all of this time, are you?"

Shiloh takes a deep breath and glances down the line at the boys. "From the moment each of us arrived, Duke…" She stares back at the cave, at him, her eyes questioning. Duke keeps his head down. Is he even listening? "Well, he spoke about nothing but how horrible you all were. How Will was assembling an army who could strike at any moment. He told us his personal stories about Will and what a monster he was, how he'd stop at nothing to kill Duke and all of us on his side. When Olive injured Jack and he died, we were convinced."

Tommy looks away. I shrink under my skin.

"But we know it was an accident." Shiloh's eyes soften. "Just like we never meant to hurt Annabel. Yes, we caught her and held her as leverage. The plan was to lure Will in. Duke felt if we got rid of Will, the rest of you would join us. As you know, that didn't work out. Annabel escaped and fell trying to climb up the cliffs. We agreed to claim responsibility for it, to intimate you all." Shiloh wraps her hair into a knot on the back of her head and crosses her arms in front of her stomach.

"After that, Duke changed. I mean, he was intense before, but it got worse…" Again, she glances down the line and back at the cave opening and the lump that is Duke sitting under it. "Still, he was our leader and we're loyal. Always. We'd follow him to the end of the earth and back. Maybe we did." She seems to reflect on something then sniffs and straightens her shoulders. "But now… After everything… We just want to get home."

I look to my right. Jude and Lewis nod, Charlie raises his eyebrows. I then glance the other direction. Bug shrugs her shoulders. Will nods, his jaw tight, but not in anger. His expression is one of hope.

"We have some theories on how to do that," I say.

Lewis explains the "face what you ran from" theory and tells them of my shimmering window and how it appeared sometime after I blew the horn and brought us together. He's got their full attention, because they all entered the island under similar circumstances: on the run, evading various demons. When he's finished, Shiloh stands.

"You have to see this." She motions for us to follow her into the cave.

The others look to me and I nod.

Everyone follows Shiloh toward the cave entrance. When Noah makes to lift Duke back up, Will stops him, whispering something only they can hear. Noah nods and steps away. Will lifts Duke, cradling him against his chest.

My throat closes up with emotion as a wave of goose bumps covers my body.

Duke stares at Will like a helpless child, so trusting, so vulnerable. But it's still Duke. King of the island. The miscreant who almost killed us all. The war paint under his eyes is now smeared with sweat and dirt and ash and dripping dark red like someone cut a couple of slits under his eyes — less menacing, more wounded. Will and Duke enter last, just after me. Despite the fact that they're a ways behind me, I can hear Will whispering to Duke, his words nothing but hushed secrets.

Shiloh leads us to the communal area, where we stop, standing around the fire pit. We're still in groups, taking our respective sides, but the mood is less on guard and more like we share a purpose.

Not too far behind, Will enters the space, murmuring something to Duke right before he gently sets him on the floor near the fire. Duke seems to drift right to sleep.

Will catches my eyes as his overflows with emotion. It's glossy with tears, but none fall. Instead, a strength and conviction take over.

"Okay," Shiloh says. "This way."

Tommy, Noah, and Henry stay back with Duke as the rest of us continue behind Shiloh into one of the many tunnels. A couple hallways twist in other directions, but we head down one that ends in a small cove, and I realize this place is more extensive than I thought — like a prairie dog burrow, full of infinite passageways.

Shiloh shines her torch over the wall, spotlighting one area. There, as if carved into the rock by nature — but somehow intentional — are cave hangings; large straws of rock growing down from the ceiling and up from the stone floor. But the way it's grown is like art, sculptures. What I see, and what I suppose the other's see, is a group of people — kids, in my opinion — connected and standing in a circle. In the center of the circle is one thick cylinder coming down from the ceiling, split in two, so there's a hole in it like a window.

The image is so obvious, but also not, like finding shapes in clouds — from one angle, you're certain what you see, but then you shift and see something entirely different. Because when I tilt my head, the kids become trees in a forest. And when I turn the other direction, they are a pride of lions, sitting at attention. Another, candlesticks. The only constant is the window. It's like the island knows. Has it been giving us hints all this time?

"We have no idea what it is, but it almost seems carved, doesn't it?" She glances over her shoulder and we all nod. "Anyway, when you mentioned the window… Well, you see it, too, don't you?" Again, we all nod. "Either it's natural or there were others before us. Either way, it's something significant. We've always known that much." Shiloh turns back down the tunnel.

We meet up with the rest of the Panthers around the fire in the common area and sit as one group.

"Tomorrow night is the full moon," Shiloh says, stabbing a piece of coconut with a stick and putting it over the fire. It crackles and she passes it down, starting another. Eventually, we're all chewing on toasted coconut — all but Charlie. Jude pulls something from his pocket and hands it over.

"Where I'm from, the full moon is an omen, a sign of luck and great possibility. It can also bring the opposite, but…we won't focus on that." Shiloh snatches her coconut with her teeth and pulls her eyebrows together.

I think back to that full moon gazing down on me the

night I arrived. If asked back then, I'd have said without hesitation it was a bad omen. Now, I'm not so sure.

"Seems as good a time as any," I say. "What are you thinking?"

"Well, you said you figured out theories for each of you. We'll do the same, then try our best to make each happen. Then, tomorrow at dusk, we'll go to where each of our windows should be and—"

"See if they're open." I finish her sentence.

She nods.

I nod back. "Since we just visited our arrival locations, we're all familiar. How about you guys?"

Shiloh opens her mouth, but Tommy breaks in. "Duke never let us forget it." He glances down at their sleeping, fallen leader. "He told us to remember where we came from, but never to run from it. He believed we were so much better off here. I was starting to believe it until Jack…" Tommy's eyes dart to mine.

My heart breaks into a million pieces.

"Okay," Shiloh says, reeling the conversation back in. "We remember, but could definitely use a refresher."

"All right, well, how about we split up? You all pinpoint where you entered the island and we'll recheck our windows to see if any happened to open."

"Sounds good. We can come back together on the beach mid-point between our two camps around sunset and figure out what to do next."

Everyone nods in agreement.

Once finished with our snack, we leave. Will and I hold hands as we make our way through the tunnel, but I stop at the mouth of the cave, jerking him back.

"What's wrong?" he asks.

"I need to do something. I'll be quick."

"Okay," he says, cocking his head to the side, then softening his expression, nodding.

Walking through the cave by myself is creepy. It's dark

and cool and I can barely hear Shiloh and the boys talking, figuring out who needs to do what. I enter the common area and everyone stares at me. I take a deep breath.

"Tommy?"

He looks at me, swishing his long, sandy tangles to one side, raising his eyebrows.

"Yes?"

"Can I talk to you?"

He stands.

The others disappear down one of the tunnels—to gather their things, I assume. Duke lies still next to the fire. I swear I see his eyes open, but if they were, they're closed before I can be sure.

Walking toward me, Tommy is petite, all muscle and bones, his skin lightly tanned. He's actually quite striking, and I can tell he'll grow into a beautiful man one day.

He stops a foot away but won't look me in the eye.

"I just need to tell you… I'm so, so sorry about Jack. I never meant to… I didn't know…" Hot tears surface and fall like heavy raindrops. "I have a little brother, and if anything ever happened to him…" I sniff and let out a sob.

Tommy stares straight at me, the slightest glint of tears in his dark coffee eyes. "Hey, it was an accident. And we were being jerks. If you didn't fight back, who knows?" He sticks his hand out.

I shake it. It's small, but his grip is strong.

He tightens his fingers around mine, then pulls me in for a hug, planting a quick peck once on each side of my face.

The sudden action catches me off guard and leaves me speechless. The way Tommy stares at me, I can only imagine my expression.

"Thank you," I say, because I don't know what else to say.

He nods, laughing under his breath. "It's how we show forgiveness around here… Well, that and giving you the eyeballs from the sheep after we slaughter it." He shrugs and I'm not sure whether he's messing with me or not.

"I'm glad you chose the first."

He laughs—a normal boy laugh.

Once outside, we decide to split our own group up for another window check. We're questioning all our actions now. The smallest change could possibly be the key to someone's freedom.

After talking, it's agreed upon we'll pair up by location to save time.

Jude and Bug's entry windows are pretty close, but Lewis's is far-off and in the opposite direction of everyone, even the Panthers, who have already scattered.

"I'm fine. I'll go alone. I can find it," says Lewis. "Mental map." He taps the side of his head.

"You really shouldn't go alone, Lewis—" I start.

"I agree," Will cuts in. "We know you're capable of finding it, but still, you never know—"

"I'll go with him," Charlie blurts, stepping next to Lewis.

"No, Charlie. You go with Olive and Will. I'm fine." Lewis all but shoves Charlie at us.

"Wait. Great idea, buddy. No point in three of us going to the same spot." Will crosses his arms. Is this really a mini Lewis-Will pissing match? Now? I step back and take in the show. "Olive and I can find it no problem."

"But Charlie should be there, to try to go through himself," Lewis adds, a satisfied grin stretched across his face.

"True. How about you and Charlie meet us there right after you check yours?" Will says.

"It would be easier and faster if he went with you."

"We don't mind waiting on him."

Oh, good God. This is ridiculous. I step forward. "Charlie, what do you want to do?"

Charlie raises his eyebrows. "I can wait. I want to go with Lewis." With that, it's settled.

Lewis exhales through his nose and turns away. Charlie

follows. Lewis slows to let the kid catch up and nudges his shoulder. Charlie nudges back.

The rest of us set off down the mountain and into the woods, where Will and I go one way, Jude and Bug the other.

"Be careful. We'll see you back at the beach," I call to them as we split and just as Will clasps my hand in his.

"Thanks. You, too," Bug sing-songs and then spots our hands. Her eyes go wide. "Ooh…"

Jude laughs and scruffs her hair.

Heat rises up the back of my neck, itching at my ears as I watch them disappear around a corner.

Will and I continue on our path. After a few minutes and once we're out of earshot of the others, he pulls me in closer, wraps his hands around my waist, and does that thing where he's right there, a breath away from my lips. My stomach twirls, my heart raps against my chest, and my breathing hitches right against his mouth.

Pulling me even closer — I can feel the heat radiating off of his chest — Will closes his eye, leans in so our foreheads touch, and runs his nose up the length of mine. Then back down. A fraction of a second passes when we're suspended in time, just long enough to draw things out so my breath catches once more. Then he kisses me.

It's a kiss that says so much without words. It's a kiss of contradictions… Good-bye and hello. Please don't leave and I set you free. More and too much.

We share several more kisses as we walk in silence — until a question starts nagging at me. I go over it in my head a thousand times before daring to speak it out loud. I inhale then breathe the words out. "What happens if this works?"

Will turns his head. "What do you mean what happens? We go home. Finally."

"No, I mean… Will I see you again?"

He stops, takes my other hand in his, and pulls me closer. "Olive, I don't exist in your time." Will's sight falls to the forest floor. "I don't see how… If my door ever shows up and

I choose to go through it, we'll be living in different times. It wouldn't work. And what if we forget? What if all of this feels like a strange dream? Or we have no memories of it at all?"

"You've been thinking about this, too," I say.

"Of course I have. It's killing me."

We continue walking.

I stop, pulling him into me this time.

"Come with me. To my time. Through my window. You yourself said you have nothing to go home to. I don't have much, either, but what I do have is beautiful and I'll share it. With you. If you'll come."

Now he won't look at me. His jaw flexes back and forth. I close the gap between us and run my fingertips over his eye patch. "Please. Say you'll consider it."

Again, Will rests his forehead against mine. "I can't be a burden to anyone ever again. That's all I ever was. I won't be that person. Plus, I tried to go through and couldn't."

"You're not a burden. Never. I'm asking you. And, what if we're holding hands? Maybe I can…I don't know…pull you through with me."

He smiles and laughs through his nose. "You're amazing, Olive Gagmuehler." And there he goes again, saying my name like it's a pretty thing.

"Tell me you'll think about it." I run my hands along his back.

He sighs.

"Please?"

"I'll think about it." It isn't convincing, but I'll take it.

He kisses me and I might melt away. His lips are coconut mixed with mint. It's a great distraction on his part. Point, Will.

He pulls away, gazing down on me. "Let's check on this so-called window. Keep your fingers crossed it's still there."

Mesmerized by the glimmering heat waves, I run my hand across the top of the fuzzy rock.

It's still there.

But something's changed. Where before the window was a single pane, like a flat mirror, it's now doubled. Now twice the shimmers, twice the thickness. I have no doubt another window's appeared.

But will it let Will through? If not, is it possible to pull him through with me? Because maybe it's Charlie's. The kid's done so much these past few days. We decided his equation is about finding his voice, and boy, did he ever and in so many ways.

"Whoa," Will whispers behind me. "It's gotta be Charlie's."

"You think?"

"I know." He moves farther behind me, so he must be leaning against the boulder.

I look over my shoulder.

Will's watching me.

My cheeks catch fire. "What?" I ask, laughing in a nervous way.

"Has anyone ever told you you're beautiful?"

Now my entire face and neck are ablaze. I shrug because, how do I answer that question? *My mom has.* Um, no.

"Well, I mean it. You. Are. Beautiful."

Before I can react, he's right there, holding me, and we're dropping to the ground in front of the mossy boulder and kissing. There's skin and warmth and the cool ground beneath us, the trees above us. And it's just us. Alone. No one to interrupt or try to push us over a cliff or bomb us or spy on us.

Just us.

The forest.

The sun.

Nothing happens. But at the same time, everything does.

We lie, embraced, closer than I've ever been to anyone. Will brushes my ear with small kisses and I kiss his chin. His nose. His closed eyelid. Then his injured one, concealed by leather.

He stares at me.

I stare back.

Will goes to take his patch off.

I grab his hand.

He smiles in a sort of sad way and removes it.

The swirls are there, as they were so many days ago. Lovely. Honest.

A tear streams down his cheek from his good eye and he nudges his head into the crook of my neck. "Olive?"

"Yeah?"

"What if when I go back my eye heals?"

"Well, that would be great, right?"

"No." He pulls back and stares at me. "It wouldn't be. I deserved this wound. I deserve worse. But this…" He puts the patch back on. "Is my reminder of who I was and how I can't be that person again." Another tear falls. "What if I forget?"

"You won't forget." It seems silly, but at the same time, not.

"What if I do?" His eye searches mine for an answer. But I don't have one for him because we don't know. We could go back and never think of this island and the people on it again. Or we could remember every second of our time here.

I hug him, tangling my legs with his, getting as close as I can. "I guess we have to take that chance to get home."

He tightens his embrace.

We stay like that for a while. Breathing. Being. But the task at hand forces us into reality. We unwind from one another. I pick the leaves and sticks from my hair.

He stands and walks up to the window. Looking down at me, he winks, then turns and pushes his face through the waves. But his shoulders fall—in frustration or relief, I'm not sure—and he walks through it without consequence, just as he did earlier.

"Told you it was Charlie's." Will loops around back to where I sit. "Your turn."

"We know I can get through—"

"No. I mean… *Your turn*."

I shake my head, because is he serious? "I'm not ready."

His forehead crumples. "What if it disappears? You can't risk it."

I think on that. It would be awful. I take a deep breath. But it would be nothing compared to not knowing.

"I need to know you're all okay before I can leave."

He stares, then pulls me tightly into him.

"Come with me," I whisper in his ear.

Will shakes his head so his cheek grazes mine, the scruff grown more soft than prickly.

"At least try? See if it's possible?"

"Olive, nothing happens when I go through."

"But, maybe if I'm with you…" I'm grasping at straws.

As if to make his point, he stands, shoving his hand out at me. I stand up next to him and take it. "We'll just stick our heads in."

"Just our heads."

"On three… One, two, three."

I shove my head in, and I'm overtaken by the multi-layered sensations of the carnival: popcorn, noise, the sweet smell of corn, with the bitter aroma of dirt. I glance to the side. No Will. I thrust my body backward because I'm half afraid he's going to shove me through so I don't miss my chance.

I land at the base of the boulder next to him.

Will has a peaceful smile across his face. "That one's there for one person. I couldn't go back with you if I wanted."

And those last three words tear me apart because…

Had he wanted to?

Chapter Thirty-Nine

The sun sets at the horizon, the sky awash with pinks, purples, and blues. I'll miss this. The smell of ocean. The salty breeze off the water. This family of strangers who took me in with open arms.

Everyone's back now from checking their windows. When Lewis and Charlie met us at the boulder, the little sneak was so excited to see his window had materialized, he kept sticking his hands and feet into it, making them disappear. We had to stop him from chucking stones and leaves through the shimmers. And despite his anticipation about getting home, he insisted he'd wait until Bug's window showed up. We didn't dare argue.

The fire crackles as we sit in a large circle on the beach. Duke is even in attendance, leaning against a large rock. Noah and Henry helped him make the trek, but he actually seems… almost content. Less extreme. Less angry. More present.

Bug is in front of me and leans back, alerting she may not share in my assessment of Duke. The guy still has a menacing way about him that I'm not sure ever goes away. Bug's hair tickles my neck, and I wrap my arms around her shoulders.

I glance over at Will. He smiles at us, but there's sadness in his eyes.

Shiloh stands, stepping forward.

I give Bug a squeeze and follow suit, meeting Shiloh's dark gaze across the fire.

"So?" I ask. "How'd it go?"

"Tommy's window is open. That's it. No others, but we weren't surprised based on the equation we worked out for him. It's probably been open a couple of days. Since the bomb at the cave." My eyes flash to Tommy. He holds my stare for a minute then looks away. I'm dying to know the details of his equation but don't dare pry.

"That's great news," I say.

Shiloh gives as close to a smile as I've seen from her. "He'll leave tonight."

I nod, glancing around at all the faces surrounding me, and I can't help feel it's like they're waiting for me to say something, watching me.

"Should we talk about 'what-ifs'?" I ask the group.

"What-ifs?" Shiloh questions me.

"Yeah, you know, explore our options…the possibilities if we're successful or if we fail."

She nods, her eyes glazed over like she's got too many to sort through.

I scan the group. "Does anyone have any doubts? Concerns? Questions? I don't have the answers any more than you do, but if we talk about things, put everything out there, maybe it'll help." I shrug. "Whatever the outcome, I know we need to figure this out together." Duke nods like he agrees with me, and I feel small, still timid in his presence.

Henry clears his throat. "So, if we do what we need to do and mine and Noah's window shows up, do you think we'll go back to the same time like things have been frozen for us all these years?"

"Shit," Noah butts in. "No! We'll be running for our lives!"

"All of us were in bad situations, which is why we ended up here…I think." I look to Lewis, then Shiloh, but they don't give me any further guidance. Then I remember, "Oh. I could smell the carnival food. Hear the sounds. If time hadn't stood still, it would be long gone."

Shiloh sits up. "Yes, but that was your window. We don't know they'll all react the same way. We could go back to whatever the present time is and rapidly age. It might be we end up in the exact same place and time like nothing's changed. Or, we could die because maybe we aren't meant to go back at all. Maybe it's unnatural to go back and forth."

"Olive?" Charlie whines in panic.

Bug tucks into a ball like a baby hedgehog.

Will cringes.

Shiloh sure can drop a black cloud over a Kumbaya moment.

"Now wait," I say, shooting Shiloh a *shut it* look, motioning at the young ones. "True, we don't know exactly what's going to happen, but we got here in one piece. There's no reason to think it'll be any different going back. And, besides, we can't run forever, right?"

Shiloh steps farther into the circle. "Well, what do you know, we finally agree on something." I raise my eyebrows and Shiloh laughs. It's a pretty sound, like a tinkly wind-chime. "So," she continues, "what's our plan?"

"Well, it seems there are still a lot of unknowns. Whether this theory is correct or the fact mine and Tommy's windows opened is a total fluke is yet to be seen. All we can do is work toward facing our demons and hope for the best." It sounds like too little, too late, but I keep that part to myself. This has to work. "We keep trying, keep working together, and keep checking to see if new windows open up." I punctuate it with a long sigh because that's all I've got.

"And what if no new windows open?" Yeah, that.

"Then, at least, we tried. And we can live here in peace instead of war."

"We? You mean, some of us. Whoever's left." Shiloh glances left and right, avoiding my eyes because I've got a one-way ticket home.

"If no new doors open, I'm not going anywhere." The words leave my mouth before they register in my mind. My heart controlled that sentence.

Will stands. "No. I won't allow it, Olive. You can't waste this chance."

Won't allow it?

"I agree." Lewis stands, too.

The rest follow, leaving Shiloh and Duke sitting and staring at me. All of a sudden, I respect those two more than ever. This is my call, not a group decision.

"Look, I appreciate it." I stare at Will. "Truly, I do, but this is my choice. And, who knows? Hopefully, it won't be an issue. But I refuse to leave you all here." My voice hitches with emotion, but I hold firm, not taking my gaze from Will.

He breathes a deep sigh, nods, and sits.

Lewis glares at Will like he's an idiot to give in so easily.

"Me, too," Tommy speaks up, taking a step into the circle. "Either we all go, or no one goes." He nods at me like we just made a pact. Maybe we did because I nod back.

"I'm on board with that," Duke speaks up for the first time since the bomb. Everyone's eyes flick toward him but quickly resume their previously scheduled programming as to not gawk.

"Me, too," Shiloh adds.

"All or nothing?" Will asks.

I nod.

"Does everyone agree with that?"

"All or nothing," Jude calls out, his hand over his heart.

In response, there's a collective nod and a scattering of "yes's" and "uh-huh's."

It's a beautiful moment.

All or nothing.

A breeze blows off the water, showering us with sea spray and salt, pulling my eyes down the beach to a cluster of rocks where the waves whip up and splash.

I gasp and point. It's dark, but between the fire, the glow of the full moon, and the bazillion stars, I spot a pane of shimmering waves like a large group of dim fireflies. A few yards from the rocks and just before the beach turns to forest, is a window.

Jude follows my eyes and stands. Because it's his.

"Holy shit," he whispers.

Jude pulls his face out away from the heat waves. "Dry, thin air and pine. Definitely Colorado." He sticks his head back in, then out again, his eyes wide. "This is insane."

While the others keep Jude busy with questions, I notice Duke's sitting alone back at the fire.

I approach him with caution.

As I grow closer, he glances up at me, acknowledging my presence with something between a smile and a grimace. I sit on a rock a few feet away.

"How are you feeling?" I break the awkward silence by speaking my first post-war words to Duke.

"Better," he answers not so much as glancing my way. Eyes glazed over, he stares into the fire.

"That's good." This might be the extent of our conversation because I'm at a total loss for words. I toss a couple of sticks into the flames and dig my toes into the sand, then glance over my shoulder at the rest of our group who are studying the window. Just as I stand and join them, Duke turns his head toward me.

"Why didn't you leave?"

"What's that?" I hear him, but his question catches me off guard. I reclaim my seat.

"When you found the window, why didn't you go back home? You have no idea how long you'll have the chance. Risky move." He shakes his head like he's disappointed in my choice.

"Well, I guess the benefits of staying outweighed the risk of not getting to go home. I couldn't leave without knowing everyone else has the same chance."

"Huh." He shrugs like he's not sure what to think of that.

"Plus, it's easier here, in a way. Sounds weird, but I don't have to work as hard to keep afloat." I gaze toward the ocean. "I can just be," I whisper to the dark waves.

Duke nods, breathing in through his nose. "I get that." I suppose he would. "But… I've found sometimes it's best to embrace your demons instead of battling them."

I give him a look of confusion.

"This scar on my chest? The P…" He points to the raised, discolored skin. I cringe. "This damn letter tortured me for the better part of my life. At some point after arriving here, I took charge. I used to be ashamed of this scar, but now I'm p-p…proud of it." He stammers but catches himself, taking little effort to lure it back. "I own it." He breathes in, raising his eyebrows and glancing back toward the fire. "When you accept what frightens you most, more times than not, you'll discover it was nothing but inventions of your own making, anyway. Silly doubts blown out of…proportion. And no one controls that but you. We're our own worst demons, Olive."

It sounds a lot like a riddle with strands of golden truth woven in.

"I'm sorry about your friend," he whispers, his voice raspy with emotion. "I never meant to—"

"I know." Despite the knot in my throat for Tilly, I do know. Because I'm plucking the golden threads from Duke's words. What if we're also products of ourselves? What happens when we don't own our demons? We don't keep our insecurities and doubts at ground level?

I can't help but stare at Duke from the corner of my eye because I'm pretty sure he's the result of just that.

"I'm glad you ended up here," Duke says, turning his head my way and almost, barely smiling. I know that smile.

I've plastered it on my face a thousand times. The emotion behind it is 100 percent sincere, but something deep inside stops it from shining through to the surface.

"I'm glad, too." I reciprocate the almost smile.

"Everything all right?" Will says from behind me, appearing like a ghost as if from nowhere.

"Yeah, just keeping warm." I raise my hands to the fire, rubbing them together, despite the warm night. "And talking."

"I was telling her about this P." Duke points to his chest, pronouncing "P" without an ounce of hesitation.

Will glances down at the scar. "One of the darkest days of my life, and I've had a lot, so I can only imagine—"

"I used to feel that way, but not anymore. I'm sort of thankful for it. Strange, I know."

Will leans in closer to Duke. "I'd told the others it was too much, man. Too cruel and too…well…too many other things that weren't right."

"I know. I remember the look in your eyes. It was the first time I saw you show fear. And then you stopped it, pulled the hot iron out of Johnston's hand."

Will nods. "But I should have done more… And, despite that I knew it was wrong, I kept at it." Will sets his eye on Duke.

I stand and slowly walk away, sensing this should be a private conversation.

"Yeah, well, we should all do more…" Is the last I hear before I'm out of ear shot.

On our hike back to the cave-tree, Will leads the way and Jude lags behind the group with me. He's quiet, but the harshness in his jaw, how he keeps peeking over at me, tells me he wants to talk. Naturally, since it's Jude, I initiate.

"How are you feeling about going home?" I ask.

He keeps his eyes ahead as he answers. "I'm all right. Half excited, half scared-shitless. I'm cooking up a sort of loose plan for my life, though." He sighs, slowing his pace. "I don't

think we can trust the windows will stay open indefinitely."
He glances ahead, then back at me. "I know you don't agree,
but we may need to seize the opportunity and go as soon as
possible. Just in case."

I shake my head. "I meant what I said. All or nothing."

"Damn it, Olive. Now's not the time to be stubborn. Three
windows have opened in the past forty-eight hours. Four,
including..." Jude trails off with a sigh. "It's only a matter
of time before the rest open as the others do whatever it is
the island feels they should." Did he just say the island *feels*?
Guess I'm not the only one who thinks there's more to this
place than rocks, trees, and sand. I can't decide if it's more
settling or unsettling.

Jude's words hang between us as we walk along, the
others chatting and laughing about who knows what several
steps ahead.

"You know... You changed us," Jude says, eyes ahead.

"How so?" I'm not sure I want to know.

"Well, despite everything that's wrong with this place, the
air is lighter since you got here. Before, sure, we had good times,
but they were few and far between the misery. And, I'll admit,
I didn't want you here at first—I *really* didn't want you here—
but you sparked something when you arrived." If it wasn't for
the half smile gracing his face, I'd be unsure whether it was a
compliment or an insult. "You brought us hope." He snorts
under his breath. "God, that sounds cheesy, but it's true."

I laugh because, coming from Jude, the sentiment is as
good as him admitting he cares for me.

I muse over me, Olive Maxi Gagmuehler, being a bearer
of hope, when Bug makes a loud, off-the-wall comment about
how she might have one of the asshole sheep chase her out of
the forest to mimic how she was chased the day she arrived
here, and I almost choke on my tongue at the swear word
leaving her small mouth.

Jude slaps his knee, accompanied by a "Ha!" because I'm
pretty sure he taught her the term.

"Do you think it'll work, Olive?" Bug calls back to me.

"You can certainly give it a try, but it's not what we worked out for you, remember?"

She breathes in a heaping sigh even I can hear from feet behind her. "Yeah, I re-mem-ber." And I can just imagine the exaggerated eye roll she's giving me.

Bug's equation had stumped us the most. And God only knows if it's correct. She'd lived in the orphan home since birth—at least, it's all she'd ever known. When she and another girl finally worked up the nerve to run, Bug ended up here. The other girl wasn't so fortunate.

It's no secret Bug's greatest fear is solitude, a favorite punishment of those in charge at the home. It's why more nights than not I wake up with the tiny beetle by my side. I don't blame the kid. Being all alone is scary without the trauma she's developed around it. But we believe, for her, it's the answer. Though, with no family, nothing but hell to go back to, this hell might be preferable.

That's when it hits me. Am I naïve to assume everyone wants to go back?

Bug slows down until we catch up, wrapping me into a tight bear-cub hug, and then climbing up Jude and onto his shoulders like the squirrel she is. The act doesn't slow Jude's pace a bit.

I smile and Jude glances down at me.

"Just think about it?" he asks, referring back to our conversation.

I nod.

I can tell Bug wants to pry, but she bites her lip instead.

"Bat guano. Can you believe it?" Lewis shakes his head. "Why didn't I think of that? The girl's an evil genius." He's recounting how Shiloh keeps teasing him, dropping small hints into how she made the bombs. I'm sensing an increased level of respect and perhaps a new crush on Lewis's horizon.

"It's unreal," Will replies, not glancing away from the marked-up wall and all our equations. "I have to admit, though, I am glad you weren't the one developing explosives. Imagine the carnage." Will winks at me.

Lewis shoots him a, *hey!* look.

Will shoves him in the shoulder.

I glance across the room. Jude works to tame Bug's hair as Charlie lights the end of a stick, blows it out, then draws on the wall. We get on all right here; change the setting and we could be a family at home in the living room on a cold winter evening.

"Does everyone *want* to go home?" I blurt out.

They all glance up at me.

"What do you mean?" Will asks.

"Well, getting home was always the goal, but, considering some of our circumstances, it's occurred to me, it may not be right for everyone."

Bug stands. "I don't want to go back. I love it here. I love all of you. It would hurt worse to go home than to stay because this is my home now." Tears pool in her eyes, her nose and chin turning dark pink.

"I'm going back," Jude states, his voice strong as he eyes Lewis.

"Me, too," says Lewis, meeting Jude's stare.

Will takes a deep breath. "I'm undecided."

I'd known it, though it hadn't felt true until this moment. My throat closes up, but I hold back the tears.

"Home. I want home," Charlie adds.

"What about you?" Will asks me with too much hope lacing his words.

I lose the battle with the spikes in my throat. Tears burn my eyes, but I manage to choke, "I have to go home."

Will nods, his jaw flexing tightly, eye set on me and only me.

Lewis stands, then grabs a piece of charcoal. He walks to the wall and places check marks by mine, Charlie's, and Jude's names. Our windows are open. He marks question marks next to Bug's and Will's equations, then leaves his own blank. They'll get checks once their windows open.

"It's coming together," Lewis says, brushing off his hands and sitting again, satisfied grin stretched across his face. Despite the fact that he still hasn't quite pieced his own equation together, he's positive his has something to do with helping everyone else figure out theirs. On both sides.

Lewis's dad was an accomplished scientist and inventor back in his time and, according to Lewis, they didn't see eye to eye. His father was tough on him, pushing him too hard to be perfect at everything. And, as those things go, Lewis started rebelling. The day he showed up on the island, he'd rigged his entire science class's chemistry experiments to go wrong. And boy, did it go wrong. In his haste, he'd been overzealous with the activator and a few kids had gotten burned from the explosions. When his father was called to pick him up, Lewis ran. And, well, one minute he was jumping over a chain-linked fence, the next he was tumbling over several mossy rocks. His ticket home is getting the rest of us home.

When I wake up the next morning, I'm cold. Bug usually sleeps next to mc and the tiny thing is like a generator. More times than not, I awaken to a fresh, sticky sheen of sweat covering my skin. But not today. I'm alone. And it scares the crap out of me because it's not right. Bug is always curled up next to me, especially since…Tilly.

I sit up straight and bolt out of the cave-tree. "Bug?" I call, turning in a circle. "Bug!"

"What's wrong?" Will shoots out of the cave after me.

"Bug's not here." The fear in my voice throws me into a steeper panic.

"Bug!" Will shouts.

"What's all the shouting for?" a small voice whines. The voice is attached to a head of bigger than life hair peeking around at us from the backside of the cave-tree.

I run around the tree and clutch her shoulders, resisting the urge to shake her. "Where the hell were you all night?!"

"There." She points to a large, flat boulder, where her mat is spread out, rag doll flopped right on top like a tattered, patchwork cherry.

"All night?"

"Yeah, I slept there. By myself." A huge grin is stretched across her face.

"Nice work, Lightning Bug!" Will says, stepping forward and giving her a fist-bump.

"Wow." I pull her in for a hug. "That's amazing. I'm so proud of you." And I am.

Once we go in, Bug tells the story of how she couldn't fall asleep and could only think about lying outside under the stars like she used to back home. So she decided to do it. Bug explained that she knew if she didn't do it right then—strike out on her own, alone—she never would and she didn't want to miss the chance. Maybe she didn't want to go home, not yet anyway, but she still wanted the option. So she chose seclusion. An entire night's worth. And, according to her, it was scary. She feared so many things, including the asshole sheep, and ghosts, and grotesque forest zombies like her and Charlie make up stories about, but once she got past all of that, she was all right.

The kid won't be sleeping on the boulder every night—on account of brain-eating forest zombies, among other things—but it's huge progress.

We eat on the run to check if Bug's window has opened. None of us expected her to complete her equation so soon and without a fight. The excitement's palpable.

When we arrive under the cove of trees in the forest where she first stepped foot on the island, Bug walks directly toward the place she knows as her entry point: a space between two thin, papery tree trunks. We follow.

"Whoa…" Bug whispers. Her iridescent, flowy window is waiting for her like an offering for her sacrifice. For getting through a night on her own, embracing her demons, the island has rewarded her with a doorway home.

Lewis, Will, Jude, and I stand behind her in a protective arc as Bug moves closer to the waves. Like she's testing the temperature in a pool, she sticks her toes in first. Then her foot. Her leg. She takes a deep breath and jumps back, away from the window.

"Whoa," she whispers again. "It's hot and smells like home. Like burned mud and aloe plants. She leans in toward the window again.

"You don't have to—" Will starts.

"I know," Bug answers, her tone dripping of confidence, her sights set on the window and whatever she might see on the other side.

Gripping an ashen tree trunk in each hand for balance, Bug sticks her head right through the heat waves. She stays in that position, head distorted by iridescence and shimmers, for several minutes until she finally pulls herself back. Although completely out of the window, she continues staring into the heat waves.

"So?" Jude breaks the silence.

Bug's lip quivers but those June bug eyes are hard. "I've gotta go back. Soon."

Jude nods. We all do. Something about the strength of her words, while few in number, says so much.

"You're sure?" Will asks.

Bug nods. "All of the kids are trying to break free. It's like I started something by running." She sticks her face back in, then out again. "It's the same picture, over and over. The day I left. Each time I look nothing changes. Like I'm being given a chance to go back and do different." She stares at us, eyes wide. "I've gotta fight with them. For them."

We have no idea how or why or when, but none of us argue. How can we?

Bug goes on without prompting. "Something's gotta change."

God, I'm both terrified and exhilarated for her. Because, despite knowing the deeper details, she's got an uphill battle before her. It could turn out positive or tragic. And like that, things are thrust into perspective for me. We all have our demons, we're all traumatized, but I'm going back to Disneyland compared to what Bug's up against. What Tilly would have returned home to.

Bug leads the way back to the cave-tree. She walks taller, growing from child to young lady overnight on a boulder under the stars.

It's the middle of the night and I lie awake. Charlie is curled up in the corner, breathing the soft rhythms of sleep.

Bug tosses and turns.

There are two spaces in this tree and we're split into me, Bug, and Charlie in one; Will, Lewis, and Jude in the other, which doubles as the common room and kitchen.

"Olive?" Bug says. "You awake?"

"I am."

"Are you afraid of going home?"

"Yes." The truth of the word floats up toward the ceiling and into the tree like a dark cloud hanging over me.

"Me, too. I want to stay here so bad" — Bug leans up on her elbows — "but I can't. Not after what I saw today. I kind of think I've always known I'd need to go back," she confesses.

"I understand. But I've been thinking. What if we aren't meant to be here? I mean, we all kind of stumbled into this world. What if, like Shiloh said, it's unnatural for us to stay after we've done what we needed to get home?"

"Maybe." She turns over onto her back. "Olive?"

"Hmm?"

"What if the island's in charge of all of this? What if it can suck us back in any time? What if we aren't supposed to leave and it sends flesh-eating monsters after us?"

I laugh. "You've been spending too much time with Charlie."

She giggles, but I swear, even her laugh is more grown-up.

"Olive?" Bug asks again and I fear we'll never sleep. "You

love Will, don't you?"

"I do. I love all of you."

"Yeah, but him the best. Like, you looove him."

"What's your question, Bed Bug?"

"Well, will you ever see him again once you go home?"

I sigh. Because that's the bonus question no one can answer. "I have no idea."

"Sorry," she whispers.

"Me, too."

There's a shifting across the room. "I-AM-TRY-ING-TO-SLEEP-HERE!" Charlie states so loudly I jump. Bug gasps, and we all laugh, giggling in rounds into our cave-tree.

I stop to take in the moment: the warmth we've created, dying-down giggles, deep sighs, how the inside of the tree absorbs the sounds. And I realize we'll all be okay. Whether we decide to stay or go, whether our windows open or close back up. It's going to be all right. We'll find our way. I mean, isn't that what we've done so far? Sure, it's been hard, and horrible, and painful, but all of that was spaced between moments of love and light and peace.

I stare up at the ceiling. Bug and Charlie having quieted, their breathing evening into soft, lulling rhythms, either sleeping or in those far-off thoughts right before sleep takes you. I imagine the pre-island me. The Olive of several weeks ago. Such a short time for so much to happen and change. I imagine that Olive with a genuine smile across her face. She's so full of light and hope. So different than before. I work to blend her into the person I am now and wonder if it's possible. Will I be able to meld that Olive with the one who's seen and done so much? The warmth of that possibility fills my chest. It's a lot like the contentedness and safety of home, and I long to return more than ever.

That's when I know.

I need to go back.

Soon.

Chapter Forty

Mementos

Jude was right, now isn't the time to be stubborn or play the martyr. I should lead by example, take control of my fate and do what I feel is right.

Sometime between waking up and eating breakfast, Jude, Bug, and I realize we're all having the same thoughts and collectively decide we ought to get home sooner rather than later because what if there is a limit on the time the windows are open?

Not surprising, our decision is accepted without question and met with support and agreement. They'd do the same, they assure us.

The day flies by too quickly. The more I try to grasp every moment, every scent, every word, the faster time passes.

We've spent the majority of the day together. Going through belongings, divvying out mementos, assuming if we brought things in, we'll be able to do the same on the way out. And hopeful everyone will get the chance to go home, should they choose.

There are three piles: trash, valuables, and randoms. We sit in a circle outside the tree and take turns separating our things. We take what we want that is ours and put the rest in the piles. The trash pile is the smallest because out here, most everything is of use.

I keep the slingshot Jude carved for me, the bag Tilly made from my jacket, and my emerald green Lewis worry stone, then pass out the rest of my chewing gum to several sour faces who couldn't believe I'd been holding out on them. I blame Will for that one. He tries to play innocent but winks and smiles at me. The rest of the items—my gourd water bottle, Lewis's maps, my empty purse, and the small spear—I leave in the valuables pile.

"If anyone stays or anyone new comes along, these will be useful," I say, setting them on the ground with care, but I hesitate. I bend back down and pick up one of Lewis's maps, the one he drew pictures of landmarks on that were specific for Charlie's and my journey. I fold it and put it in my back pocket. Lewis watches me, a small smile spreading across his face.

Late afternoon, we return what's staying to the cave-tree and Jude, Bug, and I pack up what little we're bringing home.

It all feels too final to be real.

At dusk, we share an early dinner of fish, roots, and fruit. There's a sadness, a gratitude, and an anticipation as thick as fog hanging over us. We go around and tell stories of our favorite moments. Mine is, by far, when Charlie started talking.

After I recount it, I realize I've been holding the doubloon bracelet Will made for Charlie in my pocket since he got sick. I pull it out, walk to Charlie, and hand it over. He smiles, probably thinking he'd lost it.

"You keep this close and always remember how strong you are… And to never EVER eat coconut again." Everyone laughs under their breaths.

He jumps at me armed with a tight hug.

"Thanks," he says, sliding the bracelet onto his wrist, staring at it lovingly.

"I'm going to find you back home because you and Lucky will be great friends."

Charlie smiles, his blue eyes lighting up.

The stories continue.

Will tells of the day he found Bug and how his life changed with that smile of hers.

Lewis tells about the day he and Jude went to check the pig trap and found me passed out on the ground—how they argued about whether to leave me the whole way back as they carried me. Charlie and Bug giggle, and Jude smacks Lewis on the back of his head.

Charlie shares about playing with Bug and how she's been his best friend here. They hug the longest, sweetest hug ever.

Bug is stoic but teary-eyed as she approaches each of us, holds our hands, and looks in our eyes, speaking her feelings aloud.

"Lewis, the day I taught you how to fish. I never thought you'd do it, but you did. You caught a fish the size of a beetle. Thank you for being a part of my family." She kisses his cheek and moves on. "Jude, you're my big brother. Thank you for keeping me safe. I love you." Tears stream down her cheeks. Jude kneels down to her level and they hug. He kisses her on the top of the head. "Will. You gave me my name and taught me how to speak your language. I love you." She kisses Will on the cheek. He picks her up in a bear hug. "Charlie, you're my best friend. I'll never forget you." She starts to cry harder. I cry. We're all crying at this point. "Olive. You joined our family late, but you are my sister. Thank you for loving me." She touches the side of my head where my hair was shaved and smiles, all teeth. "I'll never forget your fancy turquoise underwear!" She snickers, raising her shoulders to her ears. I kiss her on the forehead and squeeze her into a hug, scuffing her coconutty hair, trying to memorize the scent.

With sniffles as background music, it's Jude's turn. Starting then stopping several times, he peers off toward the trees and tells of a memory involving Tilly—how whenever she was up in the middle of the night with Charlie and his nightmares, Jude would come out to tend the fire, only to find her alone, mending something before the flames. He'd sit down next to her and they would talk late into the night, then he'd play with her hair until she fell asleep. He reminds us of how lovely and special Tilly was. How she took care of all of us, cared for each one of us the way we needed. Jude doesn't cry, but breathes in, nodding at the forest like he's been holding the words in for years.

Things are quiet then.

It's a beautiful silence blaring with hope and memories and a love so full I fear I'll never know it again.

We had agreed to leave once the moon was up. And, I swear, that damn moon moves quicker than it ever has, like it mocks me with its new stealthy ways.

Before I've had a chance to breathe, my time here is over—assuming things go well tonight.

No more tears to shed, all words spoken, embraces given, Bug, Jude, and I say our good-byes and good lucks, each of us with cautious optimism and a bit of fear as we head into the unknown.

It was decided that the others will try their doors, as well. That way, we're all going our separate ways, even if some eventually return to the cave-tree.

Will, Charlie, and I watch as Lewis, Bug, and Jude walk away together holding hands. Lewis and Jude will see Bug off then go to their own entry points.

"Let's go," says Will, his voice hoarse. He clears his throat and takes my hand. I take Charlie's hand and we head for the boulder.

I glance over my shoulder, enjoying one last look at the

cave-tree, remembering our original home and how grand it was considering the circumstances.

Charlie picks mint leaves, passes them around for us to chew on, and babbles here and there along the way, but Will doesn't utter more than the occasional "uh-huh" and "sure, buddy." What I wouldn't do to know what he's thinking. My own thoughts, along with so many questions, turnover and spin like a Ferris wheel on hyper-drive. Is this it? Is this the last time I'll see him? My stomach clenches and I don't realize I'm squeezing his hand until he looks over at me, that place between his eyebrows pulled together with worry.

"Sorry," I mumble, loosening my grip.

"You all right?" he asks.

No. I am not all right.

But I nod. Because what am I going to say? Short of me staying behind, there's no way to make this work. For a minute, I consider staying... Will and I living off the island. Forever sixteen. Forever in love.

But would that be the reality or am I creating a fairytale because the last thing I want to do is leave him?

I turn to Will and open my mouth when my eye catches Charlie. He gives an impish, closed grin that mimics Lucky's same smile like nothing else.

As much as the fantasy taunts me, I can't stay here. I close my mouth. There is nothing left to say. Nothing but good-bye, because I know Will's not going anywhere. Not even if his window opens up. He's too loyal, too devoted and protective of this island he believes saved him. I can't argue with that.

My shoulders tense and my eyes harden. I grasp at a deep place of strength in my gut. It's new, that place. I'll take it back with me. Keep it safe and use it often.

Once we reach the boulder, the sun is set and the full moon is visible, shining rays down on us and coating the forest in blue and silver shadows.

The heat waves are still there, bright and shimmery as ever.

We stand in a row across from the window, Charlie between us. Will reaches behind Charlie's back and slides his fingers down my arm to my hand.

I lace my fingers between his, memorizing the warmth of his skin—how it's soft in some places, reminding me of his kind heart and honest soul, and rough in others, hardened from a tough upbringing and years of living off an island.

He gazes down at our hands then up at me, his eye glistening with tears, smiling in that sad way I've come to know so well. In a way that tells me this is it. No amount of begging or pleading, crying and bargaining will change what is out of our hands.

I give him my own version of the sad smile, desperate to keep a tight grip on that strong place in my gut. But my throat tightens and my fingers slip a little. Some things are still stronger than I am.

My nose pinches and my eyes water over.

Will's eyebrows draw together and I catch a glistening down his cheek. He parts his lips to speak.

"Wow!" Charlie shouts. "Super sparkly!" His arm has disappeared behind the double window. The shimmers are extra bright at night. Like a hundred layers of bubbles smashed together and catching the moonlight just right.

I wish I could share in Charlie's excitement, his carefree joy. But I can't.

This is going to hurt a thousand times worse than being held down and having my head shaved.

Pain.

True pain.

The kind that doesn't leave visible scars, just an empty pit in your soul.

"Well, go on, buddy," Will urges Charlie to walk through the misty window.

Charlie looks at me.

"I'll be right behind you and I'll find you. I promise."

Charlie turns around and tackles Will in a hug. Will gives

him a brotherly back pat. "I love you, big guy," he says.

"I love you, too." Charlie's wearing that same over-worn Castaway Carnival shirt, the green parrot now just a shadow, the red lettering faint whispers of what was. I get one last look at the doubloon around his wrist before Charlie hesitates then launches himself in an extra fast leap through the window. It's what Lucky would do—the faster the better.

He disappears before our eyes.

Will sighs as if relieved the kid didn't bound back at us or, worse, break into a million pieces.

"You're next, Olive Gagmuehler."

And there it is. My name. No one will ever say it like he does. Gentle. Confident. Like it's a beautiful thing and not a stinky food plus gag.

He stares at me, waiting, anxiety in his expression because I'm not moving.

My body won't budge. My hand won't let go of his.

He nods like, *Go on, it's all right.*

I glance to the window, then back at him.

"What if we stay here? Together. Just a few more days," I spit the words out before they register in my brain and I can't believe what I'm saying. But I can. That strength in my gut is dwindling, my heart, silly thing, taking over.

Will is already shaking his head before he speaks. "Olive… It'll only make things harder. How many days will pass before we realize we have no choice or the window closes? Then what?"

"Then… Then…" Crap, I don't know what.

"You have to go back." And there's something in his words. His tone. His urgency. And I have no doubt.

"You aren't leaving, are you?"

He glances away, biting his lip, clenching his jaw, then turns back toward me. "I made a promise to Duke that day I carried him back into the cave. I swore I wouldn't leave him behind alone."

I nod my head because I'm not shocked, though, having it

confirmed makes my leaving that much harder. He'll be here and I'll be there and I'll always wonder if I made the right choice.

"Please. Listen," Will says, placing his hands on the sides of my face, resting his forehead against mine. "I owe this island. And this way, Duke and I can do something good. Together. We'll be here waiting in case others come. We can help them get home. Avoid future wars. Accidents. Pain."

With the word *pain*, I'm reminded of my own and how it's boiling up from my stomach and into my throat. My heart speaks before my brain can catch it.

"I'm staying."

"You can't."

I let go of his hand and cross my arms because that's where I'm at.

"I'm not leaving you here."

"Damn it, Olive. If I have to pick you up and toss you through that window, I will."

I narrow my eyes at him.

Tears, real tears, not just flashes of a tear or glimpses of moisture, stream down from the corners of his eye.

I drop my arms to my sides.

Seeing the pain within him finally surface only pulls it further from me. My chest closes and my throat tightens, but not in the hyperventilation way, in the I-am-breaking-way. Tears flow like rivers from my eyes, streaming down my cheeks, underneath my chin, down my neck.

I know I can't stay. And he knows I know I can't stay.

"What will you do here once it's only you and Duke all alone?" I manage, followed by a small sob.

He sniffs, wiping his face and all signs of sorrow. I don't know how he does it. "Don't you worry about me. I'm more at home here than I've ever been anywhere else. I'm pretty sure Duke feels the same way. We belong here, but you—"

"I don't."

He nods, taking my hands in his.

I look down and shut my eyes. They burn behind my eyelids and overflow before I even open them again. When I do, water spills over like fountains, making the rivers from before seem like small creeks.

Will pulls me in, wrapping his arms around me. My face in his neck all salty and wet, I set everything I can about him and this moment to memory. His skin smells of the forest, a mixture of sweet flowers and rusty earth. His hair is overgrown since Tilly's last haircut attempt and curls delicately along the tops of his ears. I pull back and look at his face. There's dark sporadic scruff along his jawline and chin, over his top lip. The once black eye patch has faded to a crackled gray. I touch the edges of his cheekbones, his nose, memorize the curves and angles. I do the same to his lips. He closes his eye, brow pointed downward.

He feels the pain, too.

Will's arms tighten around me, pull me in. The warmth from his chest radiates into me like his heart wants to memorize me, as well.

"I'll be here. At this exact spot"—he glances to the sky—"every island full moon. If you ever need to…" He swipes another tear from his eye. "That weird, amazing window between your world and this island?" Will nudges his head toward the heat waves. "We don't completely understand it, but it's linked. And, sure, we may not be in the same physical place and time, but we're still connected, you and I. Always."

It's the saddest, most beautiful thing I've ever heard. A small sob escapes me as I nod.

Then Will moves closer and we kiss. It's mixed with both our tears, the ocean air, the silvery moonlight, pain, hope, and a hint of mint.

It's over too soon as we mutually pull away.

I memorize the perfect sage color of his eye. "I love you," I whisper before my voice hitches.

Will squeezes my shoulders. He glances away and wipes more tears from his eyes. His jaw tightens and he looks back at me. "Go." He motions toward the heat waves. It's still shimmering but is less visible through the tears flooding my eyes.

"Go," he says again with increased urgency, taking my hand and nudging me forward like if he doesn't push me away, he'll change his mind.

I breathe in, then out, and step toward the window.

I turn away, feel a final squeeze of my fingers, and let go.

But I stop and glance back.

Will smiles and nods, but there are tears again. He rakes his fingers through his hair then puts one hand up in a motionless wave good-bye.

I don't dare look back again.

The buttery, salty scent of popcorn overwhelms me.

Chapter Forty-One

LATTES AND LIFE

I'm in the corn maze tunnel on hands and knees. I allow myself one look back.

The window is gone. Vanished. As if it never was.

Tears plop down onto the dirt and leaves as I crawl.

I pull out my phone. Despite the fact that it's worn to the bone, it works as if it hasn't been exposed to saltwater air for a month. The words HILLINGS, TEXAS plus an image of a partly cloudy sky and the temperature, seventy-six degrees, shines brightly on the screen.

When I reach the end of the tunnel, I stand. The end of the maze is in sight.

I turn in a circle, dazed.

It's like time stood still.

But it didn't.

The bag Tilly made from my jacket is slung over my shoulder, and my mouth still tastes of mint and coconut. A tingling lingers at my lips from Will's kiss. And if I try hard enough, I can smell the forest still clinging to my shirt.

But nothing will ever be the same again. I'm hit by an all-consuming anxiety to get back to the island, like I forgot something important there.

Despite my earlier declaration of "only one look back," I stop, drop to the ground, and peer into the tunnel. Nothing but bent corn stalks. No heat waves. My mouth runs dry, and my breath quickens. What have I done? It's gone. He's gone. Just like that.

I left too soon. It all happened too soon.

In an instant and with one decision, I've lost so much.

I take it back.

I beat the ground with my fist. "I take it back." Tears squeeze from my eyes, fleeing more violently now that it's done. Over.

But, as if he's sending a message over time and space, Will's parting words fill my head, *"We're connected, you and I. Always."*

I rub my thumb over my necklace, checking for the crude etching, proof it wasn't all a dream.

Just Be. The indented words scratch my thumb.

Inhaling a shaky breath, I scrub the saltwater away from my face with the back of my hand.

"You can do this. You can do this," I chant, then stand up. Straighter. Taller.

I stride through what little is left of the maze and out the exit.

I'm completely unprepared for the scene I encounter.

Tawny holds Lesley in a headlock, scattered, spilled lattes, and the hair clippers littering the ground around them.

Hannah and Dillon are nothing but silhouettes, running toward the parking lot.

"Let me go, you hippo!" Lesley screams at Tawny.

I walk closer, and when they see me, they both freeze.

"Olive! Are you all right?" Tawny asks, practically dropping Lesley to the ground.

I nod, taking in the carnage.

They stare, jaws lax, wide-eyed. I can't imagine how I must look.

Seizing the momentary pause, Lesley untangles herself from Tawny's arms and bolts.

When Tawny realizes her arms are empty, she shouts after Lesley's sprinting form, "That's right, you better run!"

Tawny's eyes flash to mine and she bounds into me, wrapping me up in a glorious, Tawny hug.

She takes a deep breath in. "What the hell happened in there?" she asks, glancing back toward the maze.

"I..." I shake my head because, really, where do I even begin?

Rubbing my back, she wraps her arm around my shoulders and urges me forward. "We'll chat it out tomorrow, babe. Let's get you home." She breathes in. "You smell like shit!"

We both laugh.

The scent of my mother's vanilla candles never smelled better.

Home.

I go to my room. Flop onto my bed. Hug warm, fluffy Hazel.

My mother will never believe the state of my clothes and my boots so I decide to tuck them away along with my Tilly bag in a box at the back of my closet, hoping the island stays on them as long as possible.

Reveling in the longest shower in the history of showers, once the hot water runs cold, I reluctantly get out and dry off, then kiss my flannel pajama pants and clean T-shirt before putting them on. The fresh material feels like heaven against my clean skin.

I then pad down the hall and climb right next to Lucky in his bed, curling under the printed spy-gadget quilt. Parrot tucked under his arm, his hair still smells of popcorn and there's dried cotton candy caking his mouth.

I wrap my arms around Lucky's small body and breathe

him in until I drift off.

Monday morning I have a new haircut, a new perspective on pretty much everything, and a plan. Funny how—relatively—quickly things can turn.

With the side of my head freshly shaved, I head straight to the office and into the sound booth.

I'd emailed Shane, the "announcements guy," Sunday night, asking him for a couple minutes of his air time. He stares up at me from a pile of papers with huge, dark eyes, a slouchy cap that's definitely against dress code, flopping to one side. "You ready?"

"As ready as I'll ever be."

He nods and pulls the hat down over his ears, all business.

I take the seat across from him.

He pushes the microphone toward me.

The bell for first period rings.

I take a deep breath.

Shane counts down, "3...2..."

He switches the mic on.

It rings in a horrible, screechy way.

Eyebrows raised, Shane adjusts a knob and mouths, *Sorry*.

"Good morning, Sinclair High," I start, keeping my voice steady, pretending I know what I'm doing. "This is Olive Maxi Gagmuehler." Inhale. Exhale. "I know"—I laugh under my breath—"it's a mouthful."

Shane smiles. It literally lights up his eyes, the white of his teeth bringing out the warmth of his dark skin. It momentarily distracts me, reminding me of sweet, little Bug, forcing me to swallow the lump in my throat.

"My name has sort of been an area of...bad luck for me the past few years. Do any of you have something you consider to be the bane of your existence?"

"I know I do," Shane cuts in. "It's my teeth. I have a gap."

I'd never have noticed, but when he flashes me an over-exaggerated grin, I see a small gap between his front teeth. It makes me think of Shiloh and makes his smile all the more engaging, but also makes my stomach sink from the loss I can't deny.

"Yeah. It could be something obvious or something no one else would ever notice or guess, but it's hard. And it sucks."

Shane's eyes bulge and he gives me the "they'll slit your neck" sign referring to my language.

I clear my throat. "Anyway, I — Olive Maxi Gagmuehler — will be in Courtyard A, under the pecan tree, during lunch conducting an…experiment of sorts. I hope you'll stop by."

I push the microphone across the table to Shane and fall back into my chair. As he finishes his announcements, I pull my hair up into a ponytail.

He flips the switch to OFF.

"That was awesome."

I smile. "Hey, thanks for letting me crash your gig."

Shane laughs an airy laugh that makes me do a double take. He motions toward the shaved side of my head. "Hey, I dig the new look."

"Thanks." My cheeks grow warm.

"See you at lunch," he says, holding the door open for me.

I'd seen it done on the internet. Someone blindfolds themselves in public, exposing what they're most insecure about.

Left completely vulnerable.

Forced to trust.

I stand in the courtyard, barefoot, scarf tied over my eyes, several metallic Sharpies splayed in one hand. I'm wearing a black T-shirt and matching leggings.

There's a sign before me that simple states: *Olive Maxi Gagmuehler =* _____. *Fill in the blank and graffiti my shirt and pants.*

At first, no one comes.

It's just me and I feel incredibly small and, honestly, kind of stupid. But I stay tall, concentrating on the spot where the etching *Just Be* lays against my chest, reaching inward, and holding that place of strength close. It's Bug and Jude, Lewis and Tilly, Will and Charlie, the island, Duke and the Panthers, all rolled into one bright light no one can ever take away from me.

Even if I stand here all day and no one writes a word, I did it. Put myself out there. Like I did on the island. Embraced my demons. *That* name.

If I give one silent voice hope, it'll be worth all the humiliation in the world.

But then something happens.

I hear the door creak open and snap shut.

Footsteps.

Someone gently takes one of the Sharpies from my hand.

It's so strange not being able to see. I think of Will, living on that island with only half his sight.

I take a shuddered breath.

The person softly squeezes me on the right shoulder then proceeds to write what seems to be one short word.

"You're amazing," the voice whispers, and I'd know that lovely rasp anywhere. Tawny.

I smile. Because I promised myself I wouldn't speak.

Warmth rises from my neck into my cheeks.

The door opens again.

And again.

More and more footsteps descend upon me.

Several pens disappear from my hand, and my palm is inexplicably empty.

People write on me and I can sense their respect, their collective intrigue and questions and how they somehow get it. We're connected.

I fleetingly wonder if any teachers come by and what they must think. I'd worried this experiment would be shut down, but if anything, they probably think it's some sort of performance art project for a class.

Pretty soon, all of my Sharpies are gone and my clothes must be covered in words. One girl even asks if she can draw something on the shaved part of my head.

I nod.

Because why not?

It's quiet.

Solemn.

Like this space is sacred.

Tears stream down my face, saturating the scarf covering my eyes.

Then, as quickly as it all happened, it's over.

I'm alone again.

The bell rings.

I wait a few minutes before removing the scarf, savoring the quiet. The breeze. The bizarre scent of Texas in autumn: dry leaves, long extinguished fireplaces, and the hinted warmth of summer refusing to concede.

When I untie the scarf, I glance down.

I'm covered.

Head to toe.

Words like *strong, badass, beautiful, amazing, brave,* and *rebellious* stare back at me.

The tops of my feet are graffitied with the words *love* and *live.*

I pull my mirror from my purse. On the side of my head in purple metallic Sharpie is a small heart over my ear.

I change into my uniform but leave my leggings on under my skirt.

Today, I smile at more people than I ever have.

Chapter Forty-Two

Moon Phases

Sometimes what happened feels more like a dream than anything, like I need to pinch myself from time to time to remember the island, that those kids were real.

Eventually, I set out to see which, if any, of my fellow castaways I can pin-point on this side of the glimmering heat waves. I wasn't sure at first. What if I found nothing? Or, worse, discovered things went horribly wrong for some of my sweet, island family. In the end, I decided knowing was better than always wondering.

Without last names, it was difficult, but I found Tilly. "Young girl disappears during bomb raid. Feared dead." Then Charlie. "Nine-year-old Hillsboro boy gets lost in famed corn maze. Found soon after, no worse for the wear." A photo of him, faded Castaways Carnival shirt, familiar bracelet tied around his wrist, impish grin across his face, stares back at me.

The others? Lewis, Jude… They didn't leave enough of a public mark for me to find anything, which I've decided to take as a positive. That "no news is good news" saying my mom always uses.

Then Duke and Will. "Teen boys go missing from small town carnival. Assumed runaways." I make a copy of the photo of Will. It's black and white and must have been a school picture because he's wearing his uniform, which isn't so far off from the ones we wear today. And, despite the fact that he has both eyes, less scars, is so much softer around the edges, there's a real sadness there. A blankness I don't recognize from the Will I came to love. Still, I keep the photo near. Always.

The only person I've told about the island is Tawny—of course, I couldn't hide it from her.

To keep her from organizing an intervention, I printed up the paper from when Will and Duke went missing and the article about Charlie, and then showed her the contents of the box in the back of my closet.

Tawny says she believes me, but the most telling proof is how I've changed.

"It's like you went through that maze one version of Olive and came out another. Who the hell are you?" she constantly asks me with a hint of respect mixed with classic Tawny humor.

I just laugh and shrug.

Some things are better kept tucked safely away.

It's a Saturday afternoon. My latest honors English assignment is nestled between my palms, and I've just read and reread the line, "The thing is, fear can't hurt you any more than a dream," over and over until it's lost all meaning.

I'm distracted.

Nervous.

I can't stop twirling my hair between my thumb and forefinger, digging at the hole in the thigh of my jeans.

The doorbell rings.

"I got it! I got it! I got it!" Lucky races past me, a blond blur.

The door swings open then slams shut.

"Hi, Olive!" Charlie yells as one blond blur becomes two. Lucky's bedroom door closes with a bang. I won't see them for hours. It's the new norm around here, and I wouldn't change it for anything. Well…most days anyway.

Tonight's the first island full moon. It was tricky figuring out the moon cycles of a place that only exists in my memories, but with a few books and internet searches, I started charting based on when I know the last island full moon was, which, as it was last month, coincides with a thin, crescent moon here.

It's actually not the most boring stuff, astronomy. And my new hobby prompted me to join the astronomy club. Me, the stars, the club? We've been hanging out lately. Still, I can't get past the deep longing and empty space in the pit of my stomach. The sadness in my heart that I've lost something so very precious, it can never be replaced.

Hours crawl past, dusk finally approaches, and I tell my parents I'm going for a walk before dinner—a routine I've taken to.

By the time I reach the abandoned field it's nearly dark, the sky awash with purples, dark blues, and hints of orange. The dim, silver crescent moon looms high in the sky like a crooked smile. I can't help the feeling it knows I'm only kidding myself.

It's been twenty-nine and a half days. The maze is long gone. Nothing but a distant memory, just like everything else. Nothing is left but decomposing remnants of brown, dried-out corn stalks and leaves littering the space. A certain carnival racket apparently doesn't take the *Don't Mess With Texas* thing seriously.

I try my best to imagine the maze and the place where the tunnel would have been. I'd be lying if I said I hadn't wandered back several times before now. Whenever I find myself questioning, unsure, or in need of something this world can't quite provide, I end up here. And, yes, maybe sometimes I childishly hope and pray to be swept away to the island by a certain handsome, beautifully complex, eye-patch wearing guy with a smile like sunshine baked ocean and an embrace to match.

Sure, I imagine all of that, too.

And then a car horn honks, a group of kids pass, dogs bark, and I'm forced to come to my senses.

As I roam the field, searching for the two large-ish rocks I placed on the ground to mark the spot where the window to the island should be, the weight in my gut tells me it's fruitless. There won't be a shimmering door waiting for me. And if it was there, really, would I venture through it?

Charlie and I have talked it over at length. We believe the island lures kids to it. Kids who need help, who could learn and grow and be better for being stuck there. Like a second chance. It's as if we were sought out.

And I'm certain we can't go back. Ever.

"Crap!" I trip, stubbing my toe on a certain large-ish rock. I stare down to find it has a twin.

I lay the plaid throw from my bed out next to the rocks and sit, my eyes searching for anything that shimmers or has the slightest glint of a heat wave because I still want to believe it's possible.

There's nothing.

Tears stream down my face. First, they're slow, falling one by one in a chase down my cheeks. Then, spurred by that emptiness in my chest, the dread that I know I'll never get back what I lost, they flow more freely. Not bothering to wipe my face dry, I lie back and stare up at the stars, the moon. I run my fingers over the ground, pretending it's not dry, cracked dirt and dead grass, but soft, warm grains of sandy soil.

I take a deep breath, pull a handful of weeds from the ground, and grind the sprigs between my fingers. I breathe in the heavy Texas air, listen to airplanes flying overhead and the hum of traffic from the freeway in the distance, and search for the beauty I know is right here surrounding me.

Once I find it, I close my eyes and imagine Will sitting in the same place, but under a different sky, leaning against the moss-covered boulder, doing the same thing. Finding the beauty in his world.

I take in a shaky sob, biting the inside of my cheek to keep from crying more loudly.

A stick cracks loudly not too far away. I jump then sit straight up, expecting to see a stray dog.

The tall, dark shadow of a person looms mere feet away.

Behind him is a pearl-shimmery window that vanishes as quickly as it appeared.

"Sorry it took me so long." Will steps closer. Bends down next to me.

Shocked into silence, I bring my hand to his face and run my thumb over his eye patch, making sure he's real.

As if to drive in the point, he wraps his fingers around my wrist and pushes my hand closer, more firmly to his face. He's all warmth and coconut and mint and saltwater…all the things I've longed for, but more.

"You're here."

He nods.

"But how?" I search his eye, his perfectly not-perfect nose, the way his jaw is tightening from emotion.

Will places his forehead to mine, speaking the words I've wished and dreamed of every day since I left the island. "After you left, I was scared I'd never see you again. Terrified that I'd never get to tell you…" He glances away, then back again. "I went to the boulder and swore to the island that if I ever got the chance, I would find you. That, even though I owe the island so much for saving me, *you*"—he stares into me—"sustain me. *You* make me better." Will sits down next to me and takes both my hands in his. "A window appeared there this morning, and I knew I couldn't hesitate for even a second. I had to go through it. I had to be with you."

"But what about Duke?"

"Shiloh decided to stay. To take on that role I'd thought was meant for me." He laughs under his breath. "They practically shoved me through the window themselves…not that they needed to."

I open my mouth to speak, to ask more questions and to say all of things I've wanted to say every second of every day since I stepped through that window, but he places his fingers over my lips and leans in so our noses just barely touch.

"I love you, Olive Maxi Gagmuehler."

Fireworks explode in my chest and butterflies flutter deep in my stomach as he wraps his arms around my waist and brings me closer. Our lips finally breach that tiny breath of space between us and we kiss. It's swirly and minty and full of hope and possibility and it's just Will and me under the stars in a vacant field of broken corn stalks, crescent moon smiling down on us.

He pulls away, but not far, thankfully staying so his lips linger just on the other side of mine. I put my forehead to his. "I love you, too."

I lean back so he can see me fully. His face is flush and his mouth is upturned in that proud, crooked grin I can't get enough of. He reaches across the tiny space and brushes his thumb back and forth over the shaved side of my head.

A sweet and honest warmth moves up from my chest like sunrise, spreading, surfacing as a smile — one that tightens my cheeks and tugs at my eyes.

A real smile.

All teeth.

Epilogue

Is it possible to smile too much?

It's a question I've asked myself over and over again the past year. I don't dare answer for fear I might get too caught up in the details and miss something. Something that might have made me smile.

I've learned to enjoy how my cheeks grow sore. How, if I haven't kept my lips sufficiently glossed, especially with a constant stream of kisses, they'll crack. Most of all, I've realized that each smile is fleeting. I try to absorb and relish in each one, but if I don't, if I get caught up in the moment, it's okay. There's always another just on the other side.

The wind whips my hair across my face, and I sense the tiniest of hints that autumn is near. Reveling in the *almost* cool breeze, I turn my head toward Will. He's driving the beat-up old truck Mr. Lawley, bless him, helped Will piece together. And it's perfect, chipped paint and all.

Eye on the road, still, Will senses my gaze because his mouth turns upward. He finds my hand and entangles his fingers with mine like a perfectly lovely knot.

"So, where are you taking me, again?"

He shakes his head. "Nope."

"Come on… You know I hate surprises!" It's a total lie. I'm just impatient.

"Liar." Will side-eyes me and squeezes my fingers.

I lift his hand then drop it like stone and punch him in the shoulder.

He laughs.

Will's been working pretty much nonstop since the day he stepped through the shimmery doorway off the island and back into my life. He landed a great gig in exchange for lodging with the Lawleys, a sweet couple who have run a fruit and bakery stand at the weekly farmer's market for ages. They own several acres of land, a random mix of animals, plus a decent-size apple, peach, and pecan tree orchard and were short-staffed. At first, Will did small tasks like cleaning and yard work and helping out with the animals, and in turn, they let him stay in the efficiency apartment above their garage. It was only to be temporary, but Will's sort of become their live-in groundskeeper. Now he puts in full days of work at the orchard and runs their stand at the farmer's market.

The best part? He's blissfully happy after a good day's work and says, in an odd way, it reminds him of being on the island. Plus, he forever smells of some form of apples or peaches and always comes bearing treats from Mrs. Lawley's home bakery.

I take a sip of the latte Will handed me about an hour ago when he picked me up, mischievous grin smacked across his face.

We've been driving for a while now and, try as I might, he won't even give me a hint into what we're doing or where we're going. I can't even imagine because we're literally in between a cow field and a rundown grain mill.

But he keeps driving.

And before too long, he exits and drives down a lonely road and into a small town not too different from Hillings. I'm still without a clue. Until he rounds a corner and pulls into a dirt lot.

It's dark when we drive up, but the yellow glow of the lighted sign leaves me without a doubt. The Castaway Carnival.

"Shut up." I face Will. "How did you…"

He winks and pulls me closer. "I tracked it down."

It was months ago when I read the story in the local paper about how The Castaway Carnival would no longer be held in Hillings. Not only had the town sold the vacant field, but because of cost, upkeep, and business decisions, its fate was unknown. I hadn't heard anything since.

The news had hit me harder than I'd thought it would. I mean, it was just a stupid, cheesy carnival. A death trap.

But not really. Not anymore. It had changed my life. And something about it vanishing, ceasing to exist, made me fear my new life, like the experiences I'd had might also vanish or somehow mean less.

"Come on," Will says, his grin gentle, meaningful.

Unsure of what to say, I answer by stepping out of the car, still pretty dazed and a little confused because I'd kept my feelings about the carnival not returning to myself.

Hand in hand, we walk up to the ticket booth.

"Two, please," Will says.

"That'll be ten dollars, son."

The minute I recognize that raspy, old twang, I shove Will over to get a peek, and I'm inexplicably relieved it's the same leathery man from last year. I smile, despite there's no way he'd ever recognize me. He shoots me a wink that forces me to reconsider his memory.

Once we're officially inside the carnival, Will pulls me to a bench. The scents—all sweet and salty, popcorn and cotton candy and hotdogs with undertones of exhaust from the rides—take me. It's strangely nostalgic and sad and exciting at the same time. Something hits me and I check the date on my phone.

"One year. To the day." Will turns and faces me, taking

one of my hands in both of his. "This year has been... I don't even have the words. When I left the island, I did it without hesitation or looking back or regret, but I can't say I wasn't fearful. I was honest-to-God afraid, Olive. What if I couldn't make a new life here? What if I failed? What if you realized you didn't want me off the island? That you didn't like this version of me? What if—"

I place tentative fingers over his mouth to hush him. My throat is a tight knot, aching from the tears stuck in the corners of my eyes. "Shhh..." is all I get out before a couple of drops squeeze through my lashes without my permission.

Will wipes the wet away, allowing his hand to linger at my cheek, his thumb grazing my jaw. Back and forth. He nods. "I know. This past year has been all I've ever wanted and more. You... Your family... That small town I used to hate so much... You've all welcomed me with open arms. Honestly, I don't deserve any of it."

"You do, though." I push my face into his hand to get closer. "You especially do."

Will pulls me into him, wrapping me up in his arms, against his chest, that place where all things warmth and apples and sandalwood hide in a tantalizing mixture I can't resist. As if it's beyond my control, I breathe in deeply.

He laughs airily against my head.

"How did you know?" I say, my words muffled.

"I've picked up some serious detective skills from Lucky."

"Will..."

Again, he laughs.

"I found the newspaper article on your desk. It was worn like you'd read it a hundred times and had a few tear stains on it."

I glare up at him. "Sneak."

"It's beyond my control. Blame that evil genius brother of yours."

I couldn't help but laugh right back.

He sits up, forcing eye contact and giving me no choice

but to vacate one of my favorite places in the world. "I need closure, too."

With those four words, that knot creeps back up, and I can tell he's got one too because he clears his own throat.

I can't help but glance over his shoulder. The maze is mere paces away. I glance at Will then back at the maze.

He turns to see what it is I'm staring at then looks at me, the same determination I'm feeling reflecting in the way his jaw has gone slightly tight.

I straighten my shoulders. Zip up my hoodie. "Let's do this."

Eyebrows raised, I can tell Will isn't sure whether to laugh or stand up and march to the entrance of the maze. Honestly, I'm not 100 percent sure, either. So, I mix the two. I give a satisfied, determined smile, stand, grab him by the hand, and lead him to the maze.

On cue, he presents me with two doubloons.

I hand them to the worker manning the entrance, and he begins to give us his speech on all things "World's Largest Corn Maze," but Will stops him mid-sentence. "Thanks, brother. We've been here before."

I grab a lantern and we walk past.

The wind howls through the stalks and the dried leaves jingle in rounds. There's a half moon high above, and it shines down from a cloudless sky in a backdrop of darkness bursting at the seams with stars.

Hand in hand, we venture deeper and deeper into the maze. And the more twists and turns we take, the more disoriented I become, and the more my skin pricks of goose bumps and déjà vu.

It isn't until I spot the place where the tunnel had been that I expect my monster to spike. I drop the lantern to the ground and stop dead so abruptly that Will's jerked backward by my hand. He stops, realizing what I'm seeing. The tunnel.

I don't speak.

And I don't hyperventilate.

I don't cry or freak out or dive into an anxiety attack.

I'm absent any reaction except memories.

I glance up at Will and allow my mouth to curve upward.

He launches himself into me, soundly placing his lips against mine and kisses me. We've had countless kisses this past year. Innumerable versions and circumstances, all with different details and tiny hints to remember them by. This one, though, is so very us. It's spiced with Will's cinnamon gum and the scent of popcorn mixed with earth and the freshness of the wind. It's all about sharing in the memories, good and bad. Experiencing closure separately and together.

At the same time, we pull away, but Will keeps his forehead pressed against mine. "Thank you."

"What? No. Thank you. This was everything I didn't know I needed at the perfect moment."

He breathes out a laugh, showering me with cinnamon. "I know exactly what you mean."

Will leans down and picks up the lantern, taking my hand in his. "Shall we?" He motions ahead—toward the path I never took.

"Definitely."

Acknowledgments

Publishing a book, I've found, is so much more than getting words on the page. Writing the story? That's the easy part. But editing, preparing, re-editing, copy editing, cover designing, marketing, formatting, final editing… A lot of really amazing people with exceptional skills and talents made this book you hold in your hands possible. First and foremost, I have to thank my editor, Theresa Cole, who has been a champion of my work, a thoughtfully brilliant editor, and such a presence of support. Also, much thanks and appreciation goes to the team at Entangled Publishing and Entangled TEEN: Liz Pelletier, Stacy C. Abrams, Melissa Montovani, Crystal Havens, and Anita Orr. A huge thank you to the copy editors and proofreaders who, honestly, had their work cut out for them, as well as to the amazingly talented Erin Dameron-Hill, whose gorgeous cover design literally took my breath away.

Huge piles of hugs and kisses and chocolate to the writing community. I'm not sure where I'd be in this journey without the continued support of my writing/critique/beta groups. Special thanks to my doppelganger and writing BFF, Jeannette

Smejkal, for always being there no matter what. Whether I've been in need of a pep-talk, a series of goofy .gifs, or to bounce ideas off of, you're my 'right hand man' and I love you for it. To Fiona McLaren who never hesitates to drop what she's doing to fit in a quick read and give me the most excellent feedback. And to the MG Readers who are ever a wealth of insight and inspiration. Special thanks to the friends and family who took the time to read *The Castaways* and gifted me with valuable feedback. Also to everyone who continues to offer me unconditional support and encouragement for this writing dream of mine. Extra special thanks goes to my soul sisters Megan Cordaro (My very first critique partner and cheerleader), Dani Bird (My college roomy and go-to public speaking pep-talker), and Sarah Stith (My go-to encourager) who are always up for a story of mine. You gals are the bee's knees!

There would be no book without a story and no story without a cast of characters who, beyond all logic, chose me to tell their tale. Special thanks to this beautiful and confusing universe, to creative freedom, and to all the strangely wonderful ways inspiration and muses present themselves.

Another thank you goes out to the tireless efforts of organizations like Kind Campaign and Stomp Out Bullying, among others, who continue to educate and advocate and speak out against bullying in all forms.

Mountains of love and respect to my parents, Joan Martin and Robert Fleck, who raised me to express myself, embrace individuality, to love big, and to always follow my heart and my greatest passions. (A special note to Mom: You've shown me how a strong, brave woman is also a compassionate and generous and kind woman. You've taught me how to embrace change and challenges with an open heart and mind and even more determination. I love you big as the sky.)

Finally, to my daughters, A.E.S and S.R.S, thank you

for inspiring me to start writing when I needed art back in my life. You two are endless sources of smiles and moments and adventures and you make me a better version of myself. You'll always be my proudest, greatest creation. I love you to the moon and back.

Last but certainly not least to my husband, Wade. You have been my biggest supporter, greatest love, and best friend. You are the most loving father to our children and the best partner in crime a girl could ask for. I love sharing this crazy adventure with you. I wouldn't choose any other way. To quote Eliza Hamilton from *Hamilton* on Broadway, "Look around, look around at how lucky we are to be alive right now."

About the Author

Jessika Fleck is a writer, unapologetic coffee drinker, and knitter—she sincerely hopes to one day discover a way to do all three at once. She loves writing novels for young adults and her work verges on fantastical and dark with a touch of realism. She currently calls rural Illinois home where she lives with her sociology professor husband and two daughters and is learning to appreciate the beauty in cornfields and terrifyingly large cicadas.

Discover more Entangled Teen books...

ISLAND OF EXILES
a *Ryogan Chronicles* novel by Erica Cameron

On the isolated desert island of Shiara, every breath is a battle. The clan comes before self, and protecting her home means Khya is a warrior above all else. But when obeying the clan leaders could cost her brother his life, Khya's home becomes a deadly trap. The council she hoped to join has betrayed her, and their secrets, hundreds of years deep, reach around a world she's never seen. To save her brother's life and her island home, her only choice is to turn against her clan and go on the run—a betrayal and a death sentence.

FANNING THE FLAMES
a *Going Down in Flames* novel by Chris Cannon

Being a shape-shifting dragon has its perks, but being forced into an arranged marriage isn't one of them. If Bryn McKenna doesn't say "I do," she'll lose everything. Good-bye flying. Good-bye best friends. Good-bye magic. But if she bends to her grandparents' will and agrees to marry Jaxon Westgate she'll lose the love of her life—her knight.

GARDEN OF THORNS
a novel by Amber Mitchell

After years of captivity in the Garden—a burlesque troupe of slave girls—Rose finally finds a way to escape. She flees one captor only to find herself in the arms of another, this one as charming as he is dangerous. Rayce has a rebellion to lead, and Rose's connection to the Gardener, a known government accomplice, is just what he needs for leverage. But her pull on his heart has him questioning whether her freedom is worth more than his political gain.

CPSIA information can be obtained
at www.ICGtesting.com
Printed in the USA
LVOW10s1257040517
533192LV00005B/15/P